Proposals in Paris

A duet from
USA TODAY *bestselling author Parker J. Cole*

Saint-Domingue heiresses, sisters Evena and
Sophiette Baptiste take Parisian society by storm
when they arrive in Louis XVI's court ready to find
worthy—and preferably titled—husbands!

In **Marriage Bargain with the Comte**

Evena reconnects with childhood friend and first kiss
Dieudonné, now the Comte de Montreau,
but she's promised to someone else!
Until one fateful night changes their friendship
when they're compromised into a marriage bargain!

And look out for Sophiette's story, coming soon!

T0357405

Author Note

Some time ago, I met a Haitian author named Vacirca. Through her writings, she was the first to open my eyes to Haiti and its rich culture. When I reached out to her a few years back, I learned that she was on her sickbed; not long after, she passed away. I remember her love for her country, the unwavering pride she carried and her constant prayers for Haiti's future.

About three years ago, I met Gomer, a young Haitian American author who furthered my fascination with Haiti. He spoke about the vibrant tapestry of Haitian culture and the depth of what it means to be Haitian. As I continued my quest to learn more, Gomer directed me to a social media account dedicated to all things Haiti—its history, culture and insightful political commentary. This led me to a YouTube channel that showcased Haiti's hidden gems: mountain retreats, majestic vistas and breathtaking scenery that painted a portrait of the nation's untold beauty.

While writing this duet, Proposals in Paris, I aimed—perhaps clumsily but earnestly—to capture a personification of Haiti, the radiant pearl of the Caribbean. Evena, bathed in sunlight, and Sophiette, illuminated by moonlight, represent Haiti's spirit: strong, resilient and steadfast. They embody the dignity, honor and indomitable spirit of the Haitian people, reflecting a nation that, no matter the challenges, faces the world with grace and unwavering resolve.

MARRIAGE BARGAIN WITH THE COMTE

PARKER J. COLE

Harlequin

HISTORICAL

If you purchased this book without a cover you should be aware that this book is stolen property. It was reported as "unsold and destroyed" to the publisher, and neither the author nor the publisher has received any payment for this "stripped book."

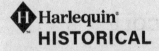

Harlequin®
HISTORICAL

ISBN-13: 978-1-335-54012-6

Marriage Bargain with the Comte

Copyright © 2025 by Parker J. Cole

All rights reserved. No part of this book may be used or reproduced in any manner whatsoever without written permission.

Without limiting the author's and publisher's exclusive rights, any unauthorized use of this publication to train generative artificial intelligence (AI) technologies is expressly prohibited.

This is a work of fiction. Names, characters, places and incidents are either the product of the author's imagination or are used fictitiously. Any resemblance to actual persons, living or dead, businesses, companies, events or locales is entirely coincidental.

For questions and comments about the quality of this book, please contact us at CustomerService@Harlequin.com.

TM and ® are trademarks of Harlequin Enterprises ULC.

Harlequin Enterprises ULC
22 Adelaide St. West, 41st Floor
Toronto, Ontario M5H 4E3, Canada
www.Harlequin.com

Printed in U.S.A.

Recycling programs for this product may not exist in your area.

Parker J. Cole is a *USA TODAY* bestselling author of historical romance who enjoys exploring history through the vehicle of romance. Consumed with a plethora of interests that keep her life busy, she lives in Detroit, Michigan.

Visit her Amazon page at : www.amazon.com/stores/author/B007ZSEDE4.

Books by Parker J. Cole

Harlequin Historical

The Duke's Defiant Cinderella
A Marquis to Protect the Governess

Look out for more books from Parker J. Cole coming soon.

To Ayiti

Chapter One

⁜

Baptiste Plantation, Belot Mountains, twelve miles outside of Kenscoff, Saint-Domingue (present-day Haiti), August 1769

'Where is he?' Evena Baptiste burst through the door of her family's house, her voice echoing in the grand entrance hall. Sunshine flooded from the tall arched windows above and filled the space with light.

Her feverish emerald gaze sparkled as she rushed forward, her feet clicking on the terracotta tiles. 'Where is he?'

'Where's who?' Her mother, Liusaidh, emerged from an archway to her right that led to the drawing room. 'I don't believe I know who you're talking about,' she teased.

'Maman!' Evena unpinned the straw hat resting on top of her *tignon* and handed it to a waiting servant. 'I know he's here!'

Liusaidh lifted her shoulder. 'I'm not quite sure what you mean.' She spun around and entered the room, the lines of her island gown flowing around her in a graceful sway.

Evena followed her, ignoring the polished gleam of the mahogany furniture and the ornate sofa coverings as she sought her quarry. 'He must be here.' Folding her arms across her chest, she sank her teeth into the flesh of her lower lip. She couldn't be wrong, could she?

'I saw the carriage outside,' she went on. 'And thought—'

'And thought what?'

A shiver went down the centre of Evena's back at the sound of that deep voice. She whirled around, mouth falling open, eyes glittering like gems. 'Dieudonné!'

The silhouette of broad shoulders and a well-honed physique impressed upon her subconscious before she ran and threw herself into his waiting arms.

'*Mon cher!* I missed you!'

Three years had passed since the last time she'd seen him, when she was a girl of fourteen and he a lad of eighteen. His family visited Saint-Domingue every few years, since it was his mother the Marquise de Lyonnais's birthplace. They'd both been born on the island and it was impossible for him to stay away from it entirely, despite now living in France.

From the strength of his embrace, and the hardness of his chest as he crushed her to him, Evena could feel how much he had changed. Gone was the lanky boy, replaced by this tall, muscular man who lifted her with ease, dangling her feet off the ground.

To say they shared a bond would be an understatement. They shared a connection rivalling that of siblings—but siblings often drifted away from each other as they matured. Life forced them apart as each went their separate ways. She and Dieudonné had drawn closer as they got older, despite the gaps in years between seeing one another.

Evena tightened her arms around his neck and drew in a deep breath. His masculine scent, a mixture of sun and earth and something that was distinctly Dieudonné, filled her nostrils. It was familiar and yet different this time. More potent. It stirred an alien response in her she couldn't quite understand. Some part of her wanted to get closer, burrow herself into his body and—

And do what?

'Ah, there's my *sirène*.'

His warm breath tickled the shell of her ear. His head dipped along the column of her throat. Faint bristles of facial hair scraped against her skin, and a peculiar tremor rippled through her. It awakened something in her she couldn't identify.

Evena blushed and pushed against his hold. It all happened in the blink of an eye, but she felt as if time stood still in his arms. A casual observer would have seen a simple fond embrace, but an outsider lacked understanding of the depth of what she and Dieudonné were to each other.

Once he set her back on the floor, Evena wagged her finger at him. 'Dieudonné, don't call me that. It's not appropriate.'

The glow in his ash and indigo eyes warmed her insides like smouldering coals.

What was going on?

Her eyes roamed over him. Dieudonné carried the inbred hauteur and arrogance of those born into wealth and prestige. Though dressed in the casual elegance typical of island men, that innate quality of nobility enhanced whatever he wore.

Strands of curly dark brown hair drew attention to the angular lines of his face—the strong jawline, the high, slanted cheekbones, that patrician nose and full, sensual mouth.

The white linen shirt emphasised his broad stature. His band collar framed the strong column of his throat, his prominent Adam's apple pressed against it. A gold-trimmed pearl button clasped it shut while a keyhole opening underneath teased her eyes with a narrow stretch of golden bronze skin.

Bright green breeches trimmed in gold ribbon and tied

at the knee moulded his lean, powerful thighs while white stockings emphasised his muscular calves.

Evena found her breath lacking as she studied this man she'd known most of her life. Yet she was discovering something about him that wasn't familiar at all.

'Now that you are here,' Liusaidh drawled from behind her, jerking Evena's thoughts away from their unexpected musings, 'perhaps my daughter will be calm once more. You've always had such a soothing presence.'

Dieudonné chuckled, the sound rich and deep. 'It's because Evena will do whatever she wishes and woe to anyone who dares try to compel her otherwise.'

Evena welcomed the shared laughter between her mother and Dieudonné. It took away that disturbing awareness.

She reached out and gripped his fingers. He was here! After so long, he was finally here again!

Liusaidh sat and motioned the servant to set the tea service on the mahogany table before her. 'Are your parents coming soon?'

'They'll be here tomorrow, Madame Baptiste.' His long fingers tightened on hers. 'Mère was struck ill during the last half of the journey, so Père wanted her to rest in Port-au-Prince tonight.'

A wrinkle appeared on her mother's brow. 'Hopefully nothing serious?'

Dieudonné shook his head. *'Non, madame.'*

Evena gave her mother a pointed look. Truly she was grateful that the Marquise de Lyonnais would recover sufficiently to extend their visit tomorrow. Right now, she didn't care. She wanted to spend time with Dieudonné before he and his family went back to Paris.

Could they cease with these social pleasantries?

'Am I intruding, *p'tit fi*?' Liusaidh peered over her teacup with a knowing look as she sipped. 'After all, you should be properly chaperoned as you are no longer a young girl, and your friend is a man.'

Dieudonné cleared his throat. 'I was always a man, Madame Baptiste.'

Evena snorted. 'Except when your voice broke, and you squeaked like a baby bird.'

Dieudonné glared at her, but his mouth twitched. 'That only happened once when I was a boy.'

'It was enough. I shall never forget it, nor will I let you.'

They both laughed. Oh, it was so good to have her friend back again!

Liusaidh sighed. 'Go on, you two. I trust you to behave at least, *monsieur*. Unlike her twin sister, Evena spends her time making the eligible men of the island fall at her feet. Why, it was only a fortnight ago that—'

'Come, Dieudonné,' Evena interrupted. For some unfathomable reason she didn't want her mother to finish that particular story. 'We'll be back soon.'

She dragged Dieudonné towards the door, and out into the sunshine.

Like carefree children, they raced across the earth separating the Great House from the foot of the mountains. They had played this game many times over the years.

Dieudonné's long-limbed stride soon outmatched hers, swallowing the ground with each step. He reached the base of the narrow upward trail her father had carved out almost twenty years ago. It led to a small clearing that overlooked their plantation.

'Aren't you going to wait for me?' she called to Dieudonné as he began to climb.

'Of course not!' he tossed over his shoulder.

Evena grinned. Dieudonné's confidence outweighed his

ability. He'd forgotten that she had climbed this trail dozens of times. He hadn't. He would tire before long.

As Evena predicted, halfway up the steep incline, Dieudonné's pace slowed. His strides grew more measured and his breathing more laboured. It wasn't long before he stopped and sank down onto the soft moist earth, head bowed.

When she quickly caught up to where he rested, she crouched down by his side. 'Are you all right?'

Dieudonné glanced at her, a twinkle in his eye. 'It seems I may have misremembered the mightiness of this mountain.'

'Ah, Belot has conquered you. Not me.'

She patted his shoulder and started up the trail once more.

'Aren't you going to wait for me?'

His incredulous tone made her chuckle as she scrambled up the side of the mountain like an agile goat. 'Of course not!'

Shaking his head, Dieudonné Godier, Comte de Montreau, watched as Evena swiftly left him behind. He should have known she'd react like that. If Evena had a chance to best him, then she would.

He leaned back and closed his eyes, breathing in the air around him. Bliss flooded his body.

The Belot Mountains boasted some of the richest, most fertile soil in all of Saint-Domingue. Dense foliage enveloped him, while all around the mountains sang, birdsong, rustling leaves and animal cries rising like a chorus. Somewhere, not too far away, he heard the distinct sounds of a waterfall gurgling its way down the deep slope.

A far cry from the urban, bustling city of Paris.

It was so good to be home with Evena.

Paris had never really felt like home to him. How could it when the noble, titled members of the aristocracy treated him like a pariah?

Wind brushed his face as if soothing his mind from his morose thoughts.

At two years of age, Dieudonné had come into the care of his uncle, André Godier, Marquis de Lyonnais, after the death of his Creole mother and her lover, André's older brother. He'd enjoyed a happy life, unencumbered by the circumstances of his blood or birth until…

A distant memory floated in his mind. His ten-year-old self bearing a cut lip and a burgeoning bruise on the right side of his face, standing before André in his study.

'What did you fight about, *mon fils*?'

He hadn't wanted to repeat the words the other boys had called him, and gritted out, 'They called me names.'

'That is no reason to fight. What did they say?'

Instead of answering, he asked a question of his own. 'Did my father love my mother?'

Looking back, Dieudonné appreciated his adoptive father's patience. Anyone else would have been unnerved by his childish rage.

André had stared for a long time into the fireplace. When he finally spoke, it was to say, 'I believe he did, *mon fils*.'

'Then why did he never marry her?'

André pierced him with his ice-blue eyes. 'What does this have to do with anything?'

'They called me a Creole bastard.' His fists clenched. Heat surged through his young self, boiling every surface of his body. 'So I hit them.'

'Dieudonné, do hurry!'

Evena's distant call jolted him from the memories. Looking up, he saw she had gained significant ground. He started up the mountain again, going slower this time to preserve his strength.

Over the years, his wealth and title were reluctantly acknowledged by his peers, but most sneered at his illegitimacy.

His lips twisted as he batted at a sturdy vine-like plant.

The mixed blood of his noble Parisian father and his Creole mother had served as a double-edged sword as he'd matured into manhood. Women wanted him for his handsome face and muscular body, but they did it behind lowered lashes and subtle invitations, as if their desire was some shameful thing to be hidden unless it was in his bed. A novelty when adultery and permissive affairs happened quite often among the French nobility.

Saint-Domingue, for all its problems, didn't try to hide anything. Being illegitimate meant very little here, and many children were born in the same state as he.

Why did his illegitimacy bother him so much every time he returned to Paris?

Stop thinking. Just enjoy being back home.

He reached the clearing, slightly winded. Evena stood close to the edge, her back to him. Dieudonné used the excuse of catching his breath to study her.

An island girl through and through, Evena dressed to match the tropical climate of Saint-Domingue. Like the nature of the island, she exhibited that same carefree and uninhibited spirit. Her exuberance affected others, drawing many with her effervescence.

Unlike her identical twin sister, Sophiette, Evena basked in the sunlight and loved the company of people. Sophiette preferred the shadows and her own company. The only other person Sophiette spent time with was Dieudonné's younger sister, Ayida, whenever they came to Saint-Domingue.

Evena was the kind of person who made friends easily and created swift bonds of loyalty.

The hem of her pale peach dress flapped in the wind.

A bright crimson kerchief wrapped around her back, and formed a knot that crossed her breasts. Her *tignon*, the colourful headscarf wrapped in a turban-like style, drew his eye.

In fact, everything about Evena commanded his attention.

As if she heard his thoughts out loud, she glanced over her shoulder. She'd grown lovelier over the past three years. Bronze skin smooth. Dark green eyes bright. Her nose snub and mouth full.

His breath lodged in the centre of his chest. Somehow, she had become a mix of playful, innocent girl edged by the sensual vivacity of a siren.

'Come see your home, Dieudonné.' Her voice had changed too. Gone was the light girlish sound he once knew, replaced by a throaty, husky tone that slid down his back like a waterfall of honey.

Like a moth to a flame, he came forward, standing by her side as they looked out at the scene before them.

Below them, the Baptiste coffee plantation stretched out. The Great House stood two storeys high, surrounded by a shady veranda that encircled most of the house. Bordering it were the outbuildings clustered around it. Eastward, rows of tender plants stood like soldiers as the workers tended to the berries that would eventually turn into the tiny coffee beans that would travel all over the world.

Unlike most, if not all, of the other plantations on the island, none of these workers were slaves. Evena's father, Claude Baptiste, had made his wealth from his time as a spice trader in his youth. When he'd returned to Saint-Domingue along with his bride some twenty years earlier, he'd bought this plantation from the son of a *grand blanc* who had died in the earthquake back in fifty-one. During the upheaval of that time, many slaves had escaped, but others had remained on the island.

Those who'd stayed had been rewarded for their loyalty to him. In exchange, they'd gained their freedom, working on the land and profiting from it as well. It helped that Evena's father's plantation was one of the few this far from Kenscoff. The soil from the mountains created a higher quality coffee bean which made Claude's plantation extremely profitable.

Evena spread out her hands, encompassing the scene before them. *'Dèyè mòn gen mòn.'*

'Behind mountains there are more mountains,' Dieudonné repeated. He stepped closer to the edge of the clearing, taking in the view. 'No matter how often I see this, it always seems new to me.'

'As home should be.'

His gaze roved over her. Her adolescent roundness had disappeared. She now carried a slimness attributed to burgeoning womanhood. Although the kerchief covered her adequately, her breasts swelled in two enticing mounds. He'd had a distracting moment or two when he'd felt their softness pressed against his chest.

He gave a start. These thoughts of Evena were foreign. She was his friend, a close confidante. They were closer than he was even to his own siblings who he'd grown up with. Granted, they were really his cousins by blood, but he loved Ayida and his younger brother, Iménel, like a brother would, just as he looked on André and Isadora as his parents.

This bond with Evena was different, but something about it was changing and it made him uneasy.

'What's wrong?'

Dieudonné blinked, not realising he had been staring at her without moving.

'Nothing.' He rolled his shoulders. 'It's good to be back.'

'Oh, is that all?' A mischievous grin lifted the corner of her mouth. 'I thought perhaps you had found your ideal bride.'

Dieudonné frowned. 'My bride?'

'Don't you remember?' Evena took a step towards him. 'When you were here last, you said you wanted to find the perfect woman who could help make you better accepted into society.'

'I did tell you that,' he replied slowly. 'I'd forgotten.'

'I didn't,' Evena said.

Dieudonné shook his head. When he'd mentioned it, the nebulous idea hadn't yet formed fully in his mind. He wanted a wife who would fully accept his illegitimate birth and Creole heritage. His jaw tightened. This mythical woman would also need to have enough influence to cajole society to accept him. From there, he would take his place among them, as was his right.

'Well, did you?' She took his hand. The warmth of her fingers seeped into his skin. 'Come, tell me about it.'

He let her lead him to their familiar spot at the back of the clearing. A knoll shadowed by a giant tree gave both shade and coolness. Sitting on the raised mound, Evena crossed her legs underneath her and pulled absently at the plants.

Dieudonné glanced up at the darkening sky. 'It looks like it may rain soon.'

'What of it?' Evena dismissed with an impatient wave of her hand. 'Tell me about her.'

He shrugged. 'There's nothing to tell. I've only just started my search and it will take a while.'

'Oh, there must be someone you've already considered!' she contradicted. 'Don't think I'm ignorant of the fact that such a fine specimen of manhood as yourself must have the ladies of the court anxious for your ardour, Dieudonné.'

He stiffened. 'Ardour? What would you know about that?'

She lifted her chin in a haughty manner. 'I know something of it.'

'Such as?'

Her lashes lowered as she twirled a blade of grass around her finger. 'I'm not a young girl any more.'

The muscles in his stomach tensed, but he responded lightly. 'You're still a girl in many ways, Evena.'

Her nostrils flared. 'I am not!'

'A woman doesn't have to tell anyone she's no longer a girl.'

Those dark green eyes of hers glittered. 'Oh, you!'

He laughed, although that odd tension lingered. 'I suspect, *La Sirène*, you've had maybe one or two quick kisses from some young, thin-faced boy and nothing more than that.'

At the sheepish expression on her face he laughed again, although there was an edge to it. Why should the thought of some young boy kissing Evena make him feel…out of sorts?

'There are times when I thoroughly dislike you, Dieudonné.' Evena pouted, looking very much like the young girl she swore she wasn't.

He grinned. 'Never that, *La Sirène*, no matter how often I'm right about you. Is there any man courting you?'

Evena shook her head. 'No man is courting me.'

The tension dissipated from his body. She'd probably only enjoyed a little flirting, the odd innocent kiss, but she wasn't ready for the responsibility of marriage or a man's possession.

Why should he feel so relieved?

'Is there some man you wish to marry? A young boy who sends your girlish heart aflutter?'

He hadn't really expected her to answer, so he was surprised when a secretive smile lifted the corners of her full mouth.

'Perhaps.'

Dieudonné's expression was thunderous. So, he didn't like the idea of her finding another man attractive? If he only knew!

He might go on about how well he knew her, but she knew him just as well.

Why taunt him this way? There must be some trickster god whispering in her ear, telling her to say these words.

No, that wasn't it. It was because she saw the masculine appreciation in his hooded eyes. It pleased her no end.

He wasn't the first man to admire her. Two years ago, she'd blossomed in that way women did. From there, a new sort of power had come into her possession.

Men wanted her and she admitted privately to herself that she liked the attention. What woman wouldn't?

Here was something between herself and Dieudonné that was completely different. An odd giddiness taking over her limbs.

'What do you mean, "perhaps", Evena?'

'Just that. I've not decided yet who I'm going to marry.'

A muscle twitched along his jawline. 'Is there a man your father favours?'

'Papa?' She blinked. 'He doesn't approve of anyone. He fears most men would take advantage of me because of his wealth.'

'They would.'

'He's being too protective. When I do marry, it will be my choice.'

'I see.'

'Enough of me, Dieudonné. I want to know about your bride.'

'As I said, I've only just started looking.'

Evena huffed. 'No woman has shown an interest in you?'

His tongue darted out and wet his lips. 'I didn't say that.'

She scoffed. 'Well, your name rests on the mouths of not a few of the women of Saint-Domingue.'

A dull flush coloured his cheeks. 'You mustn't believe all the gossip you hear.'

'Mustn't I?'

Dieudonné had the kind of handsomeness that drew all female eyes.

She coughed. Why was her throat so dry? 'Why is that?'

Why think of Dieudonné in that way? He wasn't the first attractive man she'd seen.

But he was the first she'd responded to.

A jolt went down her back.

'What's wrong? Are you cold?'

She tugged her kerchief around her tighter. 'Not really, but it has grown a little cooler. Go on.'

Dieudonné pursed his mouth. 'I love my family, Evena, but though I am the eldest child, I am not my father's son by blood. Though titled, I am not his heir.'

He leaned back against the mound, gazing up at the sky. She walked over and lay down next to him. He grabbed her hand and held it in his own.

'Will I ever be a part of something greater than me?'

'You will, when you marry a woman who loves you.' Her heart lurched at the thought of this unknown woman.

His fingers tightened on hers. 'I don't expect any woman I marry to love me.'

'That doesn't make any sense.'

'In Paris, it does,' he said darkly. 'Marriage is transactional. A means to an end. No, I don't expect her love. That's not important. But I do want her respect.'

'Why?'

His silence lingered for a long while. Evena kept quiet as well, knowing he would speak when he was ready.

'There's nothing I can do about the circumstances of my birth, but everyone outside of my family derides me for it.

I need a woman who can see past it, whose connections at court will allow me entrance in my own right.'

'Is it so important to be accepted in society?'

He turned towards her, eyes dark and bleak. 'Is it foolish of me to want that so badly?'

Evena pressed her lips together. 'I don't suppose so. Everyone wants to belong somewhere.'

'And when you don't, you feel hollow, don't you?'

'I can see that,' she agreed.

'The hollow feeling leaves me every time I come back to this island, because I belong. Yet, although I'm at home here, I live in Paris. My business interests are there, my family is there. The woman I marry will help me construct a bridge of acceptance. Not just for myself, but for our children too.'

Her heart ached at the anguish and hurt in his voice.

'I would never want my children to experience the things I have. To be forced to bear the brunt of cruel sneers and taunting. To know the pain of emptiness. Of loneliness. The feeling of not being enough. Of playing by all the rules and still never winning the game.'

Dieudonné's sadness permeated the air. Wanting to make him feel better, Evena lifted herself onto her elbow and looked down into his melancholic face. 'I don't care if you're illegitimate. You will always belong, Dieudonné. Here, with me. Always.'

He grinned then, causing two deep dimples to appear on either cheek. 'Always with you,' he whispered.

Reaching up, his large hand cupped her cheek. 'Do you know, there is no one who knows me as well as you do, Evena?'

'I do.'

His eyes narrowed as she spoke, his gaze homing in on her

mouth. The look in his eyes darkened. 'Your mouth is fuller.'
He took the pad of his thumb and pressed it against her lips.

Heat surged through her like flame.

'I know no one has courted you yet, but have you granted
any man—not a boy—a proper kiss from that lovely mouth
of yours?'

The skin at the back of her neck prickled at the tone of
Dieudonné's voice. It carried a warning that something primal and instinctive inside her reacted to. Evena went to pull
away from him when his hand shifted and cupped the back of
her head and neck, holding her still. His face hadn't changed
expression. If it wasn't for the marked difference in his eyes,
she could almost believe they were having the most casual
of conversations.

'Why are you trying to run away?'

'I'm not,' she lied.

'Then tell me. How many men have you kissed?'

'It doesn't concern you, Dieudonné. Why are you acting
so oddly?'

'Me?' His eyebrows arched. 'Let's cease with these games,
Evena.'

Then, with a swift movement, he curved his other arm
around her and shifted, drawing her under his body faster
than she could object. Using his weight, he pressed her into
the soft earth.

Her heart jumped up and lodged in the centre of her throat.
Not from fear, but from excitement.

For some reason, her tongue felt too long for her mouth,
and she stammered, 'What…what are you doing?'

Evena had known Dieudonné for years, ever since his first
visit to the island as a young boy when their parents had met
and become friends. They'd played together, argued together,

laughed and cried together. They'd shared secrets and intimate thoughts of the world around them.

Never, in all her days, had she seen Dieudonné like this!

Gone was her youthful friend. In his place was a man exhibiting a foreign air of leashed masculinity. A peculiar type of tension emanated from him, evoking an answering call in herself.

Her eyes drifted to his mouth.

'I asked you a question, Evena.'

Why couldn't she speak? Why couldn't she move?

A knowing look came into his eyes, and he bent his head. *'La Sirène,'* he whispered against her ear. 'Why are you so quiet, hmm? Has anyone kissed you like this?'

The hot press of his lips against the side of her neck made her stiffen like a board. She knew she should push him away, tell him to get off her.

But she didn't want to.

In fact, she wanted to arch her neck for him, and encourage him to do it again. Something feral erupted from within and she didn't know what to do with it.

He moved against her suggestively, sending sensations swirling across her skin. The hardness of him was a delightful discovery, a tantalising glimpse into a forbidden realm that lay outside of her experience.

'Dieudonné, I—'

A nip at her collarbone just under where he'd pressed his lips pulled a strangled cry from her mouth.

Beyond the pounding of her blood against her ears, she heard a low roll of thunder.

He lifted his head and stared down at her. 'Has any man tasted you like this, Evena?'

His mouth finally captured her gasping one.

Evena stopped breathing as flames licked across her body.

She couldn't believe this was happening. The arm around her waist gathered her closer, cleaving her to his taut body. Without being quite aware of it, her back bowed, thrusting her breasts into his chest.

More.

Her arms wound around his neck. Her restless hands thrust into his hair and pulled mindlessly at the leather thong that kept it tied. His hair got tangled up in her fingers and she tugged without conscious thought.

A violent tremor went through Dieudonné at the same time that another rumble of thunder sounded overhead. He murmured something against her mouth, but she couldn't hear what he said just as the rain began to fall.

His mouth coaxed her lips apart and his tongue drove into the moist interior. The rain came down harder, drenching them both.

A river of fire coursed through her, and she moaned against his devouring mouth. Her legs wound around his hips. Heat emanated from his body despite his drenched shirt. She wanted to be closer, feel the touch of his skin, and—

Dieudonné ripped his mouth from hers. A devastating sense of loss overwhelmed her.

Rain pelted her without the protection of his body and Evena gasped, finally thrown out of the spell his kiss had cast.

Dieudonné pulled her to her feet. 'We have to get back,' he shouted, the words nearly lost to the storm.

They slipped and slid down the side of the mountain, their clothes soaked through and muddied by the time they reached the base. Lightning streaked above them as they ran back to the Great House.

The servants were already there to attend to them. Above their heads, she and Dieudonné shared a shattered look. Things would never be the same.

As a robust crack of thunder shook the house, she couldn't help but notice that their friendship had suffered a similar blow of the sweetest kind to its foundation. A potent kiss, shared amid earth and rain.

She wasn't the woman he wanted, but could she still be the friend he needed?

Or had that kiss destroyed everything?

Chapter Two

Palais du Gouvernement, Port-au-Prince, Saint-Domingue

Rows of lantern lights illuminated the brilliant façade of the Government Palace as the carriages drew near. Sweeping steps hugged the centre spire piercing the night sky. Formal attendants stood on each step leading up to the entrance, while others met the guests as they alighted from their conveyances and walked up to the magnificent entrance to disappear under the tall arch of the portico.

Each time an attendant assisted a woman out of her carriage, Dieudonné's breath lodged in his throat. He waited to see if any of them would be Evena. When each lady proved not to be her his chest caved in with relief, only to seize up again the next time it happened.

Soon, he would come face to face with Evena for the first time in three days. It wasn't likely that the Governor General had neglected to invite one of the most prestigious *gens de couleur* families on the island to his soiree.

Unfortunately for his mother, although fortunate for himself, the bout of illness that had overtaken her on the ship had stayed with her longer than they'd expected. He'd used Isadora's illness as an excuse to stay away from the Baptiste plantation. And Evena.

What insanity had come over him? The question had plagued him ceaselessly.

The memory of her passionate response had kept Dieudonné awake at night. She'd gone up in flames at his touch. Crying out 'More...' in that husky, breathless voice. Grabbing hard at his hair, her limbs jittery and wild, her body offering itself to him in an invitation as old as time. He'd accepted that invitation, although he shouldn't have. As the older of the two, he had more experience, and he knew how the all-consuming taste of passion could overwhelm and tempt beyond reason.

A lick of shame lapped at his conscience. What had happened to his strength of will, his resolve? Moreover, Liusaidh *had* trusted him to behave himself with Evena. If she knew what he'd done, she would have boxed his ears, and he'd have deserved it!

Only a cruel imagination would conjure up Claude's retribution.

Still, he'd lost his own mind when Evena had gone mad in his arms. He couldn't help following her down the path of insanity.

Dieudonné shifted in his seat. For all the recriminations he'd heaped upon himself in the last three days, there was one thing he didn't feel.

Regret.

He'd lambasted his lack of control dozens of times, but felt no regret for what they'd shared, which was the most shameful part of all!

'Are you well, Dieudonné?'

He lifted his eyes to see his mother's gaze upon him.

'I'm fine, Mère.'

Isadora Godier, the Marquise de Lyonnais, tilted her head, a tiny wrinkle marring her brow. 'You don't seem to be. I would have thought you'd have preferred to stay with the Baptistes these last few days.'

He swallowed. 'I wanted to make sure you were well-cared-for.'

André squinted. 'Do you hear that, *mon bijou*? My own son doesn't believe I can take care of you.'

Dieudonné's mouth twitched at the corner as his father added, 'I'm more than capable of looking after your mother.'

'I didn't mean to insult you, Père.'

A gleam appeared in his father's ice blue eyes as the carriage moved forward once more. 'I know, *mon fils*. We have always taken care of your mother.'

A special look passed between them. They had taken care of Isadora for as long as he could remember. Dieudonné and his father were connected by their mutual love for Isadora. Though he had told Evena that he felt hollow, it wasn't from lack of love.

Still, once he'd discovered the truth from his parents, when they'd gently explained to him as a child that he was their nephew not their son, a barrier had been erected between them. It wasn't fair. He realised that. He'd been so young when his natural parents had died, his father in a duel, his mother to illness, that he had no memory of them.

André and Isadora had made certain he was their son in every way that counted, so why did he still feel as if he was on the outside?

As he'd matured, there were days when his Creole heritage and illegitimate status didn't matter. Those were the times when he was secure in the bonds of his close-knit family.

All too soon, though, the days where it *did* matter outnumbered the ones where it didn't. He'd noticed that Ayida and Iménel weren't treated as he was by their peers. Was it because of their noble, *legitimate* births? Dieudonné bore no resentment towards his siblings. He just wanted to understand what made them more accepted than he.

Over the years, as his family visited Saint-Domingue, he'd clung to the comfort of Evena's friendship. It soothed his inner turmoil as he'd tried to come to terms with his place in Parisian society. Other women had been in his life in their capacity as a lover. More recently, as a prospective wife.

Evena was his friend.

Now that was in jeopardy because of a kiss.

Dieudonné's scalp tingled in memory of the way her fingers had clutched his head to hers, as he'd opened her mouth with his so he could delve into that sweet cavern.

Par Dieu, how was he going to be able to face her tonight? Evena would inevitably confront him about what had happened. Never had they avoided each other, and she wasn't going to let him do so now.

What was he going to say when she did?

The smooth tones of Pierre Gédéon, Comte de Nolivos, the newly appointed Governor General, grated on Evena's nerves as he made introductions to his assembly of esteemed guests. 'Monsieur Claude Baptiste of Kenscoff, his wife, Liusaidh, and his daughters.' He indicated each member of her family with a polite, rather patronising smile.

After the introduction, Sophiette ran away before anyone could stop her. Evena sighed. Her sister would likely hide away in some unoccupied room like a mouse until it was time to leave.

The air was filled with the murmur of conversation of the elite—the *grand blancs*, the *petit blancs* and the *gens de couleur*—a delicate balance of France's governance of Saint-Domingue, and the island's compliance and acceptance of it. Or, rather, tolerance of it, as her father had said on numerous occasions.

Obviously, it was something the King of France recognised as a complicated dance because the Governor General knew that, to maintain order, he had to keep up the veneer of civility and harmony among the elites, thus this party.

Casting island politics aside, Evena's eyes roamed slowly around the room as she sipped on a small glass of spiced rum.

Her fingers clenched on the glass. Several feet away stood the man who had turned her world into upheaval three days ago.

She wanted to scold Dieudonné for ignoring her.

She wanted to talk to him about what had happened.

If she had experienced that kiss with anyone else, she would have gone to him to bare her soul. Why wouldn't she? He was her sole confidante.

Who could she go to about this now?

A raging passion had erupted between them when Dieudonné had fitted his mouth to hers. For the past three days, she'd relived it, closing her eyes and relishing the taste of his hard mouth, the cool rain and the scent of earth and Dieudonné all colliding together in a maelstrom of wonder.

And then he didn't come and see her so they could talk about it!

'It's a pleasure to make your acquaintance, Miss Baptiste.'

She gave a little start, blinking back to the present. Before her stood the tall figure of a man. It took her a moment to remember he was the son of an English lord and his Senegalese wife from England.

'Pardon, *monsieur*, I've forgotten your name.'

'Ranulf Grey,' the man answered in English. 'Sir Ranulf.'

'You flatter me, Sir Ranulf,' she answered back politely in kind.

He was handsome, with deep golden skin and eyes the colour of amber. His dark brown hair was drawn back into a queue and he was dressed in the sober attire the English were well known for. A darting glance about the room showed he'd gained the interest of several women.

She smiled. 'How are you and your family acquainted with Comte de Nolivos?'

'My father, Lord Hawkstone, met the Comte while he was Governor in Guadeloupe.'

As he continued to talk, she found her attention wandering. She looked towards the last place she had seen Dieudonné, but he'd gone. She frowned. Where was he? Surely he wouldn't have just left such a function as this?

'Miss Baptiste, may I ask you a rather impertinent question?'

The tips of her ears warmed. She hoped he hadn't noticed she hadn't heard a word he'd said. 'Of course.'

He leaned forward and lowered his voice. Those amber-hued eyes of his shone like twin suns. 'Why is that man standing in the corner of the room looking very much as if he'd like to run a dagger through my heart?'

Dieudonné!

Tension she hadn't been aware of till now seeped from her body, making her nearly collapse to the floor. So he was still here! Just trying to avoid her.

'I know who he is,' she replied. 'He's a very good friend of my family.'

Sir Ranulf's eyebrow arched high in interest. 'Is he?'

'Yes.' She bit her bottom lip. 'We've had an…exchange which has caused some tension. I wonder, Sir Ranulf, would you do me the kindness of escorting me to him?'

The man extended his arm. 'Who am I to deny a lovely woman?'

Evena grinned. Sir Ranulf was a delight.

They turned and walked to where Dieudonné stood. He tried to appear as if he wasn't watching them, but she knew better.

Her heart thumped a little faster. She'd always known Dieudonné drew the feminine eye. Tonight, she was even more aware of it.

Was it because he'd kissed her? It had to be. There was a new depth to her study of him.

On his head he wore a fitted white turban. The braided tail end of his queue peeked from the back of it. Dressed in a cream-coloured linen coat and pale blue waistcoat, it emphasised his wide shoulders and reminded her of his chest against her own. Breeches in the same colour fit snugly around his thighs and ended at the knees, brought the memory of his hard thighs between hers as he'd moved against her under the onslaught of rain.

All the moisture evaporated from her throat as if she'd swallowed a handful of sand.

As they came closer, she saw Ayida rush to his side, her head covered by an intricately wrapped, golden-hued *tignon* beaded with pearls and shells. Her dusky, peachy skin caught the fire's glow of the lanterns, bringing her distinctive, fine-boned features into sharp relief.

Sir Ranulf stumbled by her side, drawing Evena's attention away. A crooked smile on his face, he tried to regain his balance as his foot slid and accidentally stepped heavily onto hers.

Evena yelped like a small animal.

A second later, Dieudonné appeared, as if spirited out of thin air. Fury tightened his features as his arm clamped around her waist in a vice-like grip and hauled her against him.

Evena could have kissed Sir Ranulf for his clumsiness. Dieudonné was by her side again.

He whirled on Sir Ranulf, snarling in perfect English, 'What are you trying to do? Maim her?'

Sir Ranulf's high cheekbones flooded with colour. 'M-Miss Baptiste, I am dreadfully sorry if I've injured your foot.'

Evena's toes throbbed, but she tried to reassure him. The distress in his eyes tugged at her heartstrings, poor man. 'It's quite all right, Sir Ranulf.'

'No, it isn't.' Ayida halted by Dieudonné's side and glared at Sir Ranulf. 'He nearly flattened you.'

Sir Ranulf gazed at Ayida as if he'd been struck by lightning but, hearing her words, he snapped, 'Egad! How heavy do you think I am?'

'Enough to make it impossible for Mademoiselle Baptiste to ever walk again.'

Dieudonné groaned. 'Ayida, must you speak that way?'

Evena hid a smile. His sister tended to say the most outlandish things.

Sir Ranulf gaped. 'Are you daft, woman? Do I look like Goliath?'

Ayida's expression darkened. Sir Ranulf had unleashed the tigress and Evena wanted no part of it. She had Dieudonné and she wanted him to herself.

She gripped his hand. 'Dieudonné?'

Without a second's pause, Dieudonné spun away from the bickering pair and led her across the room to the doorway leading to the hall.

She limped along, grateful for Dieudonné's arm keeping her upright until they were outside.

The balmy night air brushed her face and she inhaled a deep gulp of it. The pulsating soreness in her foot had lessened, but Dieudonné still kept his arm around her until they reached the covered section of the veranda. Wicker chairs were strewn about, and he pulled one forward and set her down with gentle care.

Kneeling before her, Dieudonné took her foot into his hands and pulled off her satin slipper. His fingers stroked over her skin with deliberate care.

Tingles prickled up her leg. Her breath hitched in her throat. His hands felt so good on her skin. As he massaged her foot, her eyes closed in ecstasy, and she suppressed a groan.

If his touch was this heavenly on her foot, what would it feel like to have him caressing other parts of her body?

'Are you all right?'

Evena's eyes snapped open. With more force than she intended, she blurted out, 'I will be once you look at me, Dieudonné.'

His head lifted. 'Evena.'

Moonlight slanted on his face, highlighting his eyes. Dieudonné was just as confused as she was.

'*Mon cher*, what happened?'

Dieudonné didn't pretend to not know what she was referring to. They'd always been honest with each other. Maybe he should thank that bumbling idiot for stepping on her foot.

'I've been trying to figure it out for the past three days.'

'So have I.'

He studied her foot again, seeing its slender length. It wasn't as dainty as a lady's foot in Paris, nor as highly cared for, but Saint-Dominguans wouldn't avoid the feel of the earth under their feet. They were connected to nature. To be separated from it was to cut a part of themselves away.

He tried to ignore the warmth of her shapely calf as he examined her foot. Her skin slid beneath his palms like hot silk, and he was hard-pressed to not place a kiss behind her knee and trail his lips down to her toes.

He brought himself up short, shocked by the direction of his thoughts. Why was this happening? He'd never had these ideas about Evena before.

The moonlight caught the edge of the long-healed scar that had left its mark on Evena's foot, from the base of her third toe almost to her ankle.

When Evena was a child, she'd fallen onto some sharp rocks and slashed the top of her foot. He'd done his best to stop the bleeding, carrying her in his arms for what seemed like hours before they arrived back at the Great House.

That was one of a thousand memories. An almost uncontrollable urge to press his mouth along that scar nearly overwhelmed him. Dieudonné lifted his finger and traced it.

Evena hissed.

He jerked his finger back. 'Did I hurt you?'

There was a pause of silence. '*Oui*, Dieudonné,' she said in a pointed way after a moment. 'You did. When you avoided me.'

Carefully, he placed her foot back into her shoe and looked up at her face. 'I didn't know what to say or do. We've never done that before, *La Sirène*.'

'I know I taunted you, Dieudonné. Perhaps I'm to blame for placing such a challenge before you.'

'You're not to blame for anything,' he interrupted her fiercely. The last thing he wanted Evena to feel was some sort of misguided guilt over their kiss. 'The only one at fault is me. I shouldn't have allowed things to go so far. And you weren't a challenge for me to conquer.'

'But what we shared was wonderful. I have never experienced that before.'

No shyness or coyness. Just the blatant honesty he'd always expected from her.

His eyes closed. 'Neither have I,' he admitted.

Before that oaf had nearly broken her foot, he'd been unable to keep his eyes off her and he'd drunk in her loveliness with a new appreciation.

The *tignon* on her head was new, yellow sewn with beads and pearls. Her dress glowed in the lanternlight, with a fitted bodice and flowing skirt, short sleeves trimmed with lace and a red ribbon edging her neckline, drawing attention to her voluptuous breasts.

Dieudonné suppressed a groan. He wanted things to go back to the way they'd been before. Had things stayed the same, he would have spent the past three days with the Baptistes. And tonight he would have taken her arm and danced them around the room.

Instead, he'd stood in the corner, remembering their kiss.

That was the problem. He couldn't stop thinking about it, and he had to. He had a goal in mind he had to see through.

Evena wasn't part of his plan, even if he wanted her to be. She understood that as well as he did.

His heart whispered, *She's the woman you want.*

His head argued back, *But not the woman you need.*

'Dieudonné?'

He looked straight into her eyes. 'You know it can't ever happen again.'

Who was he saying that to—her or himself?

'Why not?'

A jolt went through his body. Evena couldn't be implying that they should see where that one kiss might lead, could she?

No, that wasn't it. Evena would be genuinely curious, but not interested in pursuing such a thing with him.

'Did you not like the kiss we shared?' she pressed.

He hadn't just *liked* it. The strength of their mutual desire had nearly taken him over. If he hadn't pulled away, using the last vestiges of his restraint, he would have done much more than kiss her.

That was what made him uneasy. How simple it would have been to explore more of Evena's body. In the darkness of night he'd wondered what might have happened if he hadn't stopped. The endless possibilities had formed sweat on his brow.

At the same time they made him ashamed.

Lust was not a substitute for their friendship. He wouldn't risk destroying that bond in exchange for a few moments of brief, transitory bliss, however heady.

Standing, he grabbed a chair and sat in it. Reaching over, he took her hands and squeezed them. 'Evena, you know what my plans entail. I need to find a woman in Parisian society who will help me to cease being an outcast. I can't buy that connection, but I can marry into it.'

A distinct pause. 'I know that.'

'You are dear to me, Evena. This is not a secret. I have cherished our friendship since the moment I met you and I don't want what happened between us to change that.'

A painful tightness settled in the centre of Evena's chest as she listened to Dieudonné's words. They were both sweet and heartbreaking at the same time.

What he'd said was true. He'd made it clear he wanted a certain type of woman to gain the respect of his peers. She remembered the tales he'd told of how people either ignored him or sneered and completely dismissed him. How he was treated like some sort of leper to be kept on the outskirts of society.

A man who only wanted to belong.

Could she fault Dieudonné for that desire? Of course not.

Her own acceptance of him had gone a long way to soothing the throb of his hurting heart.

A sad smile lifted the corner of her mouth. She was woman enough to know she couldn't give him what he needed. A lesser woman might try telling him to stop working towards that goal. But she wanted his happiness above all else.

Even if it meant he'd live his life without her.

Just because they'd shared a kiss, it didn't mean he wanted to change the dynamics of their relationship. Until this moment, some unspoken wish had lodged in the back of her mind, so far in the recesses of her hidden desires she hadn't articulated it to herself.

That maybe, just maybe, he would put aside his quest to find this paragon of womanhood who would help him obtain the respect he deserved and focus on building something...with her.

Could she have been any more foolish?

'That's why you avoided me,' she replied quietly. 'You didn't want to seem as if you were trying to take advantage.'

'I wasn't, Evena. But I should have discussed it with you. I just didn't know what to say.'

Evena drew in a deep breath and let it out in slow degrees. She'd rather die than give Dieudonné a reason to feel unhappy. He was her closest friend, and she wanted the world for him. Besides, as charming and handsome and wealthy as he was, it wouldn't take long for him to win the cooperation, maybe even the heart, of some fortunate noblewoman who would aid him in a way she could not.

As for herself, that ache in the centre of her chest would go away. Eventually.

'It's all right. We've discussed it now. You'll always be important to me, Dieudonné, but we should forget what happened. We won't speak of it again.' Evena forced a note of lightness into her voice. 'In fact, I'm glad we talked about this. Now, things can go back to the way they were.' Lifting a shoulder in a nonchalant manner, she added, 'Besides, you're not the only one with plans.'

Dieudonné arched a brow. 'Oh?'

'You don't expect me to stay in Saint-Domingue for ever, do you?' She shrugged. 'I want to travel and see other places. Then, one day, I shall fall in love with a man. We'll marry and have lots of children.'

An odd, unsettled look appeared on Dieudonné's face. 'You will, of course.' A strained smile lifted his mouth. 'What a fortunate and blessed man he will be to have you as his wife.'

'Very fortunate,' she quipped.

They both laughed. Evena finally felt the tension dissipate. It was over. Though they had kissed once, it would never be repeated.

April 1774, five years later, Baptiste Plantation

The afternoon warmth wrapped itself around Evena as she sat in the shaded part of the veranda, fanning herself with a peacock feather fan she'd received from one of her many admirers.

Over the years, she'd ceased to gain pleasure from the blind admiration of men. They no longer had the ability to impress her. If she were honest with herself, she had felt like that since Dieudonné had left the island and returned to France, never to return.

Behind her, the door opened and her mother said, 'Evena, I must speak with you.'

She looked at her expectantly.

Liusaidh came forward and sat in the wicker chair. 'I've heard from Seigneuresse de Guise Elbeuf.'

A cold hand clutched Evena's heart. 'What did she say?'

'They want us to come to Paris to continue discussions.'

The tension eased from Evena's chest, but the dread lingered. 'Then they haven't agreed to your proposal yet.'

'I didn't expect them to.' Liusaidh clasped her hands together in her lap. 'Meeting to discuss this in Paris won't be an issue once the sale of the plantation is complete.'

'Then we'll—'

'We'll see.' A forced smile came to her mother's lips. 'Maybe your father will be better by then and my plan won't be necessary.'

Neither of them believed that, but faint hope was better than none.

'Perhaps,' Evena agreed.

Ten months ago, her father had announced his desire to sell the plantation and emigrate to France. Three months later, he'd fallen ill, subject to odd swooning spells. Since then, his condition had grown worse. Her mother had sought help from every corner of the island. From the priestesses and the shaman to the island doctors, no one could determine what was causing these spells.

Then, Liusaidh had met Seigneuresse de Guise Elbeuf, an older woman from France who was staying at the Government Palace as a guest of the current Governor General, since Comte de Nolivos's departure. The two women had struck up a rapport at their first meeting and, from there, a burgeoning friendship.

When the woman had returned to France a letter exchange began. In those letters, the Seigneuresse had revealed the true state of her family's circumstances. Though noble, they were impoverished. Soon, they would lose everything. The threat of public humiliation and shame had been giving the Seigneuresse nightmares.

It was then that Evena's mother, desperate and worried about her own husband, had come up with a plan she hoped would be beneficial to both families.

Marriage to one of her daughters would bring the French family much-needed capital. In return, Seigneuresse de Guise Elbeuf would use her connections at court to obtain Evena's father an audience with the King's physician. There was no guarantee the man would see a Saint-Dominguan former spice trader and planter, however wealthy he was, but they at least had to try.

When her mother had first proposed the idea to her, Evena had known her hand would be the one offered to the Seigneuresse's son. Sophiette would sooner drown herself.

Throughout their exchanges, Evena had been given only glimpses of the kind of man this potential future husband, Gérard de Lorraine, Seigneur de Guise Elbeuf, was.

As far as Liusaidh was concerned, the Seigneur had an excellent pedigree and was therefore the perfect man for her daughter's hand. He was the equivalent of an English lord, with a noble line that stretched back many generations, giving him seniority in the French court. A member of a cadet branch of a now dissolved house, he still retained the honour the association retained.

Now, the next stage of their talks would be in Paris.

Evena worried the flesh of her lower lip. If those talks went well, would she be able to do what needed to be done? Marry a stranger for her father's sake?

'I forgot to mention,' her mother said, drawing Evena back to the here and now. 'Isadora has written to me, *p'tit fi*. It seems Dieudonné has finally become betrothed.'

Evena stilled, shocked. A moment later, she fixed a smile

on her face. 'Has he? Well, that's wonderful.' The words coated her tongue like ash.

Liusaidh went on. 'Depending on how things go, we may be able to attend his wedding.'

She'd rather hop the slopes of Belot. It took all her acting ability to reply in a light voice, 'If we can, I look forward to it. It's been so long since we've seen the Godier family.'

'Ever since the earthquake four years ago, the Marquise has been reluctant to return.'

Evena couldn't blame her. The earthquake of seventy had destroyed most of Port-au-Prince and had rocked the island. Many plantations had been demolished or damaged. It was only by God's grace that she and her family had escaped the worst of it. The memory of the ground shaking beneath her feet, the world rippling as if an ocean swayed underneath the earth, was something she would never forget.

Hearing of Dieudonné's engagement made her feel as if an earthquake had occurred all over again.

Evena toyed with the material of her dress, staring out at the façade of the mountains. From this vantage point, she could see the faint demarcation of the narrow trail that led up to the small clearing where Dieudonné had kissed her five years ago. She could still remember it as if it had happened yesterday.

Since then, she'd been kissed by several men, but none of them had generated the sensations she'd experienced in Dieudonné's arms. How she wished they had. It would mean that what they'd shared wasn't special.

But it was. That was the reason she couldn't even contemplate marrying anyone else, although many men had offered for her.

Hadn't Dieudonné told her he would find a bride who would have the connections he needed to be accepted by society? Although he hadn't visited in five years, she'd received occasional letters from him. In the last one, sent months ago, he'd given no hint that he had found the woman who would do for him what she could not.

She'd always known this day would come, so why did she feel as if the sun had fallen from the sky?

'Did you hear me, *p'tit fi*?'

Snapping out of her thoughts, Evena glanced over to see her mother staring quizzically at her. 'What did you say?'

'Are you all right? You seem upset.' Her mother's brow pleated in the centre of her forehead.

'It's not that,' she equivocated. 'I knew Dieudonné would eventually marry. It's just that in his last letter he didn't mention that he'd met anyone, so I'm understandably surprised.'

Liusaidh laughed. 'Well, you can't expect him to tell you everything. He's a man with his own life and interests. Those days of you and he running wild are gone.'

Her mother's light-hearted words crushed her inside.

Those days *were* gone, never to return.

The smile was brittle on her face as Evena said in a bright voice, 'Of course they are, Maman. I had no illusions about that.'

Not any more.

Chapter Three

Paris, France,
July 1774

Evena's heart fluttered in her chest. She could hardly contain her excitement. At last, they were here.

Paris!

Gone was the briny tang of the sea and the weathered planks of the ship's deck. Majestic buildings adorned with intricate architectural details drew her eye. The vibrant hues of the Parisian cityscape replaced the muted colours of the wharf.

Evena craned her neck to look around as she sat on the seat beside Sophiette in one of three conveyances hired by their father. Their parents occupied one of the other coaches. In a single line, they travelled from the dingy wharf to the bustling streets of her new home.

Her gaze darted from one sight to another. The narrow streets teemed with horse-drawn carriages, ladies in lavish gowns and gentlemen in powdered wigs. Market stalls displayed an array of goods. Charming cafés with outdoor seating. Elegant fountains with water cascading gently in picturesque squares. Fragrant bakeries. Blooming flowers.

So Dieudonné lived here. There was so much going on. It pulsed and breathed and swelled, and Evena wanted to experience it all before she had to decide if she should wed a stranger.

Her stomach fell as the excitement abruptly curdled like milk.

'Oh, it's all so very busy, *sè*.'

Blinking, Evena came out of her reverie. Turning away from the scenery, she asked Sophiette, 'What did you say?'

'I hate it. It's too busy.'

She scowled at her twin. 'Stop being so dour. Look at this place!'

'I'm looking.' Her sister's lips turned down at the corners. 'I don't like it and I want to go back home.'

'Well, you can't!' Evena's nostrils flared. 'You had better acquaint yourself with staying here. We're not going back. The plantation's sold, and I have a prospective match with Seigneur de Guise Elbeuf.'

Sophiette gave her a pitying glance. 'And that fills you with joy?'

Evena flinched. Trust Sophiette to pounce on the truth of the matter and ignore all the frills used to cover it up.

A vision of her father's wan face flashed in her mind, and her irritation melted away. This was more important than potentially marrying for status. It was to save her father's life.

Coolly, she said, 'I'm prepared to do my duty. You must do yours.'

Evena saw the mirror of her own face glaring back at her, her twin's dark green eyes narrowing. 'There's no need for you to lie down on the altar of sacrifice.'

'Sophiette, you know I have to do this.'

Her sister's face lost its defiance and crumpled. 'It's unfair, Evena.' Sophiette's voice shook. 'Why should Papa have to be the one to die?'

'We don't know that yet.' Evena rubbed her sister's shoulders in a comforting way as she tried to keep her own melancholic thoughts at bay. 'But if it is the end, then we must do what we can so he doesn't have to worry about us should... should...'

She couldn't finish the sentence and instead let it trail away.

They said no more as they continued through the streets of Paris. How different was this trip from what she had envisioned a little over a year ago when Claude had first announced their emigration to Paris. He hadn't been ill then, and she'd been excited at the prospect of being in the same city as Dieudonné.

In her mind's eye, she saw the family sitting in her father's library, discussing the plan. Her mother had joked, 'I'm sure Evena would enjoy the change. She's already caught the eye of nearly every eligible man on the island.'

She'd longed to cry out that the only man she wanted wasn't on the island, but at the amused expression in her mother's eyes, she'd responded in the expected manner.

'Ah, Paris! I shall dance and the most eligible noblemen shall woo me.' She'd clapped her hands. 'They shall fall before my feet and worship me.'

Little did her parents know the only man she wanted to woo her was Dieudonné!

It seemed incredible now to remember that conversation, all of them ignorant as to what would happen just a few months later. If she did marry, it wouldn't be because a man had wooed her. It was because he needed her money, and she needed his influence to try to help her father.

Dieudonné's words had come back to haunt her several times in the past year.

'Marriage is transactional. A means to an end.'

She understood that now with painful clarity. Though

she'd never judged Dieudonné for what he sought from a wife, perhaps some part of her had seen herself as superior. They'd been the thoughts of a foolish young girl, protected by her father, pampered by her mother, who had never experienced the harsh realities of life.

Unlike that day when Dieudonné had kissed her, she was a woman now. A woman who had to make a difficult decision and deal with the consequences of it.

Evena sighed. He must have been married for at least a month by now. The sale of the plantation had taken longer than expected, so they had missed the opportunity to attend his wedding.

Not that she was complaining.

'Are you listening to me?'

Evena jumped, catapulted out of her thoughts. She focused once more, seeing Sophiette staring curiously at her. 'What did you say?'

Sophiette gave her a knowing look. 'You're worried about meeting this nobleman.'

'I was,' she replied slowly.

'If it were a simple matter of marrying you for your dowry, then Seigneur de Guise Elbeuf would have married you by proxy. Heaven knows, it happens often enough.'

'*Oui,*' Evena answered, her teeth grinding.

'You are a Saint-Dominguan heiress, bearing the promise of much wealth to the man who chooses to marry you, in exchange for his title and influence. If the family is as destitute as his mother has implied, why didn't they do just that?'

Evena knew where this was going.

'Why do you think?' she replied.

'The nobleman needs to meet you and decide if the lure of riches would be enough to ignore certain unpleasantness.'

'And what exactly is that unpleasantness?'

'Our race,' Sophiette answered in a blunt fashion, causing Evena to wince. 'That, and society's ever watchful and critical eye. On Saint-Domingue, miscegenation is more readily accepted. In Paris, such things are frowned upon. I don't think our wealth will be enough to lure an impoverished yet proud Frenchman to mix his noble blood with ours. That would require a man with a particularly stiff backbone.'

Sophiette's words struck at the heart of the matter. Her sister couldn't know the tender spot she'd pressed her metaphorical finger on.

But she wasn't wrong. Dieudonné had spent most of his life faced with the same dilemma. She and her sister were considered two of the most beautiful women on their island, although Sophiette had found no comfort in the distinction. Would that count for anything in these aristocratic circles?

Dieudonné spoke about how different Saint-Domingue was to Paris, with its stricter protocols of conduct and expectations of high society. If she married this Seigneur de Guise Elbeuf, would she be up to the task?

An instant later, her confidence returned. Of course she would!

'You mustn't speak so, Sophiette. Look at the Marquis and Marquise de Lyonnais.'

Sophiette gave her another pitying glance that set Evena's teeth on edge. 'They are the exception, not the rule, and well you know it.'

'It may have started off that way,' she insisted, determined to find some hope in the situation. 'But they are fully accepted into society.'

Even before their father had fallen ill, her sister had been the only one to object to their emigration, citing dozens of reasons why they should remain in Saint-Domingue.

Seeing the worried look on Sophiette's face, Evena tried

to make her feel better. The words tumbled out of her mouth. 'You and I will be the envy of all those titled ladies here. They shall hate us, and I shall be glad,' she teased.

'I don't want anyone to hate me, *sè*,' Sophiette murmured. 'In fact, I prefer to be alone with my music.'

Evena snorted. 'You will not sit in some dark corner, clanging at the harpsichord and singing to an audience of no one. We are going to be the most sought-after ladies in all of Paris, whether I marry or not.'

Sophiette's skin paled. 'What a horrid idea.'

Trying to ease her sister's fears, Evena said, 'It's not all terrible, is it, *sè*?'

Some time later, Evena looked out of the window as their conveyance neared the end of its journey. The façade of the Hôtel Godier in the distance made her breath catch in her throat. Encompassed by a wrought-iron fence formed of vine and scrolls, the townhouse exuded elegance. Travelling up the curved bend, she took in the three-storey residence constructed in honey-coloured limestone.

They drew to a stop at the front entrance behind their parents' carriage. Immediately, the door opened and Isadora Godier dashed down the steps. As the footman opened their door, Evena watched with an amused glance as her mother nearly tripped over herself to exit the cab and embrace the other woman.

'Oh, Isadora, it's so good to see you again!'

The women laughed, and then the Marquise turned towards Evena as she alighted from her own carriage.

'Oh, my, look at them!'

Evena's face heated with pleasure as the Marquise glided towards her and Sophiette.

'You are both so grown-up now!' Isadora shifted her gaze from Evena to Sophiette. 'Now, let me see if I can tell the difference.' She pursed her lips for a moment, her eyes going back and forth between them. 'You are Evena, *oui*? And you are Sophiette?'

Evena shook her head, her lips tilted up in a grin.

'Oh, I could never tell the difference,' the Marquise protested.

'Monsieur Baptiste, a pleasure to see you again.'

The deeper voice, speaking in French, came from the front entrance. Evena glanced up to see the still-handsome Marquis strolling down the steps to stand beside his wife.

Evena prayed with all her heart that Seigneur de Guise Elbeuf would be at least passably attractive. It would be an awful twist of fate if the man was so hideous as to make her seek shelter in some dark corner of the bedroom.

'We have been looking forward to returning your hospitality,' the Marquis said.

Her father came forward and grasped the Marquis's hand. 'We thank you for your gracious hospitality. I hope we won't trouble you for too long.'

'Nonsense!' The Marquis clapped a hand on Claude's shoulder. 'We're honoured to have you as our guests.'

Evena winced. Did the other man know that her father's illness could come upon them at any time? What had her parents told the Godiers?

'Now, come, come,' the Marquise urged, mothering them like a hen with her chicks. 'You must be exhausted. We have prepared your rooms for you.'

Shaking off her wayward thoughts, Evena entered the townhouse along with everyone else.

Movement sounded on the grand staircase to her left, and Evena's mouth lifted into a smile as two figures darted down the marble steps.

Jacques-André Iménel Godier, Vicomte de Montbréson,

landed on the bottom of the stairs first. He resembled his father in a golden, debonair way, but his skin was a shade darker in complexion. His unbound brownish hair had blond tints to it, and his blue spectacles reflected the sumptuous interior of the mansion.

Mademoiselle Marguerite Ayida Godier was draped in rose and ivory. It complimented the dusky peach hue of her skin and emphasised her beryl-blue eyes.

'Sophiette!' Ayida reached the bottom of the steps and hurled herself into her old friend's arms. They hugged and kissed each other's cheeks, and Evena smiled at their joy.

Iménel shook his head and greeted her parents first, before he came towards Evena, placing a kiss against her cheek. 'It's a good thing my sister knows you two apart, because I thought you were her.' His mouth twisted in a wry smile. 'I don't have the same eyes as my brother and sister do.'

'It's perfectly understandable,' Evena said. 'There are those on Saint-Domingue who have known us since the womb who can't tell us apart.'

Everyone laughed, as Evena expected them to, but her eyes drifted back up the stairs. Where were Dieudonné and his bride?

'We apologise for missing your son's wedding last month. Is he still celebrating his honeymoon with his new wife? We can't wait to meet her,' Liusaidh said.

Evena bit her lip to keep herself from saying that she did not share her mother's sentiments.

Isadora's smile turned down at the corners. 'I didn't tell you this in my last letter, but the wedding…did not proceed as planned.'

Evena froze. 'Pardon?'

Isadora sent a sorrowful look in her direction. 'It's true.

It's a very sensitive subject for my son so I will not speak of it any more.'

'Of course,' Liusaidh agreed hastily. 'We did not mean to pry. Is he here?'

'Non,' Isadora replied. 'He's gone abroad for a while. He'll be back within a month or so.'

Evena felt as if she could be knocked to the ground with a feather.

He wasn't married!

Joy bubbled up inside of her, quickly followed by shame. She shouldn't be happy about Dieudonné's misfortune. Something awful had happened.

She pressed her lips together to stop herself from groaning. How cruel fate was. It would be at least an entire month before she found out what had happened!

Hawkstone Manor, Norfolk, England

Dieudonné tried to find solace in the rhythmic cadence of hooves against the soft earthen paths but, like everything else for the past month, serenity was an elusive lady.

Like Agnès.

Above him, the sky was cloudy and dreary. Against him, the wind blew chilly and squally. Around him, the landscape looked muted and dank. Beside him rode Sir Ranulf.

They stopped their horses by a small stream. Dismounting and leading their horses to drink, Dieudonné went over to a nearby oak tree with gnarled branches and leaned against the trunk.

'Hasn't gone away yet, has it?' Sir Ranulf asked in French, immediately bringing Dieudonné out of his thoughts.

A reluctant laugh erupted from his mouth. *'Mon Dieu,* spare me an Englishman's accent.'

Sir Ranulf grinned. 'I'll have you know I am perfectly fluent in Italian and Spanish.'

'Fluent? Undoubtedly. Pleasant to listen to? Hardly.'

When he and Sir Ranulf had first met, back in Saint-Domingue, it wasn't under the best of circumstances, but their fathers had got along well. After Lord Hawkstone had accepted André's invitation to stay with them in Paris, the families had quickly become friends, and Dieudonné now counted Sir Ranulf as a confidant.

Dieudonné stared out at the fields of gold and green. 'Why did she do it, Sir Ranulf?' he asked in English.

Sir Ranulf's booted footsteps came closer until he stood in front of him. Lifting his gaze, he said, 'I wondered when we would talk about her, my lord. It's been almost a month, you know.'

Agnès's image flashed in Dieudonné's mind. Long, midnight-black curls with a lustrous sheen surrounded her heart-shaped face, with glittering golden eyes. Smooth skin tinted with a hue of rose, and a tiny nose and an equally small, pouty mouth added a delicate touch to her fine features. She had a slender figure with small breasts and a trim waist further complementing her ethereal appearance.

It was strange, but although Dieudonné recognised that Marie Agnès Mercier was a beautiful woman, and he knew she was much admired in society, he didn't find her appealing to him personally. Her fragile looks were at odds with her notorious reputation as someone who didn't conform to the appropriate dictates of womanhood. Her conquests were legendary, having been seen on the arm of some of the most prestigious members of the Parisian elite.

Most importantly, her father, Baron Henri Édouard Mercier, held a high position in court as a favourite of the King.

When she and Dieudonné had originally met, she'd been

intrigued by the idea of marrying a wealthy, titled Creole man and had taken the idea of smoothing his acceptance into society as a challenge. Indeed, when she'd shown up on his arm the very first time at a well-attended ball, the room had gone quiet, myriad eyes staring at them. The incident had amused Agnès greatly. From there, he'd noticed others starting to draw him slowly, ever so slowly, into those circles.

She'd succeeded where he'd failed.

So, why hadn't she gone through with the wedding? His former betrothed had jilted him at the altar and had apparently gone to relatives in Venice. She had yet to return.

'She did not have to accept my proposal, Sir Ranulf. I did not force her to do so. Why go through the farce of being engaged to me then, if she had no intention of marrying me?'

Sir Ranulf folded his arms. 'Perhaps for the novelty. We are of mixed blood after all, my lord.' A sardonic glint appeared in his eyes.

'I was aware that she saw me as some sort of object to draw attention to herself,' Dieudonné muttered. 'We had a clear understanding of what our relationship would look like. I never made a secret of it.'

Sir Ranulf frowned. 'She gave you no inkling she would jilt you?'

'No.'

Agnès had known what their betrothal had meant to him. Dieudonné had no expectations of a love match. All he'd wanted from the marriage was to be tolerably content and for them to respect each other.

So why had Agnès betrayed him when it wasn't necessary? If she had decided to end their betrothal in private, he wouldn't be as upset. Instead, she'd humiliated him in the worst possible way.

He could never forgive her for that. He'd shared his deepest vulnerabilities with her, telling her exactly why he'd wanted this marriage. She'd seemed so compassionate about what he'd suffered in being an outcast amongst his own class.

If Agnès hadn't wanted to marry him, she didn't have to. Dieudonné had given her plenty of opportunity to change her mind, even before the contracts were signed and the date of the church ceremony set.

What was it about him that caused people to treat him this way? Was he some sort of automaton to them, bereft of heart and soul, as if he had no feelings whatsoever? He'd had to face the gleeful gossip and looks of faux pity while keeping the hurt and humiliation from showing.

His fingers curled into a fist. No, he would never forgive Agnès for this betrayal.

After an hour, they returned to Hawkstone Manor. Dieudonné freshened up and changed from his riding clothes into the dark-coloured breeches, waistcoat and jacket the English seemed to favour.

Reaching the dining room, he was greeted by Lord Hawkstone, who stood in the doorway.

'So glad you could join us for breakfast.'

Dieudonné gave a slight shake of his head. 'Of course, Lord Hawkstone. Why would you think any different?'

'My wife and I were under the impression you were indisposed.'

'Really, Father,' Sir Ranulf groaned. 'My lord suffers from a bruised ego, not a broken heart.'

'You must forgive your father, my son.' Lady Hawkstone had a beatific smile upon her mahogany face. 'He's a hopeless romantic and is certain that love is a disease that one can never be cured of. You mustn't blame him. His own love story is indisputably romantic.'

'This came for you, my lord.' Lord Hawkstone handed over a letter.

'It must be from my mother.' Dieudonné took the letter and glanced at the return address. 'Ah, not my mother. My sister.'

Opening it, he read:

Dear Brother,
I could tell you how much I've missed you since you went to England and how empty the house is without your presence. Or how often I wish hell and perdition on Mademoiselle Mercier. But that would be silly as it would only delay the inevitable joy I'm sure you will feel when I tell you this: the Baptistes have finally arrived in France.

Mother says they will be living here with us for the foreseeable future while Father helps Monsieur Baptiste search for a suitable home to purchase. So do come back soon.
Your loving sister,
Ayida

Dieudonné folded the letter and placed it in his pocket. Evena.

Their kiss was never far from his mind, even though five years had passed. The few kisses he'd shared with Agnès had never conjured up the same sort of feeling. His former betrothed, for all her popularity with the opposite sex, had left him cold. Though she had more than once intimated she was very willing to share his bed, drawn to the novelty of making love to a Creole man, he hadn't taken her up on the offer.

Dieudonné supposed if he had married Agnès, he would have done his conjugal duty, but that was all it would have been—a duty. A task to perform.

Agnès hadn't stirred one ounce of the ferocious desire Evena had.

Still, that was five years ago. He'd been twenty-one at the time. Surely, at twenty-six years of age, he wouldn't be as susceptible to her now?

'Is everything all right, my lord?'

Dieudonné glanced up to see everyone's eyes were fixed on him. 'Yes, I've just decided that I should return to Paris.'

'Oh!' Lady Hawkstone exclaimed. 'We expected to have you with us for at least another month.'

'I thank you for your graciousness, Lady Hawkstone. But I believe it's time I went home.'

Suddenly, he couldn't wait to get back to Paris.

Seven days later

Goddesses, hunters and animals swelled the ballroom of Hôtel de Godier, much to Dieudonné's amusement. Lively music filled the space and couples danced with each other behind their masks.

He'd got back just in time then.

'Dieudonné!'

The Queen of Sheba captured his attention, but behind the eye mask was the unmistakable form of Isadora as she hurried towards him.

'Mère, you did not do all this for me, did you?'

Isadora drew him down into a hug. 'Dieudonné, I thought you would be gone another few weeks at least! Didn't you enjoy your visit with the Hawkstones?'

'Of course I did, Mère,' Dieudonné said. 'But I had a longing to come home.' He cocked his head. 'Surely I don't need another reason, do I?'

Her golden eyes probed his own. 'Are you all right?'

Bending, he kissed her forehead above the mask. 'I'm fine, Mère.'

'*Bien, bien.*' She looked over her shoulder at the party going on behind her. 'You're welcome to join us if you're not too tired.'

Dieudonné nodded. '*Merci,* Mère.'

When he reached his room, he dismissed the servant after he'd set his luggage down and lit the lamps.

Where was Evena in that crowd? What had she come dressed as? Knowing her, she would be in the most unusual costume of all. Evena wasn't afraid to draw attention to herself. She craved it. Not in any selfish manner, he knew that. She genuinely enjoyed the company of people. The more there were, the better.

Going over to the wardrobe, he opened the door and dug deep into its depths for some semblance of a costume and a mask.

Dieudonné made his way back down the stairs nearly an hour later. The servants had brought him a tray of food and drink and he felt refreshed. Only Evena would recognise the significance of the costume he had changed into. Putting his mask on, he entered the bedlam in search of his prey.

Chapter Four

'I've yet to determine who you are, *mademoiselle*.' The masked figure of Jupiter, the supreme god of Roman mythology, leaned forward, the brown of his eyes emphasised by the holes of his mask.

Evena approved of this stranger's costume. The purple and golden robes flowed around him, catching the light. With the mask on his face, she'd no clue as to his identity, but it made the ball that much more fun.

Evena smiled. 'I believe that is the objective, *monsieur*.'

'No, not your identity, *mademoiselle*.' Jupiter gestured at her costume. 'I mean, who are you meant to be? I don't recognise the subject.'

'Oh.' She glanced down at herself. 'I am a goddess.'

Dressed as one of the deities of her homeland, Evena smoothed her hands over the false snakes wrapped around her. Beads and seashells adorned her hair, giving it a slight rattling sound whenever she moved. A small mirror hung from rope around her waist, one of the important accessories of the goddess. She didn't mind drawing attention to herself, and the costume worked well at introducing her to people who'd stopped and queried her attire.

'Undoubtedly. Yet that still doesn't tell me who you are.'

Delighted by his playful flirting, Evena's cheeks warmed. 'I am a water goddess named Mami Wata.'

Just saying that brought Dieudonné's image to the forefront of her mind. He wasn't married!

'What sort of creature is she?'

Mentally shaking herself, she came back to the conversation. 'A mermaid, mostly. Yet one could also call her a siren.'

Dieudonné's deep, gravelly voice echoed in her ear as if she could hear him speaking to her. *'La Sirène,'* he'd named her. She hadn't heard him call her that in far too long. When he returned next month, would he? She hoped so.

'And, like any goddess, she lures and promises ecstasy, wealth and power in exchange for a vow of fidelity to her.'

The man's light brown eyes crinkled at the corners. 'Fidelity? How can a goddess demand fidelity when she has so many worshippers?'

Evena giggled. 'Oh, but that isn't the correct way to think of it, *monsieur.*' She crooked her finger. 'Come closer.'

The man obeyed, bending his head towards her. She whispered conspiratorially, 'See, Mami Wata seduces only those that she chooses. Once they have succumbed to her charms, then she demands their fidelity, after which her worshipper is rewarded with great wealth.'

They both laughed, and Evena knew she had a new admirer from the wondering gleam in his eye.

'It's rather maddening.'

Evena tilted her head. 'What is, *monsieur*?'

'This wretched anonymity. Your company is delightful. I must know who you are, *mademoiselle.*'

Evena shook her head, but she placed her hand on the man's arm. The muscle flexed beneath her fingers. 'You shall have to wait and see. At midnight or thereabouts.'

Taking her gloved hand, Jupiter's eyes were intent upon her as he brought it up to his mouth. 'I shall be in agony till then. Unless…' The man's voice trailed off suggestively.

'Unless what, *monsieur*?' She widened her eyes, knowing that even through the holes of her mask, the flickering light in the room would make them appear like gems.

She'd practised the look long enough to ensure that effect.

Jupiter's voice deepened. 'Surely a goddess knows when a man wishes to worship her.' His innuendo was unmistakable.

'Is that what it is?' She shook her head. 'Well, Mami Wata chooses her worshippers, not the other way around.' She leaned in closer. 'And there is the tiny matter of my honour.'

'Does a goddess need honour when she is powerful enough to bestow riches?'

'Especially then.' Though the man had captured her interest, she wasn't likely to toss her skirts over her head for him. If she hadn't capitulated to temptation on Saint-Domingue, she wasn't going to do so here.

Still, Evena had no wish to offend him, so she said, 'Your offer is tempting, but—' She let her voice die out in a regretful manner.

He brought his lips to her knuckles once more. 'Of course, *mademoiselle*.' Letting go of her hand, the man slowly bowed and backed away.

Evena looked around her. Whoever he was, he wasn't enough of a diversion from what was utmost in her mind.

Dieudonné.

She still didn't know the circumstances of his doomed wedding. When she'd tried to get Ayida to tell her, she'd become uncharacteristically close-lipped. Maybe it was better this way. Once she saw him, she would find out everything.

Dieudonné never kept anything from her. Or at least he never used to keep anything from her.

She frowned. What if he'd changed? After all, five years had passed. He might not feel the same about her. The letters she'd received over the years had been few and far between.

Instead of the long, eloquent messages he used to share with her about his life in France, they had become rather perfunctory and polite. Carefully written, as if he had put a barrier between them.

Was it because of the woman who was supposed to be his bride? Or was it that he simply wanted nothing more to do with her?

A burst of laughter brought her out of her thoughts. Looking around, she could see that although their identities were concealed, she knew who most of the guests were, except for a few.

With a sigh, Evena let the laughter and conversation surround her, basking in the thrill of being a part of the festivities. She'd always loved being in the midst of things, even when she'd lived in Saint-Domingue. Right now, she needed the comforting chaos around her to keep herself from thinking too much.

On a night like this, everyone played pretend. Their masks held off the very real fact that in a few hours the fantasy would end, and reality would set in.

Evena didn't want reality to set in, though. If she closed her eyes, she could imagine that Dieudonné were here.

The hair at the back of Evena's neck prickled in warning, snapping her out of her thoughts. She turned to see if someone was paying any undue attention to her.

Cleopatra chatted with a jester, while a fox and a hunter danced to the music. All around, people were enjoying themselves, but the feeling intensified.

Evena gazed around more wildly, trying to find the source, when her eyes landed on the figure of a masked, shipwrecked sailor who was looking in her direction. Her heart jumped inside of her throat.

Could that be—

No, no it wasn't.

Dejected, Evena stood there, surrounded by people, and for the first time in a long time, she had the urge to get away from everyone.

Alexander the Great was making his way towards her. Before he could get to her, he was waylaid by a minotaur. Grateful for the interruption, Evena hurried through the throng and headed towards the door that led to the gardens.

Immediately, the fresh cool air soothed her.

Under the moonlight, Evena ambled down one of the paths, seeing that others had come out here for privacy. She grinned, seeing a swan and a pirate wrapped in an intimate embrace.

Further along she went until she came to an arbour. The trees' canopy stretched overhead and the leaves under her feet rustled. Glancing behind her, she made sure that she was alone before taking off her mask.

Evena sauntered a little farther along until she came to a bench that was almost hidden.

She didn't like the feeling of isolation that surrounded her. Sinking onto the seat, she sat and absorbed the silence. So alone and lost. How could Sophiette prefer being this way?

The cool air felt good on her heated skin, and Evena lifted her head. The breeze caressed her like a man's hand, but the only one who had done that was Dieudonné.

Blushing as if someone could read her thoughts, she bit her lip. Another few weeks to wait to see if their friendship still existed, even though they had—

The hairs on the back of her neck grew erect once more. Jumping to her feet, Evena whirled around, searching the trees for a sign. Nothing moved, but she knew she wasn't alone.

Angry that someone was trying to frighten her, Evena raised her chin and called out, 'If you're there, tell me.'

A movement from the corner of her eye made her spin

her head in that direction. From several yards away, a figure detached itself from the cover of a tall tree. For a moment a scream sought escape, but she didn't move. Instead, she affected an expression of bravado as the figure came nearer.

It was tall, certainly. A man, by the wide-shouldered silhouette against the moonlight. As he drew closer, she realised it was the shipwrecked sailor that she had seen before.

Her brows drew into a V. 'A sailor,' she whispered out loud, tasting the words, while a strange excitement started to tingle across her skin.

The light of the moon peeked through the trees and landed on his masked face as he stopped a few inches before her.

'Don't tell me you don't know me, *La Sirène*.'

Evena's eyes widened at the sound of that familiar voice. Her lips trembled as happiness she hadn't felt in such a long time filled her. All her problems, all her doubts and fears, melted away, dissipating like a thick fog under a bright, glaring sun as the man removed his mask.

That face. That wonderful, handsome face!

A moment later, she threw herself into his arms. 'Dieudonné!'

Dieudonné couldn't suppress the groan that erupted from his mouth as Evena's softness melted into him. His arms embraced her as if they acted independently of his will, crushing her to him as if they never wanted to let her go.

He was thrown back to that day on the mountain.

The rain above them. The soft earth beneath them. Her fingers tangled in his hair with wild urgency. Her legs moving restlessly, and the preternatural sense that if he kept kissing her for one more heartbeat he would never be able to stop.

The feel of her now threatened to unravel his wits, which were holding on by a thread. He dipped his head into the crevice of her neck and inhaled. A warm, spiced, womanly fragrance flowed deep into his lungs. He savoured it like the sensuous notes of the most exotic flower.

'Dieudonné.' Her voice shook as her arms wrapped around him tighter. A quiver racked her body, and he felt the impact of it against his own. 'I missed you so much.'

'I missed you too,' he murmured, knowing he spoke the truth. Nothing felt as right as being with Evena again. He hadn't felt this complete in a very long time.

How could he have let five years go by without seeing her face again? Being near her again? The hollow feeling that always seemed to exist whenever he was away from her vanished.

Whole again. Connected again.

Evena drew back, her gaze locking onto his. Whether it was a trick of his mind or not, Dieudonné couldn't tell, but her eyes seemed to glow with an otherworldly light. A small tear captured the gleam of the moon on her cheek, and he used his thumb to gently wipe it away.

Her mouth parted, and he found himself leaning forward as if being pulled towards her by something powerful and unnameable, their faces coming closer until they were mere breaths apart.

A creaking noise sounded behind him. It was enough to snap him out of the spell. Swiftly, he pulled back and cleared his throat.

Trying to regain a sense of normalcy, he croaked out, 'Evena, it's good to see you.'

Her mouth closed and she also drew away. 'It's wonderful to see you again.' She let out an airy laugh. 'I hope I didn't embarrass you, Dieudonné.'

His brow furrowed. 'Embarrass me? What are you referring to?'

She lifted her shoulders. 'I've learned, in the few days I've been a guest of your parents, that society has different rules here that aren't on Saint-Domingue.'

'We are alone now, but even that is improper.'

She laughed. 'Isn't it wonderful then that we met on Saint-Domingue? I would have never been able to make you my most ardent admirer.'

A memory flashed in his mind. He saw himself as a young lad, pouting and bowing at Evena's feet after she'd won some game or childish wager. The rather wicked glimmer in her eyes as she'd exacted her revenge.

He grinned. 'You were quite a terror, Evena.'

A well-remembered look appeared in her eyes. The haughtiness that was as much a part of her as her natural inclination for friendship. 'Shall I test your fidelity to me?'

His mouth twisted as he recalled how the Water Goddess would abduct an unfortunate sailor. Plucking at his costume, he said, 'Alas, I'm already shipwrecked. Must you beguile me too?'

Was he speaking in jest or was there more truth in that than he cared to admit?

She spun around in a circle, distracting him from the unwelcome thought. 'Oh, what foolery we got up to back then, Dieudonné. Do you remember how I used to make you bow to me as your goddess? And how I made you give me sacrifices and offerings.'

'But you couldn't bear the thought of me killing an animal. You preferred I catch some creature and then release it. As for the offerings, those were primarily gifts of jewellery, if I recall,' he remarked drily.

'Well, you can't just give Mami Wata rocks, Dieudonné,' she replied in a matter-of-fact tone.

He shook his head ruefully. 'For such a young girl, you certainly knew how to obtain my obedience.'

'A skill all women should learn.'

He chuckled at her audacity. *'La Sirène,'* he said helplessly.

As their laughter subsided, a tense silence lingered between them. The muscles in his stomach knotted. This wasn't good. Not at all.

Why was he still so aware of her? What had happened five years ago was an anomaly, a single circumstance, never to be repeated. There shouldn't be this odd breathlessness taking hold of him again. This strange awe.

It was building, whatever it was. Swelling like some sort of storm cloud. Swiftly, he tried to think of something to break the tension.

Finally, he blurted out, 'I should have known you would dress as Mami Wata.'

He took in the elements of her costume, knowing that very few would be able to recognise the water goddess Evena portrayed.

Evena glanced down at herself, before looking back at him again. 'I…thought you were still in England.'

Dieudonné inhaled a deep breath. From the careful way she spoke, he knew she had heard of his doomed wedding.

He might as well get this over and done with.

'There's no need to be mindful of my feelings. It's true. When my mother wrote to you, I was preparing to marry. But it didn't happen.'

'Why not?'

A wry twist of his lips. 'As soon as I find out, I'll be sure to let you know.'

Evena hissed, her eyes stricken. 'You can't mean that?'

'Quite.' He couldn't keep the bitterness out of his voice. 'I was just as surprised by the absence of my bride in the church as everyone else was.'

'She must have given you some hint of her change of heart?'

The memory of his wedding day rose in his mind. Waiting and waiting and waiting at the altar until it became painfully obvious Agnès wasn't coming.

He shook his head in helpless fury. 'Do you think I'm a fool, Evena?' A humourless laugh burst from his mouth. 'That I wouldn't have made certain that the woman who'd agreed to marry a Creole bastard such as myself hadn't changed her mind? That I would stand before God and man to be humiliated by her?'

Instead of making his life easier and giving him that place in society he so desperately longed for, Agnès's desertion had made everything worse.

'Stop calling yourself that,' Evena snapped. 'You're not a bastard. You're my friend.'

Her angry admonishment broke through the tide of rage he still hadn't got over. He stared into her eyes, seeing her hurt on his behalf.

Dieudonné suddenly felt weary. What did Evena know about it? She'd spent her entire life accepted, wanted and desired. How could she know? Truth was, he didn't *want* her to know what it meant to be ostracised the way he did. Still, he should have known she would defend him, no matter what.

It was time to change the subject.

Tugging the hem of his costume, he cleared his throat. 'Enough of me.' Affecting a light tone, he asked, 'And what of you? Have you or your sister found someone to marry?'

'Not Sophiette, no.'

A jolt went through him. For some reason, he'd expected her to say that she had found no one too. 'No?'

She gave a slow nod. 'I think I will be married to someone before long.'

Now he was confused. 'Someone? What do you mean? It's not as if you're going to marry some stranger.'

He expected her to agree. Instead, her lips drooped at the corners, and this time it wasn't a trick of the shadows. Her eyes dulled.

Immediately, he took a step forward. 'Evena?'

She wrung her hands together and alarm grew within him.

'Really, I shouldn't burden you with my troubles, Dieudonné.'

There *was* something wrong.

'Let's sit, Evena,' he told her, indicating the bench. Gently, he led her there and made sure she sat before he joined her.

He didn't dally. 'What is it?'

For a long while Evena said nothing, studying the back of her hand as if it was the only object in the world worthy of her concentration. Dieudonné waited patiently, crossing his ankles. Evena might love to be the centre of attention but when it came to asking for help she'd rather throw herself into the tumultuous sea instead.

When she spoke, she said the last thing he'd expected to hear.

'Papa may be dying, Dieudonné.'

The words were out of Evena's mouth before she considered the wisdom of uttering them. After five years apart and on their first meeting, the last thing she should be doing was burdening Dieudonné with her family's problems.

Then she remembered the way he'd crushed her to his body so tightly. She'd revelled in the intensity of that hold. Loved it. It was like coming home after a long time away. When he'd gently touched her cheek and wiped that single, inconsiderate tear away…

Evena let out a silent sigh. Who else could she talk to so frankly?

Her eyes roved covertly over him as he sat beside her.

For a few seconds she allowed herself to be swayed by the changes time had wrought in him. Attired as he was, how was it possible for him to seem even more virile?

The last vestiges of boyhood had been swept away, replaced by the gruff exterior of a man who had experienced life.

The loose fit of his sailor's breeches, tied at the knee with bright but worn fabric, emphasised his calves. His shirt hung in tattered rags, showing just a hint of flesh. The moonlight cast an almost bluish tinge, but Evena knew that in the candlelight it would be a golden brown. Dressed in the shipwrecked sailor's costume, he still exuded a commanding presence.

'What do you mean, your father may be dying?'

Just like that, she couldn't let her secret admiration of his masculine charms stall her any more. There was a heavy note of disbelief in the words, as if he expected her at any moment to say it was a jest of some sort.

She'd give anything to tell Dieudonné that it wasn't true about her father's failing health. The severity of their situation finally came back upon her, and she was grateful for the reminder. Too much time had been spent in the past already.

Mournfully, she nodded. 'It's true. He's been ill.'

'What happened?'

She said nothing for a moment, trying to gather her thoughts. 'I'm not sure where to begin.'

'Start at the end,' he suggested.

'The end?' Evena smiled. 'I should have known you would be practical about it.'

'Sometimes, if we start from where we are, we can then ascertain where we've been, and thus can see where we're going.'

She shook her head. 'Well said. The end is that I may indeed have to marry a stranger.'

The entire arbour seemed to become silent as all sound

ceased. Dieudonné hadn't moved, but she felt as if she'd just walloped him in the stomach.

When he spoke, he asked, 'A stranger?'

Slowly, Evena nodded.

'Who?'

'His name is Seigneur de Guise Elbeuf.'

Dieudonné jumped to his feet and walked a few steps away. Evena frowned as she watched his retreating back. 'Are you leaving?'

'I am not,' he said quietly, although his voice seemed to stretch across the distance between them.

'Then why—'

'How did you meet him?' he interrupted in a harsh voice.

'I've never met him.'

Dieudonné was silent again and then he walked a few more steps, still not looking at her. Stopping suddenly, he stood directly in the moonlight and it washed over his face. 'Go on with your story, Evena.'

The past unfolded in her mind's eye. 'Over a year ago, Papa told us he wanted to sell the plantation and leave Saint-Domingue. He sensed things were changing on the island and wanted to get away from it. A few months later, he fell. We didn't think too much of it, but it was peculiar. He'd been a sailor most of his life, and well-accustomed to an uneven terrain. At the time he'd been walking so we assumed that fall was simply an accident.

'Then he fell again. This time, he'd been standing still. He told Maman later that a swooning spell came over him and he lost consciousness, causing his legs to collapse from beneath him.'

A knot formed in Evena's throat as the image of her father appeared in her mind. Claude Baptiste had always been a strong tower of a man. To see him falling to the ground like some helpless invalid...

She wanted to stop the flood of memories, but she couldn't. 'Then came that awful day.'

'What awful day, Evena?'

'We were in Port-au-Prince, shopping. Most of the town has been rebuilt since the earthquake. That day, the earth trembled beneath our feet, and we all stood there in fright. After a few moments it happened again, more violently this time. So much so that one of the signs on the shops fell off, nearly striking my head. Papa rushed forward and thrust me out of the way.

'I've never seen terror on Papa's face as I did then, Dieudonné. His eyes bulged, his mouth quivered, and spittle collected at the corners. He was so frightened that I'd been hurt. When the earth stopped moving and nothing more happened, he grabbed and held me, kissing me in joy.'

She bit her lip. 'After that day, Papa's health noticeably declined. Until one day, we were at the home of a friend when we heard a terrible commotion. We ran and saw Papa being shaken by his friend, but he didn't respond. He was staring at his friend...but he wasn't there.'

'What do you mean, he wasn't there?'

She turned towards Dieudonné, but she couldn't see him, her mind locked onto the happenings of the day. 'Papa wasn't there. His eyes were completely empty.' The next words nearly choked her. 'It was as if his soul had gone away.'

How could she even relate exactly what that moment had been like? To see her father, so big and strong, so capable... frozen as if locked in place by an invisible hand.

'His friend smacked his face and...he came back. Oh, it was the oddest thing, Dieudonné. Papa wasn't there, and then suddenly he was. The light had come back into his eyes.'

Dieudonné gently asked, 'What happened next?'

'Maman insisted we go to the doctors on the island, but they didn't have any answers for us. Neither did anyone else.'

The rest of it came pouring out as she told him about her mother's plan to marry her off.

'That's why we're here,' she finished after what seemed like a very long time.

'I see.' There was an edge to his voice.

She made a sound at the back of her throat. 'As you once told me, marriage is transactional.'

'Are you so eager for this to come to fruition? Is it what you truly want?'

Evena closed her eyes. 'I hesitate to enter into marriage just for my father's sake, but I would rather die than not do something that might save his life. If my husband could convince the King's physician to see him…'

'The physician belongs to the King for a reason, *La Sirène*,' Dieudonné said gently. 'I don't think even marriage to a prince would be able to give you access to the King's officers.'

Her throat thickened.

'What of Sophiette?'

'Sophiette prefers her own company to that of men.'

'And you, Evena?'

The odd note in his voice caused her to look at him. Shadows concealed his face, so she couldn't see him clearly, but his mouth was turned down at the corners.

'What daughter wouldn't do what she could to protect her father?'

'Wait a moment, Evena,' he said incredulously. 'Are you saying that my parents won't help your father?'

She smiled sadly. 'My parents are proud, Dieudonné. They wouldn't want to burden anyone else with this, especially not their friends. I shouldn't have told you, but I have…'

'I'm glad you did. You can always trust me.'

'I know.'

Dieudonné said something under his breath, so low she didn't catch it. Before she could ask him to repeat it, they heard the very faint sound of a church bell.

She sprang to her feet. 'It's midnight! Everyone's going to take off their masks. Come, we must hurry.'

Together, they started to run from the arbour. Well, Dieudonné ran, and she walked as quickly as she could— her costume prevented her from sprinting in the same manner as he did. Dieudonné must have realised that because he stopped and reached behind him to curl an arm around her and help her along.

'Come, *La Sirène*.'

Evena couldn't help but smile.

'What is it?'

She shook her head. 'We're like children again, aren't we? You helping me to come back into the Great House without anyone knowing after one of our midnight escapades. Do you remember how I used to leave the window open?'

'I do.' She could hear the mirth in his voice. 'If only our parents knew exactly how naughty we were!'

They shared a laugh as they hurried back through the gardens, seeing the lights from the mansion breaking up the darkness.

Chapter Five

'There you are.' Liusaidh's hazel-green eyes lit up as Evena neared her. Garbed in the flowing *stola* and *palla* of a Roman lady, accented with golden jewellery, her mother's regal appearance drew the eye. 'You missed the unmasking.'

'My apologies.' A subtle movement caught her peripheral vision. Angling her head in that direction, she noticed the man she'd met earlier that evening dressed as Jupiter coming forward to stand beside her mother, still masked.

Evena's brows lifted. 'I thought you said the unmasking was over?'

A relaxed smile crossed Liusaidh's face. 'It is, *p'tit fi*. I wanted to—'

'Let me, *madame*,' the masked man interrupted. 'I would prefer to do this myself, if you don't mind.'

Liusaidh nodded, saying nothing more.

The man gave a slight bow. 'Mademoiselle Baptiste, I didn't want to reveal my identity until I saw you again.'

She gave a little start. 'How do you know my name?'

He chuckled and, oddly, the sound grated on her ears. Why hadn't she felt like this earlier when they were talking?

'I know almost everything about you.'

Without another word, Jupiter reached up and pulled off his mask. 'I'm Gérard de Lorraine, Seigneur de Guise Elbeuf.'

Evena's mouth formed into an O, and she immediately became flustered. 'Monsieur le Seigneur, I had no idea you would attend tonight.'

'I'm aware of that,' he said as he took a step forward. 'Forgive my subterfuge. It was intentional, *mademoiselle*, to see what sort of woman you were.'

She took no offence at his words. They were being offered to each other in this rather odd transaction.

All this time, she'd wanted to know what the man she would possibly marry looked like. Now, he was standing before her.

Without his mask, Seigneur de Guise Elbeuf cut quite the handsome figure. Tall and imposing, he stood with the authority and demeanour of a deity. His hair, a cascade of golden waves, elegantly framed his strong, chiselled face that seemed sculpted by the finest artisan.

Seigneur de Guise Elbeuf appeared perfect.

Almost too perfect, a part of her mind acknowledged.

His light brown eyes shone in the light. But there was something about them, something she'd missed earlier on. As she took in his presence, studied him, her intuition bristled.

Evena saw past the attractive façade and sensed something was…different about this man.

What it was she didn't know, but a heightened need for flight prompted her to take a step back as if she were going to do that very thing.

'I was just as surprised when I met the Seigneur,' Liusaidh was saying as if from far away and it took an effort to focus on what she was saying. 'But when he introduced himself to me a few moments ago, I was thoroughly pleased to make his acquaintance. It was gracious of him to surprise us tonight, wasn't it, Evena?'

Gracious? That wasn't the word she would use for his

presence tonight. Underhanded, perhaps. He wasn't the King or Queen after all!

A movement from behind her mother caught her eye, and she looked in that direction to see ash and indigo eyes staring back at her. Liusaidh, following the direction of her gaze, turned around and then let out a delighted sound. 'Comte de Montreau!' Liusaidh greeted with exuberance.

'It's good to see you, Madame Baptiste,' Dieudonné answered, the solemn expression on his face replaced by one of genuine joy. 'You are looking very beautiful this evening.'

Liusaidh laughed. 'You are such a flatterer. I had no idea you had returned.'

'I came back only this evening,' he told her.

Evena stole a glance at Seigneur de Guise Elbeuf and gave a little start to see his eyes fixed on her. They had a gleam within their depths. He studied her thoroughly and she could feel his gaze roaming over her body, although she didn't see any trace of lust or lasciviousness in his gaze.

Nor admiration.

Although her costume was modest enough, the few visible hints of flesh along her body now seemed to heat up as his gaze lingered on them.

There was no apparent reason why he was making her so uncomfortable. Upon this first meeting, he'd been polite and respectful.

And calculating. The fact he'd hidden his identity gave her a measure of unease. His explanation for why he'd done so was reasonable, but it didn't dispel the trapped feeling she had in his presence.

She had known different types of men on the island, some cruel and unkind, but most men could be considered decent.

What kind of a man Seigneur de Guise Elbeuf was, she didn't particularly want to find out.

But if she married him, she certainly would.

'Have I introduced you, Comte de Montreau? This is Seigneur de Guise Elbeuf.'

Dieudonné looked at her with an unreadable expression. When he spoke there was a distinct coolness in his tone. 'We are already acquainted, Madame Baptiste.'

A jolt went through Evena. Why hadn't he told her he knew the man?

'Oh, that's splendid then, I was just saying that—'

'Dieudonné!' a voice called.

Evena turned along with everyone else to see Sophiette hurrying towards them.

Dieudonné tried to tamp down the rage coursing through him. He'd seen the look in the Seigneur's eyes as he'd assessed Evena like a horse rather than his potential wife.

Of course, no one looking at the man could see his sense of superiority etched on his face. He knew how to present the exact façade he wanted people to see. Only the very astute could see behind the mask.

Inwardly, Dieudonné cursed. How was it that, of all the people in the country, Liusaidh Baptiste had selected Gérard de Lorraine as a possible match for her daughter? Surely she could tell with one glance what kind of man he was?

No, she couldn't. It had taken Dieudonné some years before he'd discovered the Seigneur was a man who preferred to observe and collect information about a person—their strengths, their weaknesses.

Their most tender vulnerabilities.

A knot formed in his throat. *Especially* their vulnerabilities. And then he would find a way to use them to his greatest advantage. He wouldn't put it past the Seigneur to guess what was in his mind now, but he wouldn't give him the satisfaction.

What Dieudonné hadn't told anyone, not even his family, was that he strongly believed the Seigneur was instrumental in some way to Agnès's betrayal and abandonment of him at the altar.

He couldn't prove it, though, and for that reason alone he'd remained silent.

'Dieudonné!'

Sophiette's voice broke through the simmering anger. Glad for the intrusion, he turned around and then smiled. 'Mademoiselle Baptiste!'

Sophiette hurried towards him, her costume little more than a plain dark blue dress with an eye mask.

As she neared, Dieudonné couldn't help but wonder once again how anyone could think the twin sisters looked alike. They had the same features, but not the same face. Their personalities were too disparate.

Sophiette was a single tongue of candlelight, steady, silent and capable of keeping away the descent of the dark. Although his relationship with Sophiette was not as intimate as the one he had with Evena, he knew enough about her to know what type of woman she was. Any man who made her his wife would need to be careful to never extinguish her gentle yet strong spirit.

Evena was a raging fire, glorious and full of fury. Any man she chose to give herself to would have to be capable of handling her volatile temperament or relish the burn with her.

Thinking of the kiss they'd shared, Dieudonné couldn't suppress a sense of masculine pride. When Evena had gone up in flames, he'd stoked them and burned up with her.

An unwanted image of the Seigneur's hands on Evena's

body flashed through his mind. *Mon Dieu*, he'd cut that man's hands off before he'd ever let him lay a finger on Evena.

The violent thought startled him. What did he mean by that exactly? If Evena wanted to marry the Seigneur, who was he to stop her? He couldn't marry her himself because she couldn't fulfil the requirements for the kind of bride he needed.

Agnès's appeal came from being in the good graces of the aristocracy. Being her husband would have pushed the boundaries but, ultimately, they would have been forced to accept him.

Now he had to start all over again, this time with the further damage to his reputation of being a jilted bridegroom.

A jilted Creole *bastard* bridegroom. Which was going to make his search for a suitable bride all the more difficult.

If he saw Agnès again, he'd be hard-pressed not to wring her neck!

A pair of soft, slender arms went around him in a hug, and he pulled himself out of his dark thoughts.

'It's good to see you,' Sophiette said in Creole. She drew back quickly. Unlike Evena, Sophiette wasn't one to express herself too openly. She was a muted, more guarded, introspective version of Evena. Still, she had an elusiveness which drew certain people to her.

'You're nothing at all like your sister, are you, Mademoiselle Baptiste?'

The Seigneur had come to stand closer to them. His eyes were fixed on Sophiette in a peculiar fashion, as if he were examining her with all the dedication of a man of science.

'Pardon me, *monsieur*.' Sophiette stepped back further, her eyes confused. 'Who are you?'

'You're nothing alike,' the Seigneur murmured again, not answering her question.

Of course, the man would be able to tell the two apart where many others couldn't. He was nothing if not observant.

'How astute of you, *monsieur*,' Liusaidh said. 'Nearly everyone struggles to tell them apart.'

It seemed to take the Seigneur a moment to pull his eyes away from Sophiette, though Dieudonné couldn't be sure. Facing Liusaidh once more, the other man declared, 'Not I. My sense of judgement has always been keen. Neither of you could fool me.'

Dieudonné's jaw clenched, while Liusaidh laughed as if the Seigneur had made a clever joke. How could he blame the woman? Her interactions with the man had been limited. Only Dieudonné knew how deceptive he was.

Evena took a step forward. He sensed the tension emanating from her, saw the slight wrinkle of worry and something more in her features. He wanted to comfort her, but that was impossible here.

Instead, he placed a calming hand on the small of her back as unobtrusively as possible. Her spine was rigid. A slight tremor quaked through her.

At his touch, she immediately relaxed. She sent a grateful look from the corner of her eye.

'*Mon frère!* I thought that was you!'

At the sound of his sister's voice, Dieudonné turned in time for Ayida, dressed as a wood nymph, to fling herself at him. She nearly knocked Evena over and he quickly moved away.

Ayida's arms wrapped around him tightly, and she squeezed as if she was trying to kill him, although he knew she was just excited to see him again.

'You're choking me!' he gasped.

'*Désolée.*' Ayida pulled back, her beryl-blue eyes warm. 'Aren't you glad I wrote to you about Evena and Sophiette? It got you away from that dreadful Sir Ranulf, didn't it?'

Why did it seem as if his sister's voice carried across the room and into the gardens?

'I am.' There was no point defending his friend to his sister; she hated Sir Ranulf, for some reason.

Ayida's eyes gleamed. 'I knew you would be.' She grabbed Sophiette's arm and clutched it tightly to her. 'Sophiette's mine, and Evena's yours.'

The room suddenly quietened, as if everyone had heard the declaration.

'Is that so, Mademoiselle Godier?' The Seigneur's eyes lingered on Sophiette, an enigmatic expression in his eyes. 'Is Mademoiselle Baptiste yours?' His voice had grown quiet, and Dieudonné had the idea the nobleman wasn't asking the question as much as challenging what Ayida had said.

His sister blinked owlishly. '*Oui*. Can't you tell?'

A flush of heat seared Dieudonné's face. 'Oh, Ayida, must you speak so?'

Sophiette laughed, unperturbed by Ayida's frank speech although her mirth subsided when her gaze clashed with the Seigneur's rather intent one, an uneasy expression marring her features.

Still, Dieudonné was glad someone could find humour in his sister's bluntness. *Mon Dieu*, his parents had tried to curb her frank and uninhibited speech for more years than he could count. Finally, they'd thrown up their hands in defeat and simply prayed for the best.

If this was any indication, their prayers were not being answered.

'What?' his sister asked. 'It's the truth.'

'I am tired, Ayida,' Sophiette said, politely covering her mouth. 'Let's retire for the night and then we shall see each other come morning.'

As if her words had given rise to the feeling, a sudden

cloak of weariness descended on Dieudonné's shoulders. With all that had happened, he'd forgotten he'd only just arrived from England today.

'It seems as if your words have reminded me that I am also feeling weary,' he admitted.

'Might I have a few more moments of your time, Madame Baptiste?' Seigneur de Guise Elbeuf had pulled his attention away from Sophiette and addressed Liusaidh.

'Of course, Seigneur. Come, Evena.'

Dieudonné watched as they pulled away from the group and headed over to a corner of the room. Around them, the rest of the guests still lingered, and it was quite possible no one would leave until the early hours of the morning.

For himself, Dieudonné knew he would have to succumb to the dictates of his body, but he longed to know what they were talking about.

He had to pass them going to the stairs. As he did so, Evena's eyes drifted towards him, and he longed to go over and comfort her. Instead, he tried to let her know with his eyes.

The slightly panicked look receded as she seemed to draw whatever she needed from him. That tightly coiled bond between them endured.

Still, Dieudonné couldn't prevent a slight spurt of anger. Tomorrow, he would have a talk with his father. He had to find out what they could do to help Claude Baptiste and prevent Evena having to marry Seigneur de Guise Elbeuf.

The next morning, Evena woke up and stretched her arms far above her head just as the maid came into her bedroom bearing hot chocolate.

Thanking the woman, she gratefully sipped the warming liquid and sighed, then leaned back against the plush pillows wondering what her plans would be for the day. Hopefully, they would include some time with Dieudonné.

An irrepressible giggle came from her mouth. Would he take her anywhere? Perhaps they could travel past the Palace of Versailles. Isadora had promised to do so when she had time, but her own schedule was full. Evena had heard so much about it, even in Saint-Domingue. She couldn't expect to ever explore that place, but certainly she could look.

A knock sounded at the door, and Evena called out, 'Come.'

Liusaidh stood in the doorway. A pearlescent *robe de chambre* of sumptuous silk decorated with delicate flowers and trimmed with lavish lacing hugged her slim figure. Her finery, however, did not distract Evena from noticing the tired lines around her mother's eyes, or the downward turn of her lips.

Calling the maid's attention, Evena handed over her empty cup and sat up. 'Maman? What's wrong?'

Liusaidh dismissed the maid and shut the door behind her. 'Nothing that can't wait, *p'tit fi.*' She lifted her brow. 'I see it didn't take long for you and Dieudonné to reunite.'

Evena looked away from her mother's knowing glance. 'I didn't know he was going to be there.'

'I know. I spoke with Isadora last night and she said as much. He'd just returned from England. But we both should have known. Dieudonné could never miss an opportunity to spend time with you, Evena.'

Thinking of the way he'd held her, Evena could feel heat singe her cheeks. Wanting to change the subject, she asked, 'How long did Papa stay at the party? He was there for a while and then I didn't see him again.'

'What did you think of the Seigneur?' Liusaidh asked abruptly.

Evena nibbled on her lip as she observed her mother's

expectant face. *Bondye bon!* She hadn't even thought of the Seigneur till that moment, her mind had been fixated only on Dieudonné. What was she supposed to tell her?

The truth always helps, a voice reminded her.

Picking at the threads of her silk coverlet, she said, 'Maman, there's something I don't like about the man.'

Her mother frowned. 'Did he do or say anything to upset you?'

'Non...' she answered slowly. 'But—'

The words died on her tongue. How could she tell her mother what she couldn't quite put into words herself? But he hadn't done anything untoward, unless it was showing Sophiette an almost undue amount of attention.

That and the fact he could tell them apart was unsettling.

'Bèl dan pa di zanmi, eh?'

Liusaidh's words quoting the well-known saying brought her back to the here and now. A sigh of relief escaped her.

'Oui, Maman. Pretty teeth don't mean friendship.'

'Or, in this case, marriage.'

Liusaidh wandered over to the window. The morning sunlight highlighted her mother's beauty, and her worry. It was there, carved in every curve of her body.

'Your father had another attack last night. Unfortunately, it was in front of Isadora, so I had to tell her everything. She sent for her physician. That was why your father didn't stay for the rest of the party.'

Evena's heart thudded hard in her chest. 'And?'

'At André's insistence, he thoroughly examined your father...and he didn't think there was anything he could do.'

A cold hand squeezed Evena's throat, choking the air from her lungs.

'When I corresponded with the Seigneuresse she gave me her assurance that they have enough influence at court to approach the royal physician. I know she can't promise he will see Claude, but if she can just ask him to consider doing so, it will be well worth it.'

Evena thought back to last night. Dieudonné had quite plainly doubted the idea that anyone, even a prince, could gain access to the King's physician. If that was true, was Seigneuresse de Guise Elbeuf lying to them? Was this some ploy to gain access to their wealth?

No, that couldn't be the case. She remembered how her mother had told her about the anguish and pain in the Seigneuresse's voice and letters. Their position at court did afford them considerable privileges. That had to count for something.

Was Dieudonné exaggerating the difficulty of approaching the physician? She knew he didn't have the same advantages as the Lorraine family, thus his plan to seek an influential bride at court.

Her head was spinning. Who was telling the truth—the mother of her potential husband, or her bitter friend?

'It pains me to tell you this, but I don't know how much time we have left. However, neither your father nor I will force you into a marriage you do not want. This was all my idea, and I drew you into it. Your father has always been against the notion.' Her mother gave a brittle laugh. 'Even if he hadn't fallen prey to whatever this is, he'd be more than content for both of his daughters to live safely under his wing for ever. Or, if not under his wing, in a convent.'

Evena grinned, although her lips quivered. 'Well, Sophiette may find comfort in a convent, but not I!'

They both shared a strained laugh that petered off into a heavy silence. Then her mother spoke. 'For my sake, can you at least try with the Seigneur?'

Everything inside of Evena recoiled at the thought of

being with the man again. Yet how could she not try? Her father's health was at stake. Wasn't the man who'd loved and cared for her all her life worth it?

'How, Maman?'

Liusaidh moved away from the window and came to sit in the chair before her dressing table. 'He'd like to take you on a carriage ride.'

'A carriage ride?' The idea of being in such close confines with the man didn't make her feel any happier. But could she afford that? If these attacks, whatever they were, were indeed getting worse she owed it to her father and herself to try to do what she could to make things easier for them all.

'Evena?'

Her mother's voice brought her back to the present. There was an understanding gleam in the hazel-green eyes. 'You don't have to tell me now. Just think on it and let me know.'

Dieudonné knew he'd find Evena in the library. Of course he did. The past five years of absence might never have been for the intuition he had concerning her. This morning he'd gone in search of his father, only to learn that the Marquis and Monsieur Baptiste had left for a morning appointment.

After eating a light breakfast in his room, he tugged on his banyan and went to search for her. When he came upon her, he stood for a few moments in the doorway, seeing how the morning sunlight gilded her seated figure.

Evena had wrapped another *tignon* around her hair, this time blood-red. It drew attention to the beautiful contrast of her bronze skin and added an island essence to the sophisticated Parisian gown. The dark gold fabric clung to her like an embrace.

The book in her hand was forgotten as she stared into the

distance. Was she thinking of last night? Or of her father? Or, worse, Seigneur de Guise Elbeuf?

'*La Sirène.*'

Her head whipped in his direction, her face exuding joy. Her eyes looked greener than usual, probably due to the *tignon* that helped to bring out the colour.

'I'm so glad to see you,' she told him as he came further into the library.

Saying nothing, he sat by her. 'What are you reading?'

'I've no idea,' she said candidly, causing him to grin. 'I must have read the same page three times, but I can't concentrate.'

'Why is that?'

Her even teeth drew in the corner of her bottom lip. 'The truth?'

'I expect nothing less.'

She set the book to one side and then angled her body towards him. 'I've been trying to decide if I should let Seigneur de Guise Elbeuf take me out in his carriage.'

The muscles in his stomach hardened. She'd just met the man last night. It hadn't even been a full day and she was already contemplating going out with the man?

'That's rather quick,' he muttered.

Evena gave him a patient, long-suffering look. 'He spoke to my mother yesterday evening and he's already waiting for an answer.'

He bit the inside of his cheek.

You're not wasting any time, are you?

'Do you really want to go with him?' The question came out harder than he intended, but he didn't care.

Evena lifted her shoulder, seemingly unbothered by his tone. 'Doesn't matter. If a man like the Seigneur wants to take me on a carriage ride, shouldn't I go?'

He couldn't keep the sarcasm out of his voice. 'Is that all

that matters? The man shows an interest in you, and you immediately allow him to see you?'

Her nostrils flared while her eyes narrowed. 'Why shouldn't I?'

He could tell they were both starting to get angry. A dull flush of red flooded her cheeks, heightening the contours of her face.

Flexing his fingers, he tried to rein in his temper as he said, 'Remember, Evena, this isn't Saint-Domingue. The men of Paris are different than those you're used to having wrapped around your finger.'

'I doubt it,' she said flippantly. 'In fact, I would say the opposite.'

'He's not a gentleman.'

'Oh? Why not?'

Dieudonné frowned. He only had his suspicions about the role the other man had played in influencing Agnès. To his way of thinking, that was more than enough for Evena to agree that he wasn't a gentleman.

On the other hand, just because the Seigneur had been one of a crowd of young boys who'd regularly taunted him didn't mean he would behave the same way to Evena. He hadn't heard any rumours about the Seigneur treating women callously.

That didn't mean he hadn't, just that there was no evidence to suggest it.

Admit it, you don't want him anywhere near Evena, far less in her bed.

The very idea almost made him choke.

'Dieudonné?'

He glanced into her face, seeing her slightly anxious expression. It wasn't fair to her. She was doing what she could for her father. Adding doubts about her suitor wasn't going to help her.

'Nothing,' he mumbled. 'I just don't care for him.'

'When I mentioned it last night, you didn't tell me you knew him.'

'We went to the same school. When we were younger, we got into more than one fight over him calling me names that I took issue with. So, I know him well enough.'

Evena pursed her lips. 'That was some time ago, Dieudonné. You can't let childish squabbles define a person's character when they reach maturity, can you? If that were true, then you and I wouldn't be here now. I was awful to you at times.'

'That's different.'

'Is it?' The words lingered for a moment. 'And besides, why are you so against my meeting him? It wasn't too long ago that you were willing to marry a woman for the help she could give you.'

Dieudonné stiffened. 'That's different.'

Her arms folded across her chest. 'Is that all you have to say?'

He was indeed starting to sound very much like a parrot. Grudgingly, he said, 'Agnès… Mademoiselle Mercier knew what I wanted from her.'

'Seigneur de Guise Elbeuf knows as well. We haven't hidden anything from him.'

Her logic was sound, but he didn't have to like it.

'Do you think Seigneur de Guise Elbeuf is the only one who might help your father?'

Her eyes widened with hope. 'Is there someone else who could help?'

Me, he longed to say. *The one who knows you best.*

Shaken by the direction of his thoughts, and how much he wanted to be the one who could help her, he went over to the shelves, staring blindly at the spines.

Suppose, just suppose, he could be the one to marry her. But complete social ostracism would be her reward for giving herself to an outcast. Evena was a woman meant for the light. Being in the thick of things and enjoying the company of others was what she basked in. As his wife, she would be forced to stay on the fringe of society. She didn't deserve that.

There had to be something his parents could do. There must be! He owed it to Evena and their friendship to try.

A gentle hand cupped his shoulder, and he turned around to see Evena's eyes had darkened to the colour of moss. 'What if we are running out of time?'

Without thinking of propriety or anything else, Dieudonné drew Evena into his arms, laying her head on his shoulder.

'Everything will be all right with your father, Evena. I'm sure of it.'

She said nothing, keeping her arms around him as if she didn't want to let him go.

He didn't want to let her go either. He felt at home with her. Always had. Always would.

When she drew back, he reluctantly released her. '*Merci*, Dieudonné.'

Words failed him as a sudden urge, a throbbing need, took hold of him. She looked so beautiful, washed in the sunlight, her skin supple and smooth, begging to be touched and caressed. Her full lower lip trembled slightly, drawing his eyes to it. He could hear her moan, 'More…' in his ear as he kissed her.

He wanted to take her lower lip, draw it into his mouth and—

'I'll have one of the servants bring you some hot chocolate,' he said in a rush, his senses whirling.

He had to get out of here right now, or he'd do something

he wouldn't regret, but that could cost them both everything they wanted and needed.

'But—'

Dieudonné ran out of the room as if being chased by demons. Most likely his own.

Chapter Six

'Where are my parents?' Dieudonné asked the servant he came upon in the hall.

'The Marquis and Marquise are in the *Salle des Miroirs*, monsieur. But *monsieur*, I don't think it's a good time to—'

'You may go,' he dismissed the man, and started down the halls to the Mirror Room. When he reached it, he pushed open the door, calling out, 'Mère… Père. I want to speak to you— Oh!'

A wave of heat slashed his face as he caught his parents in a passionate embrace. Stammering, he said, 'I'll come back later.'

'Good,' André said. 'Close the door behind you.'

'Come in and ignore your father,' Isadora countered with amusement.

'He said he'll come back, *mon bijou*.'

Dieudonné rolled his eyes. If it wasn't for the fact he was trying to help Evena he would have done as his father wished. It wasn't the first time he'd caught his parents expressing their love for each other. Over the years, it had become something of a joke with the staff about being careful before knocking on a locked door behind which the Marquis and Marquise were closeted.

On the one hand, Dieudonné was glad to know his parents' physical desire for each other hadn't diminished. He'd heard others speak of losing attraction for one's spouse as marriage went on, but the way his parents acted, he doubted that would ever happen to them.

The few liaisons with women he'd had in his life had been conducted in privacy. He might have been struck by desire, but never by an uncontrollable urgency.

The only time that had happened was on a rainy day in Saint-Domingue when…

Swiftly, he sent the thought back to the recesses of his mind. The last thing he wanted to do right now was think about *that*.

'What did you want to speak with us about?'

'You have impeccable timing, Dieudonné,' his father grumbled in a rueful manner.

'I didn't mean to…to…interrupt you,' he said.

'You did,' André disagreed with a hint of long-suffering. 'Since the time you were a boy, I could almost swear that you've had an uncanny ability to interrupt your mother and me at just the wrong moment. I solemnly pray, with every fibre of my being, that when you have your own children you will have visited on you the exact same torture.'

As Isadora laughed, Dieudonné had the impression his father meant every word he said. 'Don't be so cruel,' his mother went on. 'You're embarrassing him. Now, what is it, *mon cher*?' Her topaz eyes sparkled. 'I'm surprised to see you have torn yourself away from Evena long enough to speak to us. How kind of you.'

André lifted his brow. 'I was actually depending on your preoccupation.'

Dieudonné blinked. It was true that since yesterday he'd been glued to her side. Evena certainly hadn't minded his company. She seemed willing to spend as much time as she could with him. Although he had been to Saint-Domingue many times over the years, it was the first time she had ever been to Paris.

There was so much he wanted to show her and in the coming weeks he had every intention of doing so.

Seigneur de Guise Elbeuf be damned!

Taking a seat across from them, he came directly to the point. 'Evena tells me her father is very ill.'

Isadora's brow furrowed. 'He is. Liusaidh related the unfortunate news to us.'

'Is it true our physician has seen him and is unable to help?'

'What is this, *mon fils*?' André asked, but there was a curious expression on his face, an intentness, as if he knew what Dieudonné was going to say.

'Could you use your influence at court to aid them? Everyone knows the King's physician is the most skilled. If anyone can help Monsieur Baptiste, it would be him.'

His mother stiffened at the same time his father's eyebrows lowered over his bright blue eyes. A pointed look passed between his parents, but Dieudonné didn't understand what it meant. He hadn't asked anything so unreasonable, had he?

Isadora's voice laden with a curious caution, she tilted her head to the side. 'Has Evena asked this of you? Or her mother?'

He shook his head. '*Non*, Mère. This is my request.'

Isadora's shoulders slumped as if some weight had suddenly fallen off them. 'I see.' Again, another look of silent communication passed between his parents.

Despite Dieudonné's optimism, for surely his parents would do all they could to help, something tight coiled in the centre of his chest.

He tried again. 'Père, you know some of the most powerful courtiers in court. Surely you can speak to someone?'

Silence met his words, and the air in the room filled with tension.

André stood and dragged his fingers through his hair, shrugging the wig off his head and setting it on a nearby table. In the mirror behind him, the reflection showed his father's blond hair in a mess with faint greying at the temples.

'It pains me to tell you this, *mon fils*, but we cannot.'

Dieudonné froze. 'What do you mean?'

'We cannot, nor will we, reach out to the King on behalf of the Baptistes,' André repeated implacably. 'It truly pains us that we are not able to do more for them.'

He couldn't help a quick intake of breath as his father's words sank into his brain painfully. 'I can't believe this.'

Was he speaking to himself or his parents?

'You don't understand, *mon fils*.' Isadora reached out to touch him, but Dieudonné jumped to his feet, out of his mother's grasp.

'I don't. So explain it to me.'

André rubbed the back of his neck. 'There are things we can't disclose to you, Dieudonné.'

'These are the Baptistes we're discussing. Our friends.' He glared from one parent to the other. 'Perhaps you've forgotten that.'

'We've not forgotten anything.' André's voice had an edge to it. 'We're not at liberty to help in the manner that you want us to.'

Was this a nightmare? Perhaps he'd fallen asleep in his room and had yet to wake up.

'*Mon fils*—'

Slashing the air with his hand, Dieudonné prowled about the room like a caged animal. Evena's face filled his mind, her green eyes dark with worry and uncertainty. He had promised her that he would do what he could to try and gain access to the King's physician. How could he disappoint her with his failure?

'We've accepted their hospitality so many times over the years. They've been a part of our lives for as long as I can remember.' Gesticulating wildly to Isadora, who sat on the chaise with a frozen expression on her face, he cried out, 'You've told me more than once that the Baptistes are your closest friends.' He let out a harsh sound, bitter and hard. 'Not just *your* closest friends, but mine too. Evena is dear to me. I care for her a great deal. I can't just stand by and do nothing to prevent her from having to marry a man who isn't worthy to lick the shoes on her feet!'

'They are our friends.' Isadora looked as if she were about to weep. 'And truly, we don't want Evena to be trapped in an unhappy marriage. But we simply can't do what you're asking of us.'

'Can't?' he asked, feeling his fingers flex. 'Or won't?'

'Can't,' his father returned. 'And we're not going to discuss this any more.'

There was an implacable tone in his father's voice that he hadn't heard in a long time. As far as André was concerned, the discussion was closed.

Dieudonné stared at two of the people he loved most in the world and felt his heart shrink in the middle of his chest. His mouth tightened. How could they do this to Evena? To him? If she had to marry the Seigneur, he'd destroy her little by little, attacking her weaknesses until she was nothing but a shell of her former self.

If anyone knew what kind of havoc the Seigneur could wreak, he did. He couldn't let that happen to her.

Never had he felt so helpless and useless.

'If we could, don't you think we would have done so already?'

Isadora's words broke through the whirling chaos in his brain. A sort of madness was taking over his mind, his body.

A slight tremor took hold of his limbs and he had a hard time controlling it. 'Could?' His voice had risen an octave as his restraint on his temper started to unravel. 'What the devil is preventing you?'

His mother's eyes had a glassy sheen. She looked over at his father in a pleading way. A muscle leapt along André's jawline, and he gave a minute shake of his head.

For the first time in his life, Dieudonné realised that his parents were hiding something important from him. Never would he have guessed they could keep a secret from him.

Him! Their eldest son!

No, a nasty voice echoed in his ear. *You're not really their son, are you?*

It was like being gutted by a broadsword. Dieudonné wouldn't have been surprised if his stomach split open at that moment and his insides spilled onto the floor.

No, he wasn't their son. Just an illegitimate nephew who hadn't deserved the title bestowed upon him anyway.

Wasn't that the reason why Agnès had left him at the altar? Because she couldn't, in the end, bear the stain of marrying a man like him. It had been easier for her to leave him to deal with the humiliation of her desertion.

His blood boiled as all the injustices of the past flashed in his mind—the taunts, the shunning, the fights, the looks, the sneers.

Isadora and André knew what he had lived with his entire life. They knew, and if anyone should have been able to give him some sort of dignity, some sort of recompense for what the world had repeatedly punished him for, it should have been them. His parents. The people who were supposed to love him the most.

But no! For some unfathomable reason, they would not help him when they knew how much it meant to him.

Was he supposed to stand there and let Evena give herself to a man like Seigneur de Guise Elbeuf?

'You're both cowards.' He spoke out loud, not realising that he had until the words left his mouth. Then it was as if a dam had burst, and he couldn't stop. 'You're both despicable cowards.'

'Dieudonné!' Isadora gasped, her hand shaking as she covered her mouth.

'How can you call the Baptistes your friends? They've never asked for our help before. And now, in their hour of need, you reject your Christian duty to provide it.'

'*Soyez silencieux*, Dieudonné. You don't know what you're talking about.'

The note of icy warning in André's voice hardly broke through the maelstrom inside him. All Dieudonné could see was Evena's face. How was she going to react when she realised he had failed her?

He glared at his mother, the words spilling out of his heart filled with such pain, such anguish that he almost collapsed from the weight of it. 'You sit there, crying, as if your tears mean anything,' he accused.

A sob was wrenched from Isadora's mouth, but that was nothing to the animalistic snarl that came from André's lips before he marched over and yanked Dieudonné by the lapels of his coat, giving him a shake of fury.

'Don't you ever speak to your mother like that again,' André hissed through thinned lips. His eyes were hard like shards of ice. 'Do you understand? I don't give a damn how angry you are with us. I won't allow you to disrespect your mother.'

A tiny voice inside him told Dieudonné to stop. To consider his words.

The heat of rage and pain drowned out the solemn advice.

'She's not my mother,' Dieudonné rasped. 'Nor are you my father.'

Isadora let out a cry, the sound reminiscent of a wounded animal. 'Dieudonné, how can you say that!'

The anguish in her voice touched a small, rational part of him, trying to bring him back to the realm of reason. He couldn't enter that realm. This betrayal by the people he loved most in the world prevented that.

André's blue eyes narrowed into slits. 'How dare you?'

With a burst of strength, Dieudonné gripped those hands that had lifted him in play and embraced him with love. Without another thought, he snatched them away from his clothes, shoving André away.

Shocked anger contorted the man's face before he took a step towards him, ready to do battle, when Isadora jumped up and lay a quieting hand on André's chest.

'Don't, André,' she said. 'He doesn't mean what he's saying.' She gave a watery smile. 'Do you? You don't really mean it.'

'I mean every word… *Tante*,' he stressed deliberately. He slid his gaze over to André. *'Oncle.'*

Isadora's face paled, making her eyes look like nuggets of gold. 'Dieudonné—'

'Let it go, *mon bijou*. Let it go.'

For a moment, Dieudonné longed to take back the words he'd just uttered, but then he remembered Evena, who would be forced to bear the burden of his failure.

He couldn't forgive them for this. He just couldn't.

Silently, he left them standing there, feeling their eyes probing his back even as he slammed the door behind him.

'Are you sure I look presentable, *sè*?'

'Oui,' Sophiette answered as she patted at the *tignon* around Evena's head. 'All eyes shall be riveted to your person.'

Evena pulled on her bottom lip with her teeth and eyed her reflection once more.

The new, rather rustic *robe à la polonaise* in forest-green and gold fitted her figure in a snug fashion. Her *tignon* she'd chosen with care, making sure it added charm to her outfit. In a way, the headscarf connected her to Saint-Domingue and right now, she needed the comfort of home. Atop her head, she'd placed a green wide-brimmed hat trimmed with gold ribbon, tilted at just the right angle to shadow her eyes.

Blowing out a cleansing breath, Evena nodded to the maid who came forward with wide eyes and carefully draped a velvet-lined *mantelet* across her shoulders.

If she were in Saint-Domingue, she wouldn't think twice about what she wore. Now, she was filled with nerves.

Would she come to regret this?

A knock at the door, and then her mother stepped inside. 'You look delightful, Evena. I'm sure the Seigneur won't be able to stop looking at you.'

'*Mèsi*, Maman,' she replied.

'You must hurry, now. He said he would call for you at half past three and we are nearly there.'

Writing the acceptance to the Seigneur's offer was one of the hardest things she'd ever done. Conflicted by her love for her father and an innate sense of self-preservation, she'd capitulated for the sake of her father.

She had to give the Seigneur a chance to change her mind about him. Maybe he wasn't as terrible as her instincts told her. She couldn't expect all men to be like Dieudonné.

Speaking of Dieudonné, where was he? Had he spoken to his parents yet? Would they be able to help?

She didn't hold out much hope. Even though the Marquis and Marquise had connections, that didn't mean they could sway the new King to aid her father. She'd wanted to tell Dieudonné to stop when he'd broached the topic with her yesterday. Yet he'd insisted he could persuade his parents to help.

Evena hadn't the heart to tell him otherwise. He could be stubborn like that.

Like a lamb to slaughter, Evena followed her mother and sister and made her way down the winding staircase in her finery. The door knocker rattled just as the chime rang half past the hour.

Never had she been less excited to meet a man.

Standing in the doorway, she could at least be thankful the Seigneur was handsomely dressed in a peach-coloured frock with a high turned-down collar. Sunlight landed on his blond hair, revealing its curly texture.

The man was attractive, there was no denying that. But good-looking men were plentiful. Good men weren't.

He came forward as she arrived at the bottom of the stairs. His eyes were fixed on her, but he had impeccable manners as he greeted her mother. 'Madame Baptiste, a pleasure to see you again.'

'The pleasure is mine,' her mother answered.

'Mademoiselle...' he addressed her sister '...I trust you're well today.'

Sophiette mumbled under her breath and moved away. As usual.

When he looked at her, his brown eyes glowed with admiration. 'Ah, Mademoiselle Baptiste, may I say you look *magnifique?*'

'Merci, monsieur,' she responded, feeling some of her inner tension fade.

'I'm looking forward to our drive. I'm not sure how much of Paris you've seen, but the route I have planned will be sure to give you a lovely approximation,' he said.

Despite herself, excitement coursed through her. She'd wanted to see more of Paris. 'I look forward to it.'

His eyes lifted to her hat and he coughed. 'If I may be so

bold, there is something I must ask. The carriage is open… will your hat be…safe from the wind?'

Evena grinned. 'Oh, *oui, monsieur*. Not even a hurricane could rip it from my head.'

They both laughed, and a little more of her unease melted away. He seemed rather charming if she could get past her initial uncertainty about him. Maybe her intuition was wrong?

The hair on the back of her neck suddenly stood up on end just as she heard, 'What's all this?'

Dieudonné!

Turning around, Evena watched as Dieudonné walked towards them. The skin of his face was tight, as if he were controlling some great emotion beneath the surface of that studied blandness. He moved in a deliberate way with each step measured as he drew near.

When he came to stand next to her, the air about him reached out to her with invisible gossamer threads, trailing along her skin and sending goose bumps up her arm. She couldn't help but notice where he stood, to her side and a little in front of her as if he were shielding her with his body.

'Ah, Comte de Montreau,' the Seigneur greeted him in a cool voice. 'A pleasure to see you again.'

Dieudonné gave a curt nod. 'Seigneur.'

'We're going for a carriage ride,' Evena supplied and then inwardly winced. Dieudonné already knew that!

'Is that so?' he asked as if it were the first time he had heard about it.

The Seigneur lifted a shoulder. 'I thought it would be pleasant to give Mademoiselle Baptiste a chance to view Paris as she's never seen it before.'

Dieudonné scowled. 'We can easily do that for her. No need for you to bother going out of your way.'

Evena's eyes widened. If she didn't know better, she would think Dieudonné was jealous.

Seigneur de Guise Elbeuf's brow arched. 'Hardly a bother, Monsieur le Comte.' His eyes drifted to her and lingered. Her skin flushed at the blatant admiration she saw. 'A pleasure,' he went on, his voice low and intimate.

If Dieudonné ever looked at her that way, she'd probably melt to the floor! As it was, the Seigneur's gaze made her aware of just how warm everything seemed to be in this exact moment.

Warm enough to challenge the sun on Saint-Domingue!

A quick glance at Dieudonné showed a muscle leaping along his jawline. In a tight, hard voice, he said, 'I hope you enjoy your drive, *mademoiselle*. I shall look forward to hearing about it later this evening.'

'Oui, monsieur,' she said formally. How she longed to clasp her arms around him as she had in the library.

The other man extended his hand to her. 'Shall we, Mademoiselle Baptiste?'

Evena couldn't help looking back and forth between the two men. Her past and her potential future. One she wished to cling to with both hands, while the other she was hoping would be the honourable man she needed, who would use his influence to help her father.

Swallowing hard, she dragged her eyes away from Dieudonné's cold face and made herself take the Seigneur's arm as he led her out of the door. One last glance behind her as he helped her into the carriage showed Dieudonné standing in the doorway watching them.

At any other time, Evena could perhaps delight in the beauty and elegance of the Champs-Élysées. Instead, all she could see was the look of disapproval on Dieudonné's face.

'Tell me, *mademoiselle*, how long have you known the Comte de Montreau?'

Evena gave a start. She'd forgotten that she was supposed to be making herself agreeable to the man by her side.

Clearing her throat, she turned towards him. His brown eyes were already on her, and she found that unnerving. Why was he watching her so intently? 'I've known him most of my life, *monsieur*.'

'Is that so?'

'Oui.' An uncontrollable smile came to her face. 'He and his family often came to Saint-Domingue. The Marquise de Lyonnaise is from there and she didn't like being so far from her homeland.'

'She is Creole, isn't that so?'

'Oui. That's how the Comte de Montreau's family and mine became acquainted.'

'What makes him such a close acquaintance to you?'

Evena frowned. 'Why are you asking me these things, *monsieur*? Is there something you'd like to know?'

'There is, but I was trying to be tactful.'

Like a crocodile at a tea party.

'In what way?'

'I understand that Saint-Domingue doesn't have quite the society we have here in Paris. Certain behaviours that would be unacceptable here, for instance, may well be encouraged there.'

Evena's nostrils flared. 'Are you doubting my chastity?'

At the startled look in the man's eyes, Evena shrugged. 'I have no reason to lie to you about that, *monsieur*. If I were not chaste, my mother would not have begun talking to yours.'

'Mothers only know what their sons and daughters tell them,' he murmured in an odd voice.

'Perhaps,' she conceded. 'But my mother knows her children well.'

They sat in silence for a few minutes. She tried to enjoy the scenery again, but it blurred in her eyes.

Papa. I must do this for Papa.

'Tell me, will you be attending the Duchesse de Villers-Cotterêt's *fête du jardin* next week?'

Evena gave a slow nod. 'I will. We received the invitation yesterday.'

'Excellent. I put in a good word for you and your family with the Duchesse.'

'*Merci beaucoup.*'

He waved away her thanks. 'There's no need. It's part of our bargain after all, isn't it? The Duchesse is a *princesse du sang*, you know.'

Her heart leaped into her throat. A princess of the blood? That meant she had familial ties to the Crown!

The Seigneur and his mother had kept their word. They'd said they would be able to connect her family with the King's physician. They were one step closer to doing that.

'That's so very kind of you.'

The Seigneur took her gloved hand and brought it to his mouth. He held her gaze as he placed a kiss along the knuckles. She could feel the heat of his lips permeate the material as if she were bare-skinned.

A shiver went down her back, alien and unwanted.

'*Monsieur...*' she breathed, thoroughly confused.

There was a knowing look in the man's eyes, but when he spoke it was only to say, 'I would be honoured if you'd allow me to have the first dance with you at the Duchesse's garden party, *mademoiselle.*'

She tugged at her hand and he let her go instantly. Clearing her throat, which had gone dry, she answered the only way she could.

'The honour would be all mine, *monsieur.*'

You'll have to marry him now, a voice in her head said. *You no longer have a choice.*

Chapter Seven

The Duchesse de Villers-Cotterêt's chateau was burnished like a stone queen under the moonlight. Before the towering edifice, a row of lanterns lined the front of the residence, lending their flickering light to the cobblestone pathway leading to the massive ornate garden *à la française* east of the mansion.

As night descended, the revelry of the garden party grew in intensity. Dieudonné strolled by servants who stood at intervals with torches as he and the other guests walked along lit paths leading to sections of the garden formed in intricate geometric patterns.

His eyes took in the area that had been set aside for dancing and as the guests started to gather, the music from the string quartet began to play.

'Your envy is showing, Dieudonné.'

Rattled by her comment from his silent, brooding contemplation, Dieudonné spun around and met the flame-lit eyes of Sophiette.

'I didn't see you there, Sophiette. My apologies.' He'd hardly been aware of anyone else. His eyes drifted back to Evena; he'd watched as she'd danced with various men on the outdoor ballroom floor.

She was dressed in a gown of silver silk, beaded here and there with rubies and sapphires. A dark wig decorated with a plume of feathers topped her head. In her element, she laughed and smiled, and even the most critical women were unable to find anything wrong with her appearance or manners.

'Did you hear me, Dieudonné?'

Blinking, he refocused his attention back on Sophiette. 'Did you say something?'

Sophiette laughed. 'You can barely pay attention to anything because you're so focused on my sister.'

There wasn't any point in trying to deny it. When Evena had come back from the carriage drive with Seigneur de Guise Elbeuf she'd been subdued. Muted.

What had happened during that drive? When he'd asked her, she'd refused to answer him, saying that it was none of his concern.

For the first time in their lives, she was keeping secrets from him.

'He didn't hurt me, Dieudonné,' she'd said, as if that would reassure him. 'That much I can tell you.'

'Hurt isn't always of a physical nature, *La Sirène*.'

Her eyes had turned sad, the bright green dimming. 'No. It isn't.'

Since then, she'd pulled away from him. He hated it.

'Why won't she talk to me?'

Glancing down at Sophiette, he was struck by the quiet, gentle beauty of her eyes. Like Evena, she wore a dark wig. Unlike her sister, she had chosen a gown of olive green, rather plain, which did nothing to draw attention to herself.

Her gaze was kind and understanding. 'She wants to. There isn't a doubt in my mind she wishes to tell you everything that is in her heart.'

'Then she should. We've kept nothing from each other before.'

That was what made this distance between them so terrible. How could one go from sharing a lifetime together to nothing?

'She's trying to solve this on her own. You must allow her to do so.'

'And that means giving herself to some man who isn't fit to breathe the same air she does?'

A complicated look crossed Sophiette's face. 'She's trying to do the best thing for our father, Dieudonné. You understand that, don't you?'

He blew out an exasperated breath. 'I do, but—'

'You don't like it,' she finished for him. She touched his arm. 'Evena is doing what I cannot, Dieudonné.'

'What are you talking about?'

Sophiette grimaced. 'My mother told us that we needed to try to obtain husbands who might be able to help give my father a chance. Papa's attacks have increased in frequency and intensity, Dieudonné. We don't know what else to do. Despite it all, I can't—I just can't marry a stranger.'

Her eyes filled with tears and Dieudonné gave a soothing pat on her arm. 'No one is blaming you, Sophiette. Least of all me.'

'People frighten me,' she whispered. 'It takes a lot of effort to simply say hello. I look at them, talking and chattering, and I'm overwhelmed. Whenever I'm forced to be around them, I feel as if my soul is being pulled from my body. It takes days to recover.'

The anguish in her face distracted him. 'You're a shy soul, Sophiette. There's nothing untoward about that.'

'Why must I be so different? How is everyone in my family able to tolerate the company of others while I cannot?'

'If you were like everyone else, then I would be forced to talk to my sister a lot more than I already do.'

Sophiette gave a startled laugh, and he was glad about it.

Evena had once said Sophiette found people stressful and exhausting, but she'd never said anything about her sister being truly unnerved by their presence.

'That is true. I adore Ayida. I've only ever really been comfortable around her. And your family,' she added quickly.

'Let's not pretend. You only tolerate us because of Ayida. And yet you're here with me. Why?'

'I know you're jealous of any man who has my sister's attention. If things were different, she would have been with you right now and I would be hiding in the corner.'

Dieudonné didn't bother to deny Sophiette's words. They were true. He was jealous and it sat on him like a too-tight coat. 'What do you suppose I do about that?'

'You've been standing there for nearly twenty minutes, watching as my sister has danced with three other men, including Seigneur de Guise Elbeuf. So why not dance with me?'

His eyebrows lifted into his hairline. 'Dance with you? You just said you're terrified of being in a crowd.'

'As long as you're with me, I won't be.'

Sophiette gave him a brave little smile, but Dieudonné knew what it had cost her to approach him. Admiration welled inside him for her bravery.

Almost against his will, he found himself once again drawn to Evena's dancing figure. It was like watching a single star twinkle in the night sky.

His lips firmed. 'All right then.' He stepped forward and gave her a formal bow. 'Shall we dance, Sophiette Baptiste?'

Nodding, she shyly took his outstretched hands and as the music played they began to dance the elegant fluid steps of the minuet.

It was obvious within the first few seconds that Sophiette was having difficulty. Even in Saint-Domingue, with the livelier dances, she could never keep up with the tempo. She moved as if her feet were tangled with each other.

Still, he persisted. It was the only way for him to be close to Evena.

He watched her change partners, now dancing with his brother Iménel before partnering with Seigneur de Guise El-beuf again. It was hard to tell if she was having a good time or not. He thought not. Evena always showed her emotions. As he looked on, he could see she had her expression locked in a bland, polite little mask.

His nostrils flared. Why wouldn't she talk to him?

'It'll be fine, Dieudonné. Trust me, it will be.'

Sophiette's eyes were brimming with tears again, but be-cause she wanted to put him at ease she was willing to deal with her own fright. Setting aside his frustration with Evena, he went out of his way to soothe her twin.

After the minuet was completed, the music for the alle-mande started up. Ayida commandeered him, talking inces-santly the entire time. From there, he had an opportunity to dance with their hostess and three other women.

By the time another minuet played, he'd allowed himself to relax and enjoy the festivities.

'Mon fils?' The hesitant voice of Isadora sounded behind him. His back stiffened, but Dieudonné turned around to see her golden gaze fixed imploringly on him.

The distance between them hadn't been resolved. Over the past few days, he'd stayed away from the family home and gone to his own estate in Montreuil. This was his first time seeing Isadora in almost a week.

He sighed. Why did things have to be so complicated?

'Would you like to dance?' he asked.

Isadora came to where he stood and took his hand.

While the music played, Dieudonné struggled with what

he should say to her. Should he forgive her and André? Even though he had rejected them as his parents in the heat of the moment, he knew he still considered them as such.

When they'd refused to help the Baptistes he'd wanted to hurt them just as they had hurt him. But calling them aunt and uncle felt wrong. They were his mother and father. They always had been, and that was what he would always call them.

That desire to hurt them had faded in the time away from them, but his confusion remained.

Why were they so unwilling to help? After he'd calmed down, he'd gone over everything that had been said. Once he had considered every part of the conversation, he'd realised that his father had told him they *couldn't* help. That implied there was something preventing them from doing so. What could it be?

The music ended. Isadora looked up, her gaze steady and unwavering.

Dieudonné knew he should apologise, but a stubborn streak inside him, probably inherited from his father, refused to do so. Still, he bent and kissed her on the cheek and squeezed her hand. An understanding gleam entered her eyes.

A flash of colour caught his attention and he turned to see his father standing not too far away, watching them intently. Taking his mother's hand, he led her back to the Marquis. They stared at each other for a long moment and then he nodded. André seemed to know exactly what Dieudonné was saying. His father drew Isadora to his side in a protective gesture, but the understanding look in his eyes let Dieudonné know that the sharpness of his anger had dulled.

As had his. Would things ever be the same between them? It remained to be seen, but nothing would change the love he felt for the two people who loved him in return.

Another dance started. He straightened his shoulders and

tugged on the hem of his coat. Whether Evena liked it or not, she was going to dance with him.

His eyes roamed over the area in search of her. A frown creased his brow. He didn't see her or the Seigneur.

Frowning, he strolled through the crowd, trying to find her. At any moment now he expected her to come forward in her silver gown and take command of the scene. A few people spoke to him, but Dieudonné responded without being aware of what he said.

Where was Evena? It wasn't like her to be away from a party.

A slither of unease trailed down the middle of his back and he picked up the pace, scouring every inch of the party.

He couldn't find them anywhere.

Finally, he went over to the walled pathway that led from the garden to the chateau. Entering the narrow cavity, he started walking down it. The party sounds were instantly muted by the thickness of the walls.

Had she and the Seigneur gone into the chateau? For what purpose? Surely they hadn't gone for some kind of tryst?

Dieudonné instantly dismissed that thought. No, Evena wouldn't do that.

But what about the Seigneur?

Dieudonné quickened his steps, goaded by some instinct he couldn't explain, a sixth sense telling him to hurry.

Just as he'd nearly reached the end of the labyrinthine pathway, he heard a faint cry. He recognised it—Evena!

His heart pounded as he ran towards the source of that cry. The wall ended at the open entrance to a small foyer.

Coming to a halt, he strained his ears to listen. Where was she?

'Please, stop! Don't do this!'

Dieudonné spun around. Behind him, a room off to the side. Without a second thought, he charged into the room.

He hardly registered the picture before him as rage coursed through him. Evena's face was contorted in distress, her lips pulled back from her teeth, her glassy eyes full of fright as her outstretched hands pushed at the Seigneur's mouth, which was almost touching the skin of her throat.

Instinctively, Dieudonné lunged towards the man, grabbing him by his coat and yanking him away. The sound of fabric tearing rent the air like a wail of pain. The Seigneur stumbled back, falling onto his bottom.

Dieudonné's breath panted as his desire to pummel the villain surged. He'd been trying to force himself on Evena! Did he think he was worthy to even kiss her slippers, much less put his mouth on her flesh?

Standing between Evena and the Seigneur, he watched with hard eyes as the man glared up at him.

'Get up,' Dieudonné snapped, his voice low and dangerous. 'And get out.'

A sardonic expression crossed the man's face as he lumbered to his feet. 'Ah, if it isn't the Creole bastard coming to the aid of another of his kind,' he drawled.

Every muscle in Dieudonné's body seized at the hated taunt.

The Seigneur stood, dusting off his clothes, his face losing some of its handsomeness as it turned cruel.

Dieudonné's teeth ground together. 'It's obvious some things don't change, *monsieur*. Now you've harmed someone very dear to me.'

'She amused me for a time. But it seems as if the game has come to an end. I enjoyed it while it lasted, though.'

With that remark, the man smirked and left.

Dieudonné seethed, but he leashed his anger. He turned around to see a minute tear in the lace of Evena's gown.

She looked devastated, as if her whole world had come to an end. He knew that expression—had worn it himself, in the presence of the same man.

'Come, *La Sirène*.' Gently, he took her into his arms, wanting with every fibre of his being to expunge the film of disgust the other man's presence had left behind.

Evena shook with reaction, trying to get her trembling body under control, when all she could think about was the repugnance she'd felt when the Seigneur had tried to kiss her.

How thankful she was that Dieudonné had come in time to save her. That was exactly what he'd done. Saved her.

'Do you want to tell me what happened?'

She closed her eyes, still shaking, remembering everything with perfect clarity.

'He started to feel faint, he told me,' she said. 'He didn't want to embarrass himself, so he asked me to accompany him here so he could sit down for a while.'

It had all seemed so innocent. Although she had come no closer to liking the man, for the past week she had tolerated his presence with some measure of equanimity. Her mother had been optimistic about the match, especially when they'd been invited to this party.

'We came in here, and he changed. A kind of…darkness fell over his face. And his eyes were so…so…'

'Dead,' Dieudonné finished for her in a blunt tone.

Startled, she pulled back and looked up into his face. Bleakness suffused his features and his eyes darkened.

'The man has no soul, Evena. I've suspected it for a long time, but he's clever at hiding it. He appears to be alive but he's not.'

Dieudonné placed a warm finger on her chin and gently

lifted it up. In his eyes, she saw not condemnation for being such a foolish woman, but compassion.

'You knew it, though, didn't you?' he asked softly. 'Some part of you knew he was evil, even though you were trying to avoid the truth, hiding it even from yourself.'

Tears filled her eyes. '*Oui*, Dieudonné. I did.'

There was nothing but silence for a few moments. Then he lowered his lashes, veiling his eyes. 'I told you that I've known him since I was a boy and he was one of those who taunted me about my illegitimacy. But it's more than that now.'

'What do you mean?'

His chest shuddered as he inhaled. 'I met Mademoiselle Agnès Mercier almost a year ago.'

Evena glanced away.

'At our first meeting, we found that we enjoyed each other's company. Over time, she kept paying special attention to me. I realised then that her interest lay in the fact she liked the attention she received by being seen with me. I used that to my advantage and eventually I asked her to marry me.'

His arms tightened around her.

'There was no love between us, Evena. Just opportunity. Although her family isn't as impoverished as the Lorraines, she wanted what my wealth could give her. Although her father, Baron Henri Édouard Mercier, is a favourite of the King, favourites of royalty risk falling out of favour at any time.'

'You don't have to explain it any more. I truly do understand.'

Dieudonné was willing to marry a woman who only saw him as some sort of unique trophy to show off to her friends. He'd been willing to live life in her shadow as long as her influence would make him accepted amongst his peers. To anyone else, it would seem as if it were ill-advised, but Evena understood. A woman like Mademoiselle Mercier would be the ideal candidate as the kind of wife he needed.

'But you told me you didn't know why she left you at the altar.'

He was quiet for a moment, and she listened to the thrum of his heart beating. Then he spoke. 'That's partly true, Evena. But I do have my suspicions.'

'Which are?'

'Seigneur de Guise Elbeuf is her cousin through their mothers. I think he convinced her to humiliate me.'

Evena gasped and pulled away, staring up in shock at Dieudonné's face. 'Why didn't you say anything to me?'

'Why would I?' he countered in a low voice. 'It didn't have anything to do with your possible engagement.'

'*Au contraire*, it has everything to do with it!' She pushed away from him, anger washing away her anxiety. 'Do you think I would have gone this far with that man if I'd known he was actually related to the woman who betrayed you?'

'You've been trying to do everything you can to save your father,' he replied.

'But my loyalty is to you, Dieudonné.'

A look crossed Dieudonné's face then, but she was too disturbed by what he'd just told her to make much sense of it. He looked as if she'd struck him in the chest. She almost wished she had. How dare he keep this from her? Did he think her father would be comfortable with the knowledge that in order to find the help he needed he'd take assistance from a man who had hurt a close friend so badly?

Why hadn't Dieudonné told her? It would have made things so much easier. She could have told her mother to cease talks with the family, could have cut the Seigneur off.

'I can't be that selfish, Evena. Your father needs all the help he can get. Why would I stop you?'

She whirled on him. 'You should have let me decide what I wanted to do. If you had, I wouldn't have—'

Thinking of his grasping hands and the hard, determined expression in the Seigneur's eyes, she shivered again in revulsion. She wanted to take a bath and rid herself of his touch.

'I can't prove any of this, but his connection to Agnès was the only thing I could think of to explain why she jilted me. For goodness' sake, the marriage contracts had been signed. It was a mere formality by the time the ceremony had come.'

'Why would he tell her to not marry you?'

His eyes narrowed as his nostrils flared. 'Why do you think? He hasn't changed from the boy he was. He was never going to accept having a Creole bastard taint their noble bloodline.'

'Did you really think I'd mix my noble blood with inferior stock like yours?'

The memory of the ugly words the Seigneur had whispered in her ear as she'd fought against his superior hold made her skin crawl all over again. He'd never intended to marry her, just as he'd prevented Agnès from marrying Dieudonné. Whatever his mother wanted, he'd only ever seen her as some sort of exotic doll to play with. A virgin Saint-Dominguan woman he could take advantage of without worry of consequences.

Her lower lip started to quiver and her vision blurred. 'You should have told me about their connection, Dieudonné. Should have trusted me.'

Without saying a word, he drew her deeper into his arms and held her close. Tears of fear and relief leaked out from under her eyelids and she sobbed against his coat. She didn't blame Dieudonné for what had happened—that rested solely with Seigneur de Guise Elbeuf.

But the fact he hadn't told her let her know without a shadow of a doubt that he hadn't believed she would support him.

That hurt. *Mon Dieu*, it hurt. Evena sobbed harder.

'I'm here,' Dieudonné whispered against her hair. 'I'm here.'

'Of course you are,' she wept into his coat. 'Of course you are. You've always been here.'

But never close enough, no matter how much I wish you were!

His arms tightened around her and she let herself wail against his chest, expelling the tumult of emotions she'd experienced while in the Seigneur's presence.

'I truly think he would have forced himself on me if you hadn't come, Dieudonné.'

The muscles underneath the fabric of his clothes tautened. 'Then I would have killed him.' From the darkness that entered his voice, Evena knew he spoke the truth.

For a short time, she simply let him hold her as the terror of the moment dissipated.

Then she became aware of their intimate position. Alone, in a tiny room that overlooked the lavish gardens, but still secluded from prying eyes.

She became aware of Dieudonné's physical presence. The hardness of his body, his scent. She became aware of the thudding of his heart against her cheek as it increased in tempo, thrumming along his breastbone. She became aware of her breathlessness and the wicked way her thoughts had started to change.

Slowly, she gazed up into Dieudonné's face to see the same need reflected in those masculine features.

Don't be foolish, a voice in her head screamed as the blood roared in her ears and her breathing escalated. *Nothing can ever come of this.*

Suddenly, Dieudonné's mouth descended on hers, and Evena moaned in ecstasy at the taste of him just as she went up in flames.

It happened too quickly, without any sort of graduality. Her fingers clasped his head and clutched him to her. She wanted to taste every crevice of his mouth, feel the strength of his kiss, and know beyond any kind of doubt she could only feel this way with him.

Dieudonné groaned in the back of his throat and he moved, pressing her against the wall, making her mewl in pleasure, which only fuelled the desire blazing through her. He kissed her, taking her mouth again and again, stoking the fire inside.

The past five years had led to this moment, this place. Like any prisoner who'd lost their will, Evena surrendered to the molten fire that pooled in all the sensitive spots of her body. No, nothing could come of this, but right now, none of that mattered. She was willing to accept what she could.

Her breasts felt heavy, swollen and tender. Eager for something she'd never had, but knew instinctively Dieudonné could give her.

As if he heard her thoughts, his fingers stroked her breast through her gown, circling her nipple until it hardened and then lightly tugged at it.

She hissed in agonised delight, and Dieudonné opened his mouth to swallow the sound. His hand slid into the neckline of her dress. When his fingers lightly pinched her nipple, a violent, restless, hungry thing sank low into her belly.

Evena forgot. She forgot that, just moments earlier, she'd been shaking with fury and fear that the Seigneur had tried to take her despite her refusals. The fact they were in a secluded room in the chateau that would be visible to a watchful eye from the garden slipped her mind. She didn't care about anything else. Didn't care that she'd have to begin her search for a new potential husband to help her father all over again.

This would likely be her only chance to feel this way with Dieudonné. It wouldn't go to waste.

She forgot everything but his taste. The way he knew her body's responses that she had no idea what to do with, and simply let herself float adrift in their sea of mutual desire. She didn't understand the sensations storming through her, thundering in her veins and sending lightning streaks of want all around her body.

A sudden sound, alien and intrusive, disturbed the cocoon that surrounded them. Dieudonné murmured something against her mouth, but she didn't want to hear what he had to say. She wrapped her arms more tightly around his neck and lifted herself up onto her toes, pressing her breasts into his chest.

A violent shudder went through him, and he nearly crushed her against him.

'Dieudonné! Evena!'

Buckets of ice-cold sensation washed over her, startling Evena out of her desire.

Dieudonné tugged his mouth away. They stared at each other. His face was drawn tight, stark and harsh. Her lips felt swollen, and she still had the taste of him in her mouth.

When she finally dragged her gaze away from Dieudonné, it was to see not only Isadora, who'd called their names, but the Duchesse de Villers-Cotterêt as well.

The Marquise came forward with a brilliant smile. 'I see we've interrupted an intimate moment, but that's to be expected following such good news. I'm so pleased you've accepted my son's offer of marriage, Mademoiselle Baptiste.'

Chapter Eight

Dieudonné knew he should never have kissed Evena. Certainly, he shouldn't have allowed that wild, leaping thing inside him to take control the moment his mouth touched hers.

But he was starting to realise he was weak when it came to Evena. Some of it could be chalked up to their friendship, but it was becoming clear there was far more to it than just that. There was something not related to their friendship that made him want to give her everything she ever needed or wanted.

In those moments, she'd wanted him with a fervour he'd never experienced with another woman. One touch and they had practically attacked each other.

'*Mon fils?*'

With the greatest effort, he dragged his eyes away from Evena's flushed, passion-filled face to see the smile on his mother's face, and the pointed look in her eyes. Only then did he become aware of the other woman in the room.

The Duchesse, who was studying them with a shrewd eye.

Just then, like a distant echo from a bell, he recalled what his mother had just said.

Marriage. To Evena.

'*Oui*, Mère,' he uttered in as calm a voice as possible. 'Mademoiselle Baptiste did accept my proposal.'

He glanced down at Evena to see the colour had fled her

face. She looked as if a feather could knock her over. In that silver dress and wig, it made the pallor of her complexion even starker.

'That's wonderful news,' the Duchesse said briskly as she came forward. 'I adore weddings. When should we expect to hear the joyous event will take place?'

'We'll be sure to let you know,' he answered after a breath because Evena looked as if she were going to be physically ill.

'I'll leave you to speak privately, but I would be offended if you didn't share this exciting news with our guests before you leave.'

Now it was his turn to stare at her.

Did this woman want him to announce their engagement in front of everyone at the party? He'd done that once before with Agnès and that hadn't ended well.

'What a marvellous idea, Madame la Duchesse,' Isadora said, clasping her hands together in seeming delight. 'We'll do so.'

The Duchesse left, leaving behind a tense silence one could have cut with a knife. His mother's smile vanished like morning mist, and she looked back and forth between them.

'*Mon fils*, you have to see that we must do it this way, don't you?'

'*Madame*, why did you—?' Evena began, but his mother held up her hand.

'Oh, *ma petite*, people noticed that you had been gone for quite some time. Not to mention the rather furious expression on Seigneur de Guise Elbeuf's face when he came back to the festivities alone and then promptly took his leave. What did you think people would say?'

'But marriage, *madame*!' Evena looked stricken.

Why did she look so devastated at the thought of being his wife? Would it be so terrible to marry him?

No, it wasn't him, he suddenly realised. It was because of her father.

She had wanted marriage to the Seigneur because of his connections that could lead to an appointment for her father with the King's physician.

Could he do that for her? No.

Not for the first time in his life, Dieudonné was ashamed of his birth. His illegitimacy made him a pariah. His Creole blood made him a barely tolerated outcast. If he had been of legitimate birth, he could have helped her. His mother could have gained respectability if his father had married her. He'd only wanted the same thing for himself and yet now he'd never obtain it.

He clasped his hands behind his back to keep the fact they were shaking in fury from observant eyes. Never had he felt so helpless and so pathetic! What sort of man, having been shunned and rebuked his whole life, would willingly put a woman he cared about through that sort of thing? What about his children? It would be cruel to them as well.

Yet there wasn't any way he could go out there and say that he and Evena were not betrothed. Her reputation as a chaste woman was all she had to stand upon. It wasn't fair, but it was the way of society. She already had her race as a strike against her.

Still, this was his dear friend. He'd sworn to himself that he would do what he could to help her.

Was compromising her helpful?

The nasty voice in his head made him frown. Where had that come from?

Remembering how Evena had become undone in his arms, he gave himself a mental shake.

He hadn't compromised her against her will. They had both succumbed to an undeniable passion that flared up between them. It had only taken a single spark to ignite into an inferno. Just like five years ago.

If you had controlled yourself, you wouldn't be in this predicament.

The truth nearly knocked him over. He should have pulled back. She had already been assaulted by Seigneur de Guise Elbeuf. He should have comforted her, calmed her, not…

Burned with her.

He took a deep breath, trying to dispel the threads of shame crawling like worms along his skin.

There was no other explanation for it. No excuse. He was responsible for what had happened and because of that, her father's life might well now be forfeit.

Evena would blame him, and he would have no one else to blame but himself. The other problem was one he couldn't ignore either.

Evena couldn't give him the entrance into the highest circles of society he'd always craved. She couldn't pave the way for him gaining acceptance and respect from his peers. Quite the opposite. They would be tied to each other for ever, locked into a marriage that would only cause each of them great pain.

He wouldn't wish that on his greatest enemy…and certainly not his dearest friend.

How could this have happened? Evena wanted to scream.

She'd ruined Dieudonné's chances of finding the woman who would help him be accepted and belong. She was just a Saint-Dominguan heiress, with no ancient French lineage. His title and wealth meant nothing to him if no one would allow him in or respect him as a person. And she didn't have the right influence to make any difference.

'Are you all right, *ma petite*?'

Isadora looked at her with worry in her eyes. Evena wanted to reassure her, but there wasn't anything she could say.

Dieu! Why had she thrown herself at Dieudonné when he began to kiss her?

Because you wanted to.

Well, that was true. No point in lying to herself about that.

'I'm fine, *madame*. Just a little overwhelmed, that's all.'

She glanced over at Dieudonné to see a hardened expression on his face, as if he were trying to keep his emotions from showing.

He must be so furious with her! Even if he had initiated that kiss, did she have to respond so…so…

Helplessly. Utterly unable to ignore the way he made her feel.

She couldn't have suppressed her response to him any more than she could have told the moon to dim or the stars to fall from the night sky. It had been unavoidable, uncontrollable.

Destined?

'To be honest, Evena… Dieudonné, I'm not too surprised this has happened.'

Evena gasped. 'You aren't?'

The Marquise shook her head in an amused manner. 'Of course not. We knew it.'

'We?' Dieudonné asked coolly.

'Your father and me.' Isadora gave them an indulgent look, her face creased in a soft smile. 'You've been close for so long. We feel joy thinking of our families connected by marriage. Honestly, despite the circumstances, I'm rather glad. I never did approve of the other women you've pursued over the years, Dieudonné. Your father and I never did understand why you chose them, but who were we to interfere?'

Evena glanced at Dieudonné, who met her gaze as if he

knew what she was thinking. He must have kept the worst of his ostracism to himself. She didn't even have to ask why. If his parents knew the full extent of his suffering, it would pain them greatly. They probably only saw Agnès Mercier's desertion of him as extremely poor taste and manners.

Which it was, but there was far more to the story, as she now knew.

Evena felt her stomach roil. Isadora didn't have any idea what she was talking about. She and the Marquis might well express their joy at their union, but Liusaidh was going to be very disappointed.

A cold dread came over her. What was she going to do to help her father?

Dieudonné couldn't help her at all, nor could his parents. The people she had met these past weeks all seemed wonderful, but none of them would be willing to come to her father's aid. She would save her reputation, but she knew their marriage would do no good for the man who would be her husband.

'You've been good for each other over the years and we're pleased.'

The Marquise looked at Evena's slightly torn dress and said in a dry voice, 'But it does appear my son's passion is of an ardent nature, so we won't delay the wedding.'

There was no point in correcting her. It was better for the Marquise to think she was wanton than to know the truth of the Seigneur's assault.

Despite the mess she found herself in, she was profoundly thankful for one thing—at least she wouldn't have to marry that horrible man.

If she had to marry someone to protect her honour, at least it was Dieudonné. He'd always let her do what she wished, within reason, of course. It wasn't just an indulgence. Rather, it was taking her as she was without censure. Dieudonné Godier liked her as a person...but would he like her as a wife? Would he come to regret being with her?

'Let me see what I can do to repair your dress,' the Marquise was saying, bringing her back to the matter at hand. Her golden-brown eyes gleamed. 'So when we announce your engagement, no one will think it's because you're with child.'

Evena wanted the ground to open and swallow her whole.

By some miracle, the Marquise was able to repair her gown with some clever tucking and using a lace handkerchief to cover the tear. Unless one was looking closely, no one would be any the wiser.

The next half hour was a blur. She stood by Dieudonné's side and accepted the congratulations of the well-wishers. Sophiette and Ayida gaped at her as if she'd grown a horn out of the middle of her head.

She didn't even have to look at her twin to know she wasn't fooled. She'd soon be forced to tell Sophiette everything.

All the while, Evena tried to keep her expression from showing her despair. Before she had allowed that kiss to spiral out of control, Dieudonné's suspicions about the Seigneur and his possible involvement in Dieudonné's failed wedding had sent her reeling. How awful if it was true. It would have been a devastating, humiliating blow when Agnès had abandoned him at the altar in front of all those members of society whose respect he craved. Put in perspective, her lack of control seemed even more heinous.

She had ruined Dieudonné's only chance at getting what he wanted. Would this cause him to resent her for ever?

'Evena, how could you have allowed this to happen?'
By the time they had returned from the Duchesse's garden

party, it had been the early hours of the morning. There hadn't been any opportunity to talk as weariness had taken hold of them. Once the maid had undressed her, Evena had fallen into a dreamless sleep, waking only when the clink of the hot chocolate cup the maid brought forced her from slumber.

She'd barely had time to take a sip from the cup before Liusaidh had come barrelling into the room, her *robe de chambre* billowing about her like the wings of some avenging angel.

Evena had wanted more time before she faced her mother, but that wasn't going to happen. Now, as she squirmed under the direct gaze of those hazel-green eyes, she knew she had to give some explanation for her actions.

What could she say? Apologise for succumbing to Dieudonné's kisses? Beg forgiveness?

'Maman, do you know what happened?'

Liusaidh frowned. 'Isadora said that you and Dieudonné were found in a compromising position. She had to think quickly to save your reputation, for which I am truly thankful, but I don't know what to do now.'

She stared at her mother, seeing the worry lines on her face. 'Maman, that's not all that happened last night.'

Her mother tilted her head. 'What are you talking about?'

Evena set the cup of hot chocolate down on the tray. 'Dieudonné saved me from Seigneur de Guise Elbeuf.'

'What do you mean?'

'Sit and I will tell you.'

Liusaidh brought the chair nearer to the bed and sat as Evena related the story, only leaving out her response to Dieudonné. When she repeated the words Seigneur de Guise Elbeuf had spoken to her, her mother moaned like a wounded animal.

'I hoped he would be different,' Liusaidh said as Evena finished. 'That he would be an honourable man.'

'I did, too,' Evena replied. 'If you believe nothing else, Maman, please know I wished for that too.'

Liusaidh rose from her seat and went over to the window, gazing out at the morning sunshine. At the pensive expression on her face, Evena felt guilt beat a steady rhythm in her breast.

Had she doomed her father?

After a moment, her mother turned back, and her expression was surprisingly clear. 'Well, *p'tit fi*, we won't worry about it. What's done is done. Luckily, there wasn't anything formal about your association with the Seigneur. I received a message from him this morning, severing contact with us due to your "improper conduct".'

Evena almost cursed, but her mother shook her finger. 'Let it go, Evena. We will accept Dieudonné into our family as we always have.'

Evena bit her lower lip. Without looking at her mother, she asked, 'Are you angry with me, Maman?'

She heard movement and then the bed dipped as her mother got in beside her and wrapped her arms around her.

Evena closed her eyes, feeling tears smart the corners. She hadn't realised until this moment how much she'd needed her mother's reassurance.

'No, *p'tit fi*, I'm not angry with you. I'm worried about your father, that is all, but I'm most upset with myself.'

'What do you mean?'

Liusaidh pulled away, cupping Evena's face in her hands. 'I placed the burden of your father's well-being upon your shoulders. That was very wrong of me. Claude may be your father, but he is *my* husband. My responsibility to care for, not yours.'

'I don't understand.'

A gentle look came into her mother's eyes. 'You're about to marry, Evena. To a man who I know cares about you. But you are going to be his wife and that is quite a different thing than being his close friend.'

Evena's lashes lowered over her eyes. 'I am aware of the marriage bed, Maman.'

'Are you? Marriage isn't just about pleasing one another in bed. It is love and hate. Passion and pain. Melody and frightful noises. I think you are so used to seeing Dieudonné as a friend that you may forget that he is also a man.'

'I do know that.'

'A man is more than some passionate kisses. They may excite you and fill you with pleasure, as I am sure Dieudonné will.'

Thinking of how he'd touched her last night, Evena almost blurted out that she was right, but her mother kept speaking.

'You care for Dieudonné. Everyone knows that. You also desire him, as evidenced by what happened last night. But do you love him, Evena? Does he love you as a man should love his wife?'

Of course he doesn't, she longed to wail to her mother. *I'm his very last choice for his bride.*

Liusaidh leaned forward and kissed her cheek before rising from the bed. 'You don't have to answer me. Just think about these things for yourself. There's much we have to do to prepare for the wedding.'

'Will it be a public affair?'

Her mother gave her a sly look. 'Would you want it any other way?'

The door closed behind her, cocooning Evena in her thoughts.

Her mother's words made her purse her lips. Did she love Dieudonné? If she said that she did, what did it mean?

Was it the type of love poets wrote about? The all-consuming song of the heart? She didn't know. She'd never really thought about it before.

Their friendship had always been their main point of connection. Whenever he came to Saint-Domingue, that was at the centre of everything.

Until that last time, when the dynamics had completely changed.

Now, their relationship was going to change again. He wasn't going to be Dieudonné Godier, friend of the family, but her husband.

Her husband.

Something rippled through her at the thought, and she burrowed deeper into the covers. *Mon Dieu!* No longer would she be Evena Baptiste, but the Comtesse de Montreau. She felt nothing but honour at the prospect, although being Madame Godier would be equally welcome. His title didn't make him an honourable man, but his actions.

Then that niggling voice in the back of her head spoke.

She wasn't the kind of wife he needed. The kind that could open doors to the elite at court. Mingle with those who could elevate his status.

To help him belong.

Dieudonné didn't need her wealth. He had his own from the estate of his deceased father, and whatever benefits the Marquis would bequeath to him at some later point in the future.

What could she do for him as his wife?

Nothing. Nothing at all.

Evena pushed the covers away and got out of the bed. Padding over to the window, she stood before it as her mother had done, looking out and seeing the distant figure of a statue in the gardens.

She recalled how closed-off Dieudonné had been last

night, standing by her side and yet so far away from her. He'd avoided looking at her, as if suddenly he couldn't stand the sight of her.

Stop it! That's not true.

Then what was it? Why had he acted so distantly? They had shared a kiss as potent as opium, touched and caressed each other with the eagerness of impatient lovers.

Why would he behave as if none of that had even happened?

Maybe he truly was furious with her.

The door burst open and Sophiette dashed in, her eyes wide. 'Leave nothing out, *sè*,' her twin said as she took a chair and pulled it towards her.

'Really, Sophiette! You look like a cat salivating over a mouse.'

Her sister looked nonplussed. Gesturing with her hand, she asked in an incredulous tone, 'What did you expect I would do, *sè*?'

What, indeed? Without another word, Evena told her everything that had happened. Sophiette listened with rapt attention, transfixed by her every word.

After she'd finished, Sophiette was quiet for several minutes. Evena knew she was considering everything she'd heard.

Finally, Sophiette asked, 'What were they like, *sè*?'

Evena pretended not to understand. 'What was what like?'

'Dieudonné's kisses?'

She opened her mouth to admonish her sister and tell her that she was treading on thin ice, when she stopped herself. Closing her eyes, she relived the whole experience.

When she opened them, Sophiette's eyes met her own. 'Beautiful. Passionate. Overwhelming. I didn't want them to end.'

Sophiette let out a wistful sigh, staring off into the distance at something only she could see. 'I wonder if I shall ever experience such as that. A man's passion. What would it be like to be swept into his arms and taken away to wherever he goes?'

Evena couldn't believe what she was hearing. Sophiette had always avoided talk of a sensual nature, like some people avoided curses. 'You surprise me, Sophiette.'

Her twin gave her a rather sly look. 'What do you think Ayida and I talk about? Dresses?'

She blinked. 'I never really considered it.' Coughing delicately, she added in a pointed fashion, 'It would require you to be in the presence of men. Not hiding in corners playing the harpsichord.'

Sophiette's shoulders slumped. 'But people frighten me. Still, I long for a husband and family of my own. Could a man ever want a woman like me?' Her eyes widened in fear. With an audible swallow, she tugged at the sleeves of her dressing gown. 'Well, isn't it a good thing that you will be his wife soon? When he takes you to bed, it won't end until both of you says it does.'

Evena couldn't prevent the hitch in her throat at the image her sister's words conjured. The possibilities stole her breath away.

'*Oui*, Sophiette,' she whispered. 'It's a very good thing.'

The moment Dieudonné stepped into the garden, an orchestra of sensory delights enveloped him. The sweet fragrance of blooming flowers mingled with the earthy scent of the freshly trimmed hedges. A gentle breeze whispered through the trees and rustled the leaves, bringing a refreshing coolness to the warm day.

He longed to enjoy it, to bask in the pleasure of the moment, but the rocks sitting in the pit of his stomach wouldn't allow it.

How was he going to approach Claude Baptiste about marrying Evena? Would the man resent him?

There was only one way to find out.

It didn't take long to find Claude. Ever since he'd come to Paris, whenever the man had wanted to rest and reflect, he'd gone to the gardens, to sit before the statue of the goddess Minerva.

He found him there again. Claude must have heard him coming because he stood as Dieudonné approached.

Looking at Claude, no one would think he was having a crisis of health. With his feet planted firmly apart and hands clasped behind his back, his bearing was reminiscent of the sailor of his youth.

'I knew you would come to see me, Comte de Montreau.'

The man's deep voice somehow bridged the gap between them. Dieudonné felt the tension leave him in slow degrees. For as long as he could remember, Claude had referred to him by his title. On Saint-Domingue, it didn't matter as much, but he appreciated the respect.

'Monsieur Baptiste, it's not a surprise why I am here.'

The older man sent him an enigmatic glance. *'Non.'*

All the words of the speech he'd prepared for this moment fluttered away like butterflies. He couldn't think of anything to say.

Claude lifted a brow. 'I'm listening, *monsieur.*'

'I'd like to offer my sincere apologies for compromising your daughter. I hope my offer of marriage shows you how highly I value her reputation.'

It sounded formal and pompous, but it was the best he could do. He was sure the words he'd rehearsed were far better.

The older man said nothing for a few moments, simply

studying him with an impenetrable gaze. Then, 'Won't you take a walk with me, *monsieur*?'

Dieudonné gulped. 'Of course.'

They started down one of the many paths that meandered through the garden.

'I spoke with my wife, and she told me that my daughter was saved by you, *monsieur*.'

Dieudonné gave the man a curt nod. 'Seigneur de Guise Elbeuf had tried to take advantage of her. I came to her aid before much damage was done.'

'So how was it that you were the one who offered marriage to her?'

I could barely keep my hands off her.

Dieudonné coughed. It wasn't likely he could tell the man *that*. There was such a thing as too much honesty. Besides, did Claude want to hear how his dreams last night had been invaded by visions of Evena? Or that he'd awakened with a clawing desire to have her in his bed so he could finish what they'd started in that little room?

That was something at least. Agnès, for all her beauty and birth, had left him utterly cold.

A cold bed is preferable to a cold reception in society.

Stop it! he told that nasty little voice.

There was little point in rehashing what could have been or what might have been. What was done was done.

He pushed all that to the side.

'*Monsieur?*'

Dieudonné came to a halt, and Claude did the same, eyeing him in an expectant manner.

How had he got here? Never in his wildest imagination had he pictured himself in this moment. His memories were wrapped and entangled in Evena, but Claude was there too, a distant authority figure whom he respected almost as much as his own father.

'I allowed my feelings to override my duty to protect her virtue. I apologise to you for that.'

'Why are you apologising to me? Are you truly sorry?'

Dieudonné swallowed the sudden lump that came to his throat. How to answer that?

No, he wasn't sorry he'd experienced bliss in Evena's arms. What man would regret finding a woman as passionate as her? Was he supposed to forget that he'd drunk the sweetness from her mouth with all the need of a desperately thirsty man?

What good was that when everything he had worked for was gone? If they had children…

Sacre bleu! If they had children, they would be subjected to the same treatment as he. Rejected, and left out in the proverbial cold. Forced to bear the vitriolic gossip and castigations. No, he wouldn't bring a child into the world forced to live like that. No matter how tempting and sweet and fiery Evena was, he could not allow their union to bring forth a child.

Tugging at his collar, he answered, 'I am aware Evena wanted to try to obtain the hand of the Seigneur because of his connections with the King.'

'That's true.' Claude rubbed his cheek in a thoughtful manner. 'It was my wife's idea. I had no desire to burden them with my troubles.'

Dieudonné pursed his lips. '*Monsieur*, do you know Evena told me about your attacks?'

Now it was Claude who gave him a cautious, wary look. 'I do.'

'Would you permit me to ask about the nature of these attacks? She said you've fallen, and you experience swooning spells. I will not speak of it to anyone. I'd just like to under-stand what is happening to you.'

Evena's father rocked back on his heels. 'Well, *monsieur*, it happens without warning at times. At others, I am given some warning. A sense of nausea, and a distinct sourness at the back of my throat. Then the room, the world even, spins. Wildly. I can't stand upright. It spins so badly that I...'

Claude stopped talking, a bleak expression on his face. 'Can you understand what it is like for a man who has sailed on troubled waters to be unable to stand on solid ground?'

Dieudonné could see how badly it affected the man. 'I can only imagine it, *monsieur*.'

The other man nodded. 'Lately, the attacks have become more frequent. Just last night, I suffered two of them. It is very disheartening to know there is nothing I can do.'

Dieudonné could see Claude's anguish and the guilt that lingered within him sank deeper inside. The thought churned in his mind, billowing and swelling like debris in gusts of wind.

His desire for Evena had flared out of control, robbing him of common sense. At the time, the idea of not touching her had felt as if it would be tantamount to sacrilege.

Now, her father would have to pay the price for his actions.

His parents said they could not help, and he did not have the standing or access to the King to try to plead on Claude's behalf. It was a far stretch to think that the King would lend his physician to Claude, but to not even try...

If something happened to Claude, if help could not be found in time, Evena would surely hate him for taking away the chance to find the man who could be of assistance to her father.

She would hate him for the rest of her life.

Chapter Nine

It was a curious sense of *déjà vu* Evena experienced as she and Dieudonné entered the Parisian home of the Duchesse de Villers-Cotterêt. Hôtel Villers-Cotterêt was smaller than her country chateau, but no less luxurious.

Around her, the grand foyer, with its marble floors and a sweeping staircase, gleamed under a majestic crystal chandelier.

To her left, she could see the salon, its high ceilings capturing the conversations of those who gathered under it. Everyone was dressed well, so she didn't feel her attire was out of place.

'I don't want to do this,' Dieudonné said under his breath as the attendants removed their outer garments. 'We should go back.'

Looking at his face, Evena could see the lines of strain there, a bleak expression in his ash and indigo eyes. Her heart broke for him. How often had he come to an event like this, only to be ignored or gossiped about or even insulted to his face?

Her lips firmed. Well, he wouldn't have to deal with that any more. She was no Mademoiselle Mercier, but she was Evena Baptiste.

His dearest friend.

'We have to do this. Hold your head high, Comte de Montreau, and beard the lions in their den.'

He gave her a startled look, but then he smiled, revealing those deep dimples she hadn't seen in such a long time. His hand found hers, bringing it to his lips and placing a gentle kiss there.

Evena's heart thudded in the centre of her chest.

'As you wish, *La Sirène*.'

That odd breathlessness came over her once more. Lately, she'd seemed more aware of him. Whenever Dieudonné came into her vicinity, even for a moment, her body would stiffen, the blood would pulse, and she'd have a difficult time controlling her responses.

What was this new sensation curling through her? *Mon Dieu*, she'd known Dieudonné her entire life, but sharing his kisses had awakened something else inside her she had a hard time coming to terms with.

For the past fortnight she'd received an intimate understanding of what these people thought of him. According to Ayida, everyone was talking about them since the engagement had been announced.

Isadora had fielded some of the worst gossip, inviting some of the less acerbic nobles for dinner to ensure they saw Evena and Dieudonné as a legitimate couple. Among those who had accepted was the Duchesse. The noblewoman, for some unfathomable reason, had taken Evena under her wing.

It was as if the Duchesse's approval had opened more doors for Evena and she finally understood what Dieudonné had always longed for. She had wanted a robust social life when she'd thought she might have to marry Seigneur de Guise Elbeuf, but this was something else entirely.

The Duchesse's social calendar was quite active, making Evena's privileged and affluent life in Saint-Domingue pale in comparison. Whenever Evena could, she joined the woman, using the opportunity to speak highly of her future husband.

Because the Duchesse had taken to her, Evena tentatively began to form a closer bond with the woman, opening up about her life on Saint-Domingue, discussing the various issues and complexities of the island, while praising its natural beauty and its people.

Slowly, ever so slowly, she could see a barrier begin to fall. The other woman began to ask questions and listened with an eager ear. As far as she could tell, the Duchesse didn't have much interaction with the King himself, but she had a notable place among the court.

Maybe, just maybe, she could use the Duchesse's connections to her advantage and still help her father. So she'd kept at it. Even her usual limitless stores of energy had been depleted in the past two weeks, but she didn't complain. There was so much at stake.

Her upcoming marriage, so she could be the wife Dieudonné needed.

Her father's health, so he could be seen by the very best physician.

One night, when she came home late from some event or other, Sophiette had laughed at her, though not unkindly. 'I am glad it's you and not me. I would have hurled myself off the highest tower by now.'

Evena had laughed dutifully at her sister's joke, but she knew what she had to do.

Dieudonné had given up, but she hadn't. She had to do what she could to make the proper connections with the right people. If she could somehow use her natural talents of conversation, and show her skill at being a potential hostess, it would surely ease his way.

So she dazzled with gaiety, listened with keen ears and mingled without being overly intrusive. Strategically, she aligned herself with other women she sensed she could trust in some manner. Her nature was not to be deceitful, but she was honest enough with herself to understand that the likelihood of developing an intimate friendship with anyone here was low. Still, she did want to cultivate a genuine, mutual relationship with women of status she might depend on in the future.

Although it was taking some time, her efforts were finally just starting to come to fruition. Dieudonné might regret marrying her, but it wouldn't be for lack of trying on Evena's part.

Coming here hadn't been part of her plans tonight, but when the Duchesse had invited them at the last minute to her salon, Evena had known they had to attend. For one thing, it was the first time she and Dieudonné had been invited together. That had to be a good sign.

By the skin of her teeth, she'd bathed and dressed in enough time to meet him when he'd arrived at the door. He'd gazed down at her, but she had no idea how to read his face. Had he come to resent her, despite all her efforts? Did he wish he'd never succumbed to the passion that leapt between them at the chateau?

Perhaps she was indeed a wanton because, despite all the recent turmoil, she clung to that memory with both hands. They had been close for many years, but she'd sensed things would be different from that day on. They already were.

'Are you going to trust me?' she asked now.

Something in his ash and indigo eyes softened. He took her hand and led them inside.

A brief silence met their entrance. *Exactly* what she'd wanted.

Evena knew she and Dieudonné made a bold sight among the French nobility. The titled, illegitimate Creole comte with his Saint-Dominguan wealthy heiress on his arm.

She'd dressed with care, donning a patterned *robe à la française* in dark blue linen chintz with small crimson flowers. Ayida had pinned a large-petalled flower to nestle just underneath her breasts, while wrapping a gauzy blue kerchief around her shoulders. She'd tied a bright red *tignon* around her head and allowed the tail end to drape over her bare shoulders in a playful manner.

Dieudonné looked debonair in his own attire, unknowingly matching her in tone with a dark blue ensemble and his hair pulled back into queue. If nothing else, they looked like well-appointed members of society. In France, where clothes made the man—and the woman—it was important to look their best.

The murmurs began again, this time with people looking at them. Just as she went to take a step forward, she heard a frighteningly familiar voice.

'A pleasure to see you again, Mademoiselle Baptiste.'

She came to a sudden halt, sending a quick glance in Dieudonné's direction. His lips thinned, and she knew he was doing his best to control his own anger.

How dare Seigneur de Guise Elbeuf show his face here?

Then she retracted her thought. He was acquainted with the Duchesse. Of course he would be here as well. She should have thought of that, but for the past two weeks she hadn't seen the man at all. Nor had she revealed what had really happened between them to anyone outside of her family.

In a single movement, they turned around and she felt Dieudonné's fingers clench on her own. She made no attempt to hide her contempt as she replied, her voice dripping in sarcasm, 'Likewise, Seigneur.' Anyone listening would know that was the furthest thing from the truth. Her skin prickled in memory of his touch.

The Seigneur indicated the woman by his side. 'I'm sure you remember Mademoiselle Mercier, *monsieur.*'

'Do stop it, Gérard.' A light, honeyed voice spoke from one of the loveliest faces Evena had ever seen. 'Don't make things awkward.'

Things were already awkward! Quite uncomfortable, in fact.

'Mademoiselle Baptiste, it's lovely to meet you,' Agnès greeted her as she came forward, bowing her head in a regal manner.

Evena returned her bow, all the while painfully aware of the scene they were causing. All eyes were on them in the salon. She could just imagine what everyone was thinking. The jilted bridegroom parading his current fiancée on his arm, meeting his former recently betrothed.

She had heard about Agnès Mercier while she'd been in Paris. Called a 'jewel among rocks' in the court, she had the reputation of being one of the most beautiful women in France. Isadora had also intimated as much, saying wryly that if Helen of Troy had resembled Agnès Mercier, then it was no wonder why her abduction had launched a thousand ships.

Achingly lovely would be the way to describe her. She'd styled her lustrous shining black hair in a pouf with curls held in place by diamond-tipped pins. A little false bird in a miniature nest lay nestled among her tresses.

Evena found that impractical, but there was something charming about it, and she felt her own lavishly styled *tignon* to be inadequate. Eyeing the other woman's low-cut green brocade silk gown, never had she felt so dowdy.

Staring at Agnès, who returned her own study with

shrewd, pale golden eyes, Evena could understand why Dieudonné had wanted to align himself with her. Not only was she exceptionally beautiful, but she had the influence amongst the elite that Evena didn't.

A hard knot formed in her throat, but Evena forced her mouth to stretch into something she hoped resembled a smile.

'A pleasure to make your acquaintance, Mademoiselle Mercier. The Comte de Montreau has been most kind in his accolades of you.'

'Has he?' Agnès's eyes widened. 'Well, that's rather surprising since I was quite dreadful to him. I regret I don't have the privilege of knowing you so well, *mademoiselle*.'

Evena blinked and at the same time she felt a minute jolt go through Dieudonné's body. The last thing she'd expected to hear was Agnès admitting what she'd done to him.

'Really, Agnès. There's no need to be cruel,' Seigneur de Guise Elbeuf said in a low murmur.

Her teeth ground together. The audacity of the man! He'd caused this situation. For what purpose?

'Are we supposed to pretend I didn't leave the poor Comte at the altar? That would be wrong, and I refuse to profess that such a thing didn't happen.'

'It's of no matter now,' Evena answered airily, affecting the same levity as the woman. 'How long has it been since you returned to France?'

The other woman sent a quick glance in Dieudonné's direction before answering. 'Two days. I've just returned from visiting relatives in Venice.'

'Venice—I've heard a lot about it. I hope your stay was enjoyable.'

Agnès fanned herself with a lace-trimmed fan. 'It was.'

Evena felt as if she was floundering. This evening was not going at all the way she'd expected. Before she could think of anything else to say, Agnès moved forward, standing directly in front of Dieudonné's rigid figure. 'We must talk, you know.'

'Ah, some of my favourite people all coming together.' The sound of the Duchesse's voice interrupted the moment. Gladly, Evena refocused her gaze away from the sight of Dieudonné and Agnès standing so close to each other.

'Comte de Montreau, Mademoiselle Baptiste, I'm so pleased that you both could come. I see you've all become acquainted.'

'Madame la Duchesse.' Evena gave the other woman a polite curtsey. A sneaking suspicion entered her mind that, for all their supposed friendship, the Duchesse had somehow planned this humiliation. But that didn't matter now, did it?

'May I speak to you for a moment, Mademoiselle Baptiste?'

Evena looked at Dieudonné, seeing a bland expression on his face. She wanted to stay by his side and not leave him alone. Tempted to deny the Duchesse's request, she saw Dieudonné give her a slight nod.

They stepped away from the group and walked to a less crowded area of the salon. In an undertone, the Duchesse said, 'I must apologise for this mishap, my dear. I did not know Mademoiselle Mercier would be here this evening. Never would I have wanted to cause you or your betrothed any discomfort.'

Evena felt the knot in the centre of her stomach ease. 'I thank you for telling me that.'

The Duchesse gave her a beatific smile. 'Of course. I've come to regard you well, Mademoiselle Baptiste.'

Knowing the honour the woman had bestowed upon her just then, she opened her mouth to reply when the Duchesse's manner became brisk. 'I do believe you may be familiar with a new acquaintance of mine, my dear.' The woman glanced around as if searching for someone. 'Ah, there he is.'

The Duchesse lifted a hand. Evena turned to see the striking figure of Pierre Gédéon, Comte de Nolivos, striding towards them. She was surprised to see the man as they'd heard nothing from him since he was replaced as Governor General on Saint-Domingue in seventy-two.

When he neared, he bowed to the Duchesse. 'Madame la Duchesse de Villers-Cotterêt, how may I serve you?'

The woman smiled prettily. 'Comte de Nolivos, I believe you are acquainted with Mademoiselle Baptiste?'

The Comte squinted his eyes at her. 'Mademoiselle Baptiste.'

It was neither a greeting nor a sneer, just an acknowledgement of her presence. Evena decided to take it for what it was.

'*Monsieur*, it's a pleasure to see you again.'

The Duchesse beamed at Evena. 'I invited the Comte de Nolivos to join us for my salon this evening as he's going to regale us with what it's like to live on Saint-Domingue. Your stories have intrigued me thoroughly. Not to mention, we've all been quite curious about the state of affairs after that dreadful earthquake we all heard about.'

'I see.' Evena lifted her chin. 'I look forward to your talk, *monsieur*.'

The man said nothing, but with a nod he and the Duchesse moved away.

'This is turning out to be quite an evening of surprises, isn't it?'

Evena stiffened at the sound of Seigneur de Guisé Elbeuf's voice. She spun on her foot and lifted her chin. 'Is it?'

'Do you hate me very much?'

Dieudonné's jaw clenched as he stared down into Agnès's

earnest face. All around them, he could feel many curious ears pricking up. In his peripheral vision he could see the Seigneur speaking to Evena. He longed to go to her so that she didn't have to entertain that man for a single second.

This conversation could not have happened at a worse time.

'*Hate* would not be the appropriate word to use.'

Her champagne-coloured eyes darkened. 'Then what would be?'

'Why are you here, Agnès? Why today? Why now?'

All evening, he'd felt an overwhelming sense of doom hovering above him like a dark cloud. He hadn't even wanted to come, but Evena had cajoled him into it. Several times, he'd wanted to take flight, but Evena had kept him by her side.

Now he knew why.

Of course, the moment he'd seen Agnès, he hadn't been able to control the tide of emotion that swept over him. She had come back to Paris with the same abruptness with which she had left.

There was something to be said for the fashionable surprise.

'You deserve an explanation, but I'm certain you won't like it.'

He leaned forward. 'Perhaps, whatever your explanation is, it is something you could have told me the day before we were to marry.' His words were clipped. All his loathing washed through his body like waves of fire. 'Was it necessary to humiliate me as you did? What sort of pleasure did you gain from leaving your Creole bastard lover at the altar?'

Her face flushed. At least she had the decency to look suitably embarrassed. '*Monsieur...*'

'Oh, I am fully aware of what you told others—fables of

my virility and expertise. Something you never had the opportunity to discover for yourself.'

Her eyes drifted downward, her voice lowered. 'What was I supposed to say, *monsieur*? You know how everyone likes to hang on my every word. Look at you—no one would have believed me if I'd said I wasn't taking advantage of your... charms. I thought you'd be flattered.'

'I never touched you, despite the many times you begged me to. But I allowed you to use that fiction to your advantage, for it was also to mine.'

Her lips twisted and she looked away. Following her gaze, he could see people were watching them, but trying desperately hard to look as if they weren't.

Once again, he'd been made to feel a fool in front of them all.

'There's a reason why I did what I did, but this is not the proper place to tell you. Would you do me the honour of meeting me tomorrow afternoon at Café Procope?'

'Women aren't allowed there.'

As soon as he said it, he sighed. This was Agnès Mercier. If she wanted to be there, she would be. How he would be received would largely depend on her. At the impish grin that appeared on her face, he knew that she would flout society dictates as she often did.

'Very well.'

There was movement in the room, and they both turned to see everyone start for the chairs that were situated along the far wall.

'*Monsieur?*'

Looking down at her, he saw Agnès expected him to escort her. To prevent more unwanted gossip, it might be a good thing to pretend they were still on the best of terms.

Holding out his arm, he escorted her to where the Seigneur

stood by Evena. His gaze bored into the other man. Dieudonné gritted his teeth. He wanted to strike him down. Evena looked far too pale. What had the Seigneur been saying to her?

'I see you've managed to come away from that embarrassing debacle at the garden party unscathed, *mademoiselle*.'

Evena's shoulders thrust back as she glared at the Seigneur. 'With no help from you, *monsieur*.'

'No. That was never my intention.' He lowered his voice so only she could hear his words. 'The lure of your innocence as a Saint-Dominguan woman was your true value to me, *mademoiselle*. Nothing more, not even your wealth.'

He'd never had any intention of marrying her. Well, she'd already figured that out for herself. Still, she was curious.

'Then why did you agree to discuss a marriage between us when you had no intention of going through with it?'

His brown eyes glinted in an odd way. 'I didn't agree to anything.'

'What do you mean?'

'My mother simply thought to sell me to you.' A flash of anger crossed his face. 'She didn't take my feelings into consideration, *mademoiselle*.'

'You are a man, *monsieur*. Surely you could have simply refused? I came to you in good faith, ready to be the rich, chaste bride you needed to restore your family's fortunes.'

A muscle leapt in his jaw, as if he were holding back from saying something. She didn't care.

Dieudonné's words once again haunted her. *'Marriage is transactional. A means to an end.'*

'I know,' the Seigneur said finally. 'That's what surprised me about you, Evena. Your integrity and your willingness to be true to the bargain. But you must understand, I could never be interested in a union with you.'

She glared at him. 'Then why try to...to...?'

'Take what I wanted from you?' His lips twisted. 'What man wouldn't want such a beautiful woman? And I admit it, you are a very lovely woman.'

'I'm not flattered.'

He went on as if she had not spoken. 'I thought you would be malleable enough to allow me to seduce you. After all, if you were truly concerned about your father's health, then you would have done so.'

'Obviously, I wasn't that desperate,' she responded in disgust.

'No, you weren't.' Seigneur de Guise Elbeuf stood then and straightened his jacket. 'And neither am I.'

'It looks as if everyone is starting to go to their seats.'

The sound of a female voice was a welcome distraction. Until she turned and saw Dieudonné and Agnès standing there, side by side.

What had they talked about? She longed to ask, but there was no time to find out as everyone began to settle in their seats, readying themselves for the opportunity to listen to Comte de Nolivos speak about Saint-Domingue.

Evena's thoughts could not remain focused on what the Comte was saying, although it must have been amusing from the laughter and the smiles she saw on people's faces, observing them as if from far away.

How could she concentrate when she kept seeing the picture Dieudonné and Agnès made as a couple? How well suited they seemed together. No wonder Dieudonné had wanted to marry Agnès. She was beautiful, exciting and exceedingly well connected. There was also an innate confidence in her that came from not being at all concerned with what others thought of her actions.

It made perfect sense now why Dieudonné had sought an alliance with her. She could have given him what Evena could not.

For the first time in her life, Evena found the green-eyed monster clamping its sharp teeth into her and biting down hard.

After an hour, the Comte came to the end of the first part of his story and everyone stood.

'Is there something wrong, Evena?'

She jumped, startled out of her distraction to see Dieudonné staring at her. 'I'm fine.'

'You're not. Don't hide yourself from me, Evena.'

Are you hiding something from me?

'Evena, what did he say to you?'

Remembering what the Seigneur had said, she carefully picked up her fan and swayed it in the air about her.

'Nothing that bears repeating.'

'Tell me,' Dieudonné insisted darkly, 'or I'll have us take our leave.'

Her nostrils flared. 'You're not my lord and master yet, Dieudonné.'

'Non,' he replied. 'I'm your friend and I won't have that man upsetting you.'

Like water through a sieve, her ire left as quickly as it had come. 'Truly, I'm fine.'

'What did he say?'

Evena stared into his hard face. She longed to ask him what he'd discussed with Agnès. Did he realise just how little help she could give him in his drive to acquire acceptance in society, compared with his former betrothed?

Did Agnès want Dieudonné back? Did she still want to marry him?

The thought made her skin tighten. No, she wouldn't ask

what they'd discussed. For the very first time in her life, she didn't want to know the answer. Quickly, she told him the gist of their conversation.

Dieudonné's brow drew downward. 'Then what was the point of this whole thing?'

Recalling the flinty expression in the Seigneur's eyes, she added, 'He seemed very embittered with his mother.'

'Don't tell me you suddenly feel sorry for the man.'

Evena shook her head. 'No, I'm furious with him for wasting our time and effort.'

She looked around the room, stiffening when her gaze clashed with Agnès Mercier's. The woman gave her a bright, rather sly smile, as if she were privy to some inner joke when the opposite was true.

Her fingers tightened on the handle of the fan. Why had Agnès come back? What did she want with Dieudonné? The woman's presence loomed over her like a sullen dark cloud, threatening to rain its ferocity over her.

When they were in the carriage riding back to the Godier home, she stared across at Dieudonné as he gazed broodingly out of the window, his face a hard mask.

He wasn't talking to her. They'd once shared everything and now, ever since this forced engagement, they'd stopped talking, stopped sharing. Tonight was their first engagement together; she'd seen how others had treated him. It must have been humiliating for him. No wonder he felt as he did.

Despite everything she'd ever wanted out of a marriage since she was a little girl, this union of theirs would end up being purely transactional—a marriage of convenience that wouldn't actually benefit him, or her.

Heat flushed her skin. What a horrible thing to admit, even in the privacy of her own thoughts. If it were only about her, she wouldn't have cared. But she had more than herself to think about. She had to consider her father.

Though he finally turned to her and started discussing the arrangements and preparations for the upcoming wedding, she could see the darkness in his eyes. Was it regret? Disappointment? Once, he would have told her, and now? Nothing.

Silence fell between them once more as the carriage swayed back and forth on its journey home. Now that his former betrothed had come back into his life, would the other woman's obvious suitability to be Dieudonné's bride be enough to tear their own impending vows apart?

Chapter Ten

———✦✦✦———

Rue des Fossés-Saint-Germain-des-Prés teemed with activity. Carriages clopped down the cobblestone street, vendors shouted out their wares—fresh baguettes, aged cheeses, potions meant to cure all diseases—to passersby.

Dieudonné exited his carriage and tugged on the hem of his coat. Unlike other areas of Paris, this part of the city catered to the intelligentsia of the population. Philosophers, artists, musicians, well-educated men and learned fools alike gathered in any of the numerous cafés and shops for spirited conversation.

In the distance, the historic buildings of the Sorbonne stood prominent, the streets bustling with the commotion of students and scholars. Nearby, the Pont Neuf spanned the Seine, its familiar arch capturing the golden rays of the afternoon sun, creating a scene that seemed almost painted against the vibrant city life.

As he made his way to the entrance of Café Procope Dieudonné wondered why Agnès had wanted to meet here. What was her purpose for choosing this location? It would have been simpler, and even more private, if they had gone to one of the city parks or even met at her home to have this discussion.

Instead, she wanted to have this long overdue conversation here, in the most unlikely of places. Especially when she knew women were not normally permitted within these hallowed walls.

Stepping aside for two men who exited just as he reached the door, he took hold of the handle and went inside.

Crystal chandeliers dripped from the ceiling. Gold sconces lined the walls while marble-topped tables filled the space. Fragrant with the scent of coffee and hot chocolate, the place reverberated with loud, excited voices.

It was said that Voltaire, that sharp-witted fellow, frequented this very café, along with others. Here, a man could discuss anything his mind thought to question—the nature of the world, the soul of man, the legitimacy of the Crown… or maybe why a woman would jilt a man she'd promised to marry.

'Monsieur le Comte de Montreau, do stop lolling about and sit down!'

Dieudonné's head turned in the direction of the voice, surprised that he had been addressed. For one thing, he didn't frequent this place often, and for another, he didn't recognise the voice.

His gaze landed on a small table near the back of the café, occupied by two men. He walked towards it, wondering which of them had called out to him.

One leaned forward…and Dieudonné nearly stumbled.

Agnès!

She'd done the unthinkable and dressed herself as a man.

So well put-together was her disguise that no one else would recognise her unless they knew her intimately.

She'd donned the clothes of a merchant, with a powdered wig. Neither noble nor peasant, but part of that rising class of society called *bourgeois*—new money mixed with new ideas about status. She'd even decorated her upper lip with a false moustache.

It was a perfect disguise and from the twinkle in Agnès's eyes, she knew she had outdone herself.

The woman was mad.

'Sit here, *monsieur*, and join us.' She'd given her voice a raspy edge, which was why he hadn't recognised it at first.

Trying to keep a blank face, he smoothed a hand down his coat and strode over to where she sat.

'*Monsieur*, it's been some time,' Dieudonné greeted her.

'Baron Mercier,' she said, gesturing to the man beside her.

Agnès's father! He hadn't even noticed the man until she'd made the introduction. What the devil was he doing here? And did he approve of his daughter's ridiculous actions?

Baron Mercier gave a single nod, his brown eyes shrewd. 'Ah, Monsieur le Comte de Montreau, it's a pleasure to see you again.'

Dieudonné wasn't sure if 'pleasure' was the correct word to describe this rather odd interaction. The Baron had been conspicuously absent while Dieudonné had suffered the blow of his daughter's desertion, although he'd certainly made sure to null the contractual obligations that had been signed before Dieudonné had left for England.

'I'm surprised to see you here,' Dieudonné answered instead.

The man's expression grew dark. 'It is my doing, *monsieur*,' Baron Mercier said, his mouth twisting. 'I told my daughter that if she pretended to be a man, she would be able to accompany me to meet you here.'

Now he was confused. 'I don't understand.'

'That's understandable,' the older man said, taking a bite of his *pain d'épices,* a rye bread with honey and spices. 'Yesterday evening I was supposed to accompany my daughter to the Duchesse de Villers-Cotterêt's salon, but a pressing engagement prevented that. Otherwise, I would have spoken with you directly.'

'Why?'

The older man sighed. 'It was I who told my daughter to leave you at the altar, *monsieur*.'

Dieudonné was taken aback. The Baron? Not Seigneur de Guise Elbeuf after all!

'But you were the one who approved of the match!'

'I know, and to some degree I still do, but there's a reason for that.' Baron Mercier looked down at his daughter. 'Tell him the truth.'

Agnès glanced around, ostensibly to ensure they were not observed or heard. Which would be a feat since the room shrilled with riotous conversation. Still, she lowered her voice.

'I was with child.'

Dieudonné drew back. 'You were?' It was truly the last thing he'd expected to hear.

'Do you see now why she had to jilt you, *monsieur*?' her father interrupted. 'I shall be frank. Illegitimate children can be accepted or rejected. Had you been the father of my daughter's child, you would already be wed. But it would be rather difficult to…to…'

'Pretend a child without mixed blood could ever be mine,' he concluded heavily.

For a long moment he stared into Agnès's eyes, seeing deep sorrow lodged there.

'What happened to the baby?'

'*Dieu Tout-Puissant* judged me for my unrighteous living and I lost the child,' she said, surprising him. 'I wanted it, *monsieur*. When I discovered my condition, I was happy. But then, when I made it known to my father, he demanded I tell you the truth and have you decide if you would still wed me. After all, I know how illegitimacy has overshadowed your life.'

His lips tightened. 'Go on.'

'Many times, I wanted to tell you, *monsieur*. But I couldn't. I wanted the protection your name would give me. I thought that as the baby would have appeared to have three-quarters French blood, nobody would blink an eye when it didn't look like you. It wasn't you who needed me. *I* needed you.'

Dieudonné felt the impact of her words in the pit of his stomach. He couldn't believe it!

'Had you been any other man, the knowledge would have remained a secret. Many a man has raised a bastard child, after all,' she added.

Baron Mercier pushed away the half-eaten bread, brooding down at the crumbs on the pristine white tablecloth.

'I disagreed with my daughter's logic over the baby's likely appearance. Ultimately, her indiscretion would have affected my standing with the King and I couldn't allow her to marry you and remain in society. I forcibly sent her to Venice, leaving you to bear the brunt of the public humiliation, for which I deeply apologise.'

Dieudonné stared at both father and daughter, an odd feeling in the pit of his stomach.

Agnès looked fully into his face. 'Do you hold me in contempt, *monsieur*?'

Dieudonné let out a deep shuddering sigh. He didn't know what to think or feel. '*Non*, I don't hate you,' he said after some moments, gathering his thoughts and trying to make sense of everything. 'I pity you.'

Her lashes fell. 'I see.'

His back straightened. She'd jilted him because her father thought her illegitimate child couldn't be passed off as his and the resulting scandal would endanger the Baron's position at court. Could this be more sordid?

'Please forgive me, *monsieur*.'

Why did things have to be so difficult for him? It wasn't that he would have rejected a child that wasn't his own—his uncle had taken him on, after all.

Rather, it was Agnès's audacity that, if she could have, she'd have forced him to become a father without telling him first. And her assumption that once he'd discovered the truth, he'd have remained silent because he wanted her connections to ease his way with the elite.

'*Monsieur*, please speak to me.'

Agnès's voice drew him back to the present.

'What should I say?'

'Anything, *monsieur*.'

'Rather than speak, why not accept my invitation to Théâtre des Tuileries tonight? There's a ballet I'm sure you would enjoy. Your family and the family of your betrothed shall be our guests.'

Dieudonné mulled it over. He understood what the Baron was doing. By inviting a prominent, mixed-blood family such as the Godiers, as well as the wealthy Baptistes, to the ballet, he was showing his support for them. As a favourite of the King, it would send a strong message to the elite.

Even now, knowing what Agnès had done, that constant need for acceptance still lingered. He wished he could exorcise it, cut it from his flesh, his brain, and burn it like raw meat into a fire until it blackened and disintegrated into ash.

But he couldn't.

Strangely, Evena's face floated up in his mind. He could almost feel her disappointment. Instinctively, he knew she would have taken Agnès to task for her deceit and subterfuge, so alien to Evena's own nature.

Well, he would keep this private.

With a heavy heart, even though it was something he wanted so badly, he replied, 'We will accept your invitation, *monsieur*.'

Agnès's eyes filled with tears. '*Merci*, Dieudonné.'

Looking at her beautiful face—moustache notwithstanding—Dieudonné couldn't help but wonder why her gratitude meant so very little to him?

Evena thought her teeth would crack from the pressure she put on them. If she'd known when she'd woken this morning that she would be practically sitting next to Agnès Mercier this evening, she would have laughed.

Their theatre box was occupied by her parents and Sophiette, Dieudonné's parents, Ayida and the Merciers.

Though the Théâtre des Tuileries boasted of being one of the most prestigious buildings in the city, bringing performances of popular operas or, in this case, ballet to the masses, she could hardly appreciate her luxurious surroundings when that woman was smiling at Dieudonné the same way a cat smiled at a bird.

Hungrily. Desperately.

She couldn't make her interest in him any plainer if she had crawled into his lap!

Evena's face heated. Why did Agnès have to come back now? Why couldn't she just have stayed in Venice for the rest of her life? Everything she feared about the woman— her beauty, her refinement and even her boldness, made the sharp pointy teeth of the green-eyed monster sink further into her soul.

She hated the fact she was feeling this way. Never, in all her life, had she ever felt so threatened by another woman.

Especially when she knew how much better a match Agnès would be for Dieudonné.

But then, she'd never felt this way about Dieudonné before. Never thought of the implications of having this woman being a threat to her own…stability.

Agnès had even haunted her in her sleep, smiling and gleaming, until Evena wanted to scratch her with her nails.

It made sense that Dieudonné would be more than happy to find himself back in alignment with Agnès and her father. He would be able to gain the acceptance he wanted without needing Evena for anything.

Infuriated by the direction of her thoughts, she gripped her fingers tighter around the handle of her fan. She could just see the way Agnès leered at Dieudonné, the neckline of her royal blue gown so low that if she took a deep breath, her breasts would spill from it.

The last thing she'd wanted to do, when Dieudonné had returned from wherever he'd gone earlier today, was to accept the invitation from the Merciers, but she had no choice. He needed this. Being in the company of such a prominent man as the King's favourite would not be an opportunity to miss.

How she wanted to miss it, though. She longed to take Dieudonné by the hand and run away. Run all the way back to Saint-Domingue, back to the place on the Belot Mountains where his fiery kiss had first awakened her.

Back to the place where he was her friend and she had to share him with no one.

'Are you finding the performance enjoyable, Mademoiselle Baptiste?'

Evena gave a start, seeing that Agnès had moved to come and sit by her.

'It's delightful,' she said blandly, feeling somewhat guilty that she hadn't paid much attention to what the dancers were doing.

'I think so, too,' the woman said airily. 'Although it's rather a bore when you've seen the performance as often as I have. Comte de Montreau and I saw it ages ago. It loses something with familiarity, doesn't it?'

A jolt went down her back. 'What do you mean?'

Agnès shrugged, her shoulders bare and round, reminiscent of pale, smooth stones. 'Nothing, really. It's just that when one becomes accustomed to something, the appeal of it vanishes. Soon, you wonder why you even bothered.'

Evena saw red. How dare this woman say those things? Anyone with an inkling of understanding would know Agnès was referring to Evena.

Her fingers tightened even more on the handle of the fan. When she slid her glance in the woman's direction, she could see the telltale gleam in her eyes.

It had been a deliberate provocation and they both knew it.

Evena cleared her throat. 'You would be more acquainted with repeat performances than I would, *mademoiselle.*'

Agnès's eyes widened appreciatively. 'Oh, so you do have some spirit about you, *mademoiselle!*'

Evena regretted the words as soon as she'd said them. What would happen if Dieudonné found out? If it were anyone else, she wouldn't have bothered worrying.

Another horrid thought came to her. Baron Mercier was a favourite of the King. She shouldn't risk souring a possible connection that could help her father.

But for once she didn't care. All she wanted was for Agnès to disappear so she could be sure of her own place in Dieudonné's life.

Swallowing the lump that appeared in her throat, she replied, 'All Saint-Dominguan women do. The sun beats hotter there, and the rains nurture our spirit.'

Surprisingly, Agnès said nothing to that, instead, standing up and going over to where Sophiette sat in the darkest part of the box, watching the ballet in fascination while Ayida chatted with her mother. They all seemed without a care in the world. Didn't they understand what was at stake?

Her eyes landed on Dieudonné, only to find his perceptive gaze upon her.

She wanted to tug her eyes away, but she was held captive. He didn't smile or frown, just looked at her as if she were the only thing of interest.

His mood had been subdued all evening. Not only had he dressed in dark clothes, which was unlike him, but he remained distant and on edge—and she didn't know why.

Evena felt her heart speed up and a thin layer of moisture dotted her hands.

What was he thinking about? Had he heard the conversation between herself and Agnès, and was furious about it?

Her chin lifted in direct defiance. So be it.

After what seemed like an eternity, the performance ended and she and everyone else rose from their seats and exited the box, meandering into the hallway that led to the staircase.

Lit sconces placed every ten feet or so held back the darkness. Evena found herself at the tail end of their group.

'Evena…'

Without looking behind her, she felt Dieudonné's presence as tangibly as cloth against her skin.

'What is it?'

'What were you doing? You do know Agnès's father has access to the King? She could help your father. Why did you spar with her?'

'She antagonised me first. She wanted to—'

'It doesn't matter,' he gritted out between his teeth. 'You cannot afford to make her an enemy.'

Did he want Agnès so badly then? What did she care if she were in that woman's good graces?

But what about Papa?

'Oh, I see,' she said, whirling around on the wide steps. 'You expect me to bear the brunt of her hostility, meek as a lamb, while she tears into me with all the cunning of a white panther.'

'*Oui*. I do.'

Evena almost snarled, feeling tears sting her cheeks as she turned around and stomped down the largely empty staircase. The light dimmed the further away she went from him.

'You're a fool,' she scolded. 'An utter—oh!'

Hands gripped her by the forearms and pressed her against the wall. He leaned forward until he blocked out everything but himself.

'Don't test me, Evena,' he warned her in a low voice.

It sent delightful shivers up her spine, but she tried to ignore them, instead protesting, 'I'm not, but she's making an utter fool of you.'

He grunted as if she'd struck him.

Without warning, his head bent and he captured her mouth with his. Instantly, all her anger and frustration and jealousy melted away and she wrapped her arms tightly around his neck.

It didn't matter that they were alone on a staircase with the potential of anyone coming across them. All that mattered was that his mouth clung to hers, drawing out her response with the scintillating pressure of his lips. He caged her against the wall and kissed her long and deep, his hands tracing her body with urgent, restless fingers.

'*La Sirène*, I need you,' he said against her lips. 'Open your mouth for me.'

She needed no other urging, thrilled to hear him speak thus while locked in this mad, passionate embrace that had taken them over. Why concern herself with Agnès when Dieudonné was here in the dark, touching and caressing her, Evena, like this?

He withdrew finally, lifting his mouth, causing her to

whimper in protest, only to hiss in the next moment as he trailed a line of hot, tingling kisses down her sensitive neck.

'More,' she whispered as his arms tightened around her and he drew his mouth down to the cleft between her breasts. His tongue darted out, lapping her skin as if she were a delicious treat. She let out a gasp and he groaned something into her skin.

Through the haze of pleasure and want surging through her, she heard approaching voices coming towards them.

Oh, how she wished she were a real goddess with powers. She'd send them to the sea so Dieudonné could continue to worship her most ardently.

Reluctantly, she pulled away. 'People are coming.'

He stilled and drew back. There was a dazed expression in his eyes, as if he was finally coming to after being far away. Her skin still felt the burn of his mouth upon it and she wondered if it would ever go away.

Dieudonné tugged on his coat and extended his arm. With trembling fingers, she took it, feeling the firm muscles flexing underneath her touch. They went the rest of the way in a tense silence until they reached the main floor, where the rest of their party had congregated.

'I wondered where you were,' Isadora remarked.

'I'd dropped my reticule,' Evena answered swiftly. 'But we found it.'

'Ah, *bien*. Shall we?'

Evena nodded and followed the others as they left, wondering if anyone could see the effects of Dieudonné's kiss upon her, and wishing, more than ever, that she was secure in the knowledge that Agnès would be able to do nothing to take him from her.

Chapter Eleven

The morning sunlight filtered through the stained-glass windows on Dieudonné's second wedding day as he stood at the front of the church, waiting for his bride to appear. He took comfort in the fact that Evena would not leave him at the altar.

After the explanation at the Café Procope, Dieudonné had spent several days examining what had been said. Agnès had been willing to use him to shield her condition, taking advantage of his longing for acceptance into society.

As humiliated as he'd been, and the embarrassment that had followed, some part of him was glad that Agnès had left him at the altar. That it hadn't happened the way she'd wanted it.

But why was he thinking of her now, when he should be considering the woman who was to be his bride?

Vases of flowers filled the church and added a pleasant fragrance. As the guests flowed inside, he had a sense of déjà vu. From necessity, the wedding was taking place at the same church where he'd stood three months ago now, waiting for a woman who never came.

The gazes of the marble statues of saints stared at him accusingly. Feeling uncomfortable, he tugged the edges of his jacket and waited.

'Are you nervous, *mon frère?*'

Turning around, he met the amused gaze of Iménel, who stood by his side.

'I'm not. I want this part to be over with.'

Everything leading up to this day had been a whirlwind of activity. Parisian society being what it was, there was a heightened interest in his marriage, more even than there had been with Agnès.

Soon, Evena would be coming down the aisle to become his Comtesse.

They hadn't been alone together since that moment in the theatre when he'd kissed and caressed her, sipping at the honey of her skin with all the appetite of a starving man. What caused him to do that, he hadn't quite figured out. All he knew was the rawness of his emotions, and the only good thing that had come from it was the sweet, all-consuming oblivion he'd experienced with her.

Though he'd had little sleep since then, there was something to be said for the distance. He didn't trust himself with Evena around. She tempted him as no other woman ever had.

What irony that their friendship would be strained by the upcoming bonds of marriage. That his desire for her had done exactly what he'd feared.

He'd damaged their friendship, maybe even lost it.

Claude had experienced three more attacks during that time. Each one had pierced Dieudonné's heart because he felt responsible.

Swallowing his pride, he'd even visited the few acquaintances who weren't completely dismissive of him and asked for their help in trying to obtain access to the King's physician, but to no avail. It had been an object lesson in humility. Surely he should be declared a saint!

Still, Dieudonné felt he owed it to Evena to make every

effort possible. No matter what he did, however, he couldn't gain an audience with the King. Not even Baron Mercier's attempts had been successful.

Regardless, for all his failures, the wedding preparations had continued, with the banns being read and an outward show of solidarity from those curious members of society who'd accepted the invitations his mother had sent out.

His lips pressed into a thin line.

Looking around him, he saw many of those whose approval he had sought for so long sitting in the beeswax-scented pews, stealing glances at him and whispering. This was what he'd wanted for so long, but…why did it feel so hollow? Because they weren't there as well-wishers, he told himself sardonically. They were there for the spectacle and the gossip.

They were probably talking about him even as they attended his wedding and would partake of the food at the wedding breakfast. They would drink his spirits, fill his parents' home.

Still, he would be subjected to their unkind judgement.

He waited to feel the same sense of futility as he had before. Waiting for resentment to burn in the pit of his stomach. Strangely enough, it didn't come.

For some unfathomable reason, he didn't care about any of that today. Was it because this was his second wedding day?

Or was it something more?

'It will be over before you know it,' Iménel said, interrupting his musings. 'Then you shall have a wife to plague your days.'

He turned his eyes to Iménel, who laughed. 'I only make a jest with you. You've been very silent and stoic, which is no way for a bridegroom to be. Or perhaps it is frustration, eh?'

'Frustration?'

Iménel gave him a speaking look. 'Aren't you anxious for your wedding night?'

Dieudonné stiffened. 'Do be quiet—' he scowled at his brother '—you prattle more than an old woman.'

'Oh, come now. I've seen the way you watch her when you don't think anyone is looking.'

If they weren't in church, Dieudonné would probably have boxed his brother's ear. As it was, he simply glared at Iménel while he laughed at his expense.

The truth was that Iménel was right. Aside from his failure to help Claude was the undeniable fact that he wanted Evena with something approaching the hunger of a ravenous beast. There were times when the thought of unearthing all her body's secrets titillated his mind, sending him down a sensuous path filled with buried treasures ripe for discovery.

Once during this past month, he'd taken Evena to his estate so she could tour the house and gardens, giving her an idea of what her new home would be like. Sophiette and Ayida had come along to act as chaperones during the trip.

After what had happened at the theatre, it was clear that they could not be alone together again until the wedding.

While Sophiette and Ayida had followed behind them, Dieudonné had led Evena to their adjoining bedchambers. Although their girlish chatter had intruded on most of the tour, when he'd stood in the doorway and watched as Evena walked further inside the rooms, they had disappeared from his awareness.

It was as if Evena's presence in his private quarters had cast a spell over him. A vision of her lying on the bed, her golden body nude and arching under the caress of his hands, had flashed into his mind. While she toured the large rooms, his eyes had been fixed on that phantom version of her on the bed, luring him in with her dark green eyes and smile.

When he'd finally torn his mind's eye from that delectable daydream, he'd blinked and come back to the present to see Evena staring at him. They'd shared a long, knowing look before Sophiette and Ayida had come bursting past him through the door, breaking the connection.

Now, they were going to be married. No need to restrain himself. He could fall into a kind of heaven in her arms.

But at what cost?

He still couldn't help her father, which was a harsh enough punishment. He rubbed a hand over his chest. And it would be too cruel to give Evena children who would experience the same rejection he'd endured himself...but that would mean he couldn't take her to his bed and lose himself in her. If he kept her intact, they could build a life of mutual companionship. A marriage in name only. Wasn't that fairer to her? Hadn't he hurt her enough already? He frowned heavily. But to deny her children of her own could be the worst blow of all...

'Here she is, so stop your scowling.'

He looked up just as Evena came to the doorway. Claude stood by her side, but his eyes could only see his bride.

Beautiful seemed too inadequate a word to describe her, but it would have to do for the vision of loveliness making her way towards him.

She'd dressed unconventionally, combining her Saint-Dominguan heritage with Parisian fashion. The ivory gown clung to her slender figure, a blend of silk and satin. The bodice sculpted her torso, accentuating her trim waist. Lace framed the low neckline, teasing his eyes with a subtle hint of décolletage. From the waist down it formed a bell-shaped silhouette from the panniers that sat at her hips. Hand-sewn pearls dotted the gown, each one catching the light and adding another sheen of lustre. The hem swept the ground, giving him a glimpse of silk shoes embellished with pearls and ribbons.

It was offset by the bright red *tignon* that adorned her head, tied and twisted in an elaborate fashion that gave anyone the opportunity to view her face unencumbered. On top of her *tignon* rested a wide-brimmed hat of royal blue.

He preferred her *tignon* to the wigs some women wore. It was a part of their Saint-Dominguan heritage, and he was glad she'd worn it. Dieudonné found his respect for her growing. He'd always had a high regard for her, but today it had risen to new heights. Even if they weren't fully accepted by society, Evena held on to their mutual heritage without question.

When she came abreast of him, she gazed into his eyes. He felt as if he were going to drown. Submerging himself in those waters, he saw images of Evena as a young toddler, with pudgy legs and a heart-shaped mouth trying to pronounce his name properly as she'd followed him wherever he went.

His closest friend.

The woman he desired so fiercely he almost couldn't breathe.

His soon-to-be wife.

A muscle twitched in his jaw as the depth of his failure to be the kind of husband she deserved rested upon his shoulders like a heavy weight. What should he do?

Nothing. There was absolutely nothing he could do.

Did Dieudonné have to look so unhappy?

Evena stood at her bridegroom's side and wondered if she was making the biggest mistake of her life. They were marrying to avoid scandal, but was it worth losing his friendship?

Maybe she had already lost it in the heat of the fire that had surged between them that evening at the theatre. His mouth had burned her skin, leaving the memory of his touch like an invisible brand.

She still recalled how wild she'd been. How wanton. If he had thrown her onto the stairs that day, she would have joyously given up everything in return for those dizzying moments in his arms.

Who was she trying to fool? Their friendship was already gone.

All throughout the preparations for the wedding, she'd kept a firm distance between them because she'd sensed his withdrawal from her. Gone was the closeness that had been a part of their lives for as long as she had known him. He'd been replaced by a stranger.

A stranger, not her friend.

This stranger, with his stormy eyes, would become her husband.

Her eyes stole over him. How elegant his attire, clad as he was in breeches and overcoat in colours reminiscent of Saint-Domingue: bright red and blue, with gold buttons and threading.

He didn't wear a wig, but instead wore a scarf like the ones back home. It was a perfect blend of Saint-Dominguan and Parisian aesthetics.

As handsome and remote as he appeared now, what would Dieudonné look like when they shared a bed tonight?

Her cheeks heated. Was she being too wanton in her thoughts, in this sacred place? Surely she should be listening to the priest as he went on with the ceremony. Part of her responded as it was supposed to, following the ceremony with one half of her mind while the other half was fixated on the night ahead.

When he'd taken her to his estate and they'd visited the bedchambers, she couldn't prevent the way she'd imagined their eventual coming together.

She craved his touch. There. She'd admitted it.

For a moment, Evena almost expected the stained-glass windows in the church to shatter in outrage. For the statue of the Holy Virgin to gasp and crumble at the sinful thought.

It was a fanciful idea and she couldn't prevent the tiny smile on her lips.

When they exchanged vows she glanced at his face. It was hard and closed off, refusing to let her in. Was he still angry because she wasn't the bride who could help him advance socially? Was their marriage already doomed before it had even begun?

Now that he was married to a Saint-Dominguan woman, he likely believed this arrangement was a death-knell to all his hopes and dreams.

A spark of determination lit Evena within. She'd show him. She didn't know how, but she'd show him that marrying her wouldn't disadvantage him.

Before long, they were in the carriage, husband and wife.

The atmosphere was strained. He didn't speak to her except for making sure of her comfort before staring broodingly out of the window.

'Dieudonné?'

He pulled his gaze away from the scenery and gazed at her. 'What is it, Evena?'

Evena, not *La Sirène*, as he had called her for years.

For some reason, the thought that he might be upset with her made her throat tighten. She'd much prefer that, though, to this odd formality.

'Are you…angry with me?'

'Why would I be angry with you?'

Her fingers trembled. She hated this strange timidity now. She should be able to ask him anything she wanted to know.

But this man wasn't her old friend. This was her husband.

'Because things did not go the way you intended. I know that we married to protect my reputation, and I am grateful for your sacrifice, but what about how my—'

'Let's not dwell on the things we cannot change, Evena.' An expression of pain crossed his face and she looked away, struggling to breathe, knowing she was the cause of it.

When they arrived back at Hôtel Godier, there were several carriages arriving for the reception. Only the Godiers' closest allies had been invited back to the house, and Evena felt relieved at the respite from all the whispers.

Dieudonné carefully helped her out of the carriage and then he stepped back, as if he didn't want to be too close to her.

'*P'tit fi...*' Liusaidh came forward, tears in her eyes as she kissed her on the cheek. 'What a beautiful wedding and bride.'

Her father came to stand next to her, looking well and happy. A certain strain that had been a part of his visage for so long had gone, leaving only contentment. No one observing him could ever believe he suffered from strange swooning spells.

Dieudonné's parents came forward as well, offering their congratulations, too. Everything would have been perfect if Dieudonné had looked as happy as everyone else.

Sitting down to eat, she saw that the wedding meal consisted of a mix of Saint-Dominguan dishes as well as French. Thankfully, the Marquise's chef had become accustomed to making Saint-Dominguan dishes during his years in the Godier house and had created a feast to please and entice the most reluctant of stomachs.

Including Dieudonné's.

The long reception table had been set with pristine white tablecloths embroidered with fine floral details. Gleaming silver cutlery hemmed in the porcelain plates, while the linen napkins were folded to resemble swans. An elaborate arrangement of fruit created a splash of colour as the centrepiece. The crystal glasses sparkled like gems. Each place setting had a tiny bowl of lavender-scented water and its fragrance wafted to her nose as she sat down.

The meal began with hors d'oeuvres of *pâté de foie gras*, a dish of fattened goose liver seasoned and baked in a crust, along with her favourite *accras de morue*.

Despite the way Dieudonné's silence lowered her mood, she squealed with delight as *soup joumou*, a squash soup flavoured with beef pieces and vegetables, was set before her. Back home, only the plantation owners could eat the soup, although it was served by those who were forbidden to partake of the delicious fare. She was unutterably glad that everyone on her father's plantation knew the taste of *soup joumou*. She ate it with relish. Perhaps, one day, everyone on Saint-Domingue would eat it.

From there, the main course consisted of *coq au vin*—chicken cooked and braised with wine, lardons and mushrooms—along with tiny bowls filled with *riz djon-djon*—black mushroom rice and lima beans.

The meal ended with a dessert of *pain patate*, made from sweet potatoes, coconut and ginger. Champagne and rum were both served in lavish amounts.

Had she been on Saint-Domingue, there would have been dancing and music and all sorts of revelry to celebrate her wedding day. As it was, when the meal ended, she and Dieudonné said goodbye to their guests.

Their families were the last to see them away. They had all gathered outside with the waiting carriage behind them.

Sophiette's eyes were red-rimmed as she came forward and held her close. 'I didn't know until this moment how much I am going to miss you, *sè*.'

Evena felt the same. Throughout all their preparations for this day, the enormity of what it actually meant hadn't been quite so obvious until this moment.

She was leaving her family and starting a new life with her husband.

Despite their differences, she and Sophiette had always been together. Now, for the first time ever, they were to be separated.

Sophiette held on for a long time before she drew away and left, without looking back.

Evena understood.

Panic suddenly settled in. Would her father be all right? What about Sophiette and her shyness? Would her mother be able to do what—

'*P'tit fi,*' Liusaidh said, interrupting the thoughts that galloped around in her head. 'Don't worry about anything except you and Dieudonné, do you understand?'

Her eyes smarted with tears. 'But Maman, I—'

Liusaidh cupped her face. 'Remember what I said before?' Her gaze deepened. 'He's not just a friend any more. He's your husband and you are his wife.'

Her mother's words followed her as Dieudonné gently took her by the arm and slowly led her to the carriage. When they were safely ensconced, Evena took one last look out of the window at her family before Dieudonné gave the order and the carriage set off. She waved furiously as her parents' figures became smaller and blurry.

Then she threw herself into Dieudonné's arms and wept.

Evena's sobs shook Dieudonné. Each one seemed to pierce his soul.

He hadn't expected to feel as emotional as he did, leaving

his parents' home to start this new life with Evena. His mother and father had both charged him with taking good care of her.

It was surreal. For as long as he could remember, their families had been close friends, and now they were bonded by matrimony.

For ever.

As Evena cried, he gathered her closer and kissed her forehead. He felt a sudden sense of loss. Would that he could go back to those carefree days of living on the island and innocently spending time with her.

'I didn't think it would—' Evena spoke in between tears.

'You don't have to explain,' he said. 'I understand.'

She lifted her face from his chest, her eyes wet and dark like moss. 'You do, don't you?'

He thumbed a tear from her cheek. 'With our marriage, we've both lost and gained.'

'What have you lost?' She looked up at him like a young girl, confused and sad.

'Not much, I admit. My bachelorhood, not that I was willing to hold on to it,' he joked. Then he grew serious. 'And you? What do you think you've lost?'

She bit her lip, her facial expression uncertain. 'Perhaps it's easier for men. You're all taught to forge your way in the world, while a woman is expected to stay with her parents until a husband claims her.'

'And?'

'I feel like I've lost my family, even though I know we won't be far from them, but I've never been without them until now.'

Without thinking, he said, 'You've got me, *La Sirène*.'

Evena stilled in his arms. Dieudonné waited with bated breath.

Is being with me enough?

Slowly, she lifted her hand and caressed his jaw. 'I do have you. Yes, I do.'

Her eyes filled with tears again, and Dieudonné wiped the few that escaped with his thumb once more. It wasn't the first time he'd wiped away her tears. In their youth, he'd done this on more than one occasion.

Still, this was different in a way he couldn't quite grasp. Those childhood tears had been for childish squabbles and misunderstandings.

This felt as if he were taking on a serious responsibility. That he would be the one to ensure that she never had cause to cry. Never had reason to weep for sorrow.

Not if he could help it.

Something shifted and changed within him. A new maturity born from the fact that Evena had become an integral part of his life now in a permanent way.

He didn't have to wait until he travelled to Saint-Domingue to see her. He didn't have to leave her ever again.

His stomach twisted. What did it mean, this strange new sensation inside of him?

One more single tear escaped. This one he took and brought to his lips, licking away that faint taste of salt, absorbing it into his body. His soul.

He wasn't sure why he did that, only that it was necessary. A rite of passage only he understood on some primal level that defied words.

Evena hadn't seen it, and perhaps it was best that she hadn't. He wouldn't have been able to explain his action to her even if he tried.

Though he had failed to help her father, he vowed he'd never fail her again. He needed to give them some time before they consummated their vows. It would give his wife a chance to accustom herself to his life. And he needed the space to consider if having children was appropriate for them.

A brief glimpse of a possible future flashed in his mind. He saw a young girl with Evena's face and bright eyes running towards him with her arms outstretched.

His daughter.

Something inside of him lurched in happiness, in longing. If things were different, that phantom of a child would become a reality. He'd embrace fatherhood with joy. Dieudonné could see himself lifting that young girl in his arms and tossing her in the air on the beach.

Could it be that in his fantasy he could hear the tinkling sound of a child's laugh? He glanced down at his wife.

Evena would make a wonderful mother.

But was that the right thing to do—for her, for them? They needed to figure that out before they shared a bed. They had to know what this marriage would mean before it was consummated.

For better. Or for worse.

When the carriage made its final turn, Evena gazed at her new home with all the trepidation any new bride would be expected to feel.

True to its name, Château Lumières de Montreau was an estate filled with light, strategically built to capture the best of the sunlight, no matter what time of day it was. The white stone façade was regally elegant, with large windows, sculpted reliefs and ironwork.

She knew from the last time she was here which one of those windows was her own chamber, adjacent to Dieudonné's.

Her heart fluttered with excitement. He had comforted her when she'd needed it the most and she'd found solace in his arms. When he'd called her *La Sirène*, she'd known everything would be all right now.

But what would the night bring?

As they drew up to the front entrance, servants came out to take the rest of Evena's luggage into the house. When she started up the steps leading to her new home, Dieudonné stopped her.

'What is it?'

A wicked smile crossed his face. 'Do you remember Sir Ranulf?'

It took her a moment, but when she recalled the Englishman, she smiled. 'I do. He stepped on my foot that time.'

'The same. He recommends the custom of carrying a bride over the threshold of her new home.'

'Carrying me?' Her eyes widened. 'What on earth do you mean?'

Dieudonné came closer, towering over her and blocking out the afternoon sun. Then he bent and lifted her into his arms.

Evena gasped. 'Dieudonné, what are you doing? Put me down!'

He said nothing, just grinned wickedly and tightened his grip on her. Her skirts, petticoats and panniers were all askew as he carried her up the stairs and into the house.

Dieudonné set her down gently. His ash and indigo eyes gleamed. 'What did you think of that, *La Sirène*?'

Trying to fix her clothes, she grumbled, 'I think it's utterly ridiculous.'

He laughed. 'I rather enjoyed it.'

She narrowed her eyes at him, and then looked down at her rumpled clothes. If that wasn't enough, the servants had all come to greet her as the new mistress of the house. She had to speak with each of them, while being sorely conscious of her clothing.

This was not the way she'd wanted to begin her married life as the Comtesse de Montreau.

After a while, her innate sense of humour took over. When the last servant had been introduced to her, they were sent away to go about their duties while Dieudonné conferred with his head of staff about their bridal dinner that would be ready in a few hours.

There was a special expression in his eyes as he said, 'Your maid will see to your needs, *La Sirène*.'

His words sent another ripple down her back, and she couldn't wait for the moment when Dieudonné would come to her bedchamber tonight.

Chapter Twelve

Evena opened her eyes, seeing cherubs dancing on the ceiling. For a moment, she couldn't remember where she was. Then, an instant later, it all came back to her.

She was now the Comtesse de Montreau. Sitting up, she looked around her bedroom. The morning light spilled through the tall windows, casting a soft glow on the luxury that surrounded her.

Yet, for all its opulence, the room was empty. Dieudonné had not come to her.

Evena's heart sank with disappointment.

Last night had ended with so much promise. They had spent the evening together, enjoying the food the servants had prepared with extra care and basking in each other's company. She'd used all the wiles at her disposal to let her husband—her *husband!*—know that she'd welcome his touch. It seemed none of it had been of any use.

Why hadn't he come?

She rose, the silk of her nightgown whispering against her skin. Going over to her dressing table, she sat before it. Just then, the door opened and the maid who had assisted her yesterday entered. Her eyes looked around the room, obviously hoping to see signs of her employer's presence so she could spread the news to the other servants.

So would I, Evena thought darkly.

'*Madame*, shall I help you?'

Evena gave herself over to her maid's tender ministrations as she thought about what to do. Was she going to let him treat her like this?

How did a woman go about seducing her husband?

Oh, she wished she'd listened to Liusaidh. Now, her mother wasn't here, and she'd have to figure it out for herself.

A wave of homesickness came over her, but she thrust it away. This was her home now and her life would be what she made of it.

Determination firmed her jaw as Evena prepared for the day. Adorning herself in a gown that accentuated her figure, she wrapped her head in an embroidered purple *tignon* her mother had made especially for her for when she became Dieudonné's bride.

When she was fully dressed, she went down the stairs. Dieudonné stood at the foot of them, and she halted. They met each other gazes, hers questioning, his unreadable.

'Dieudonné—'

'I'm rather famished,' he interrupted her. 'Won't you join me for breakfast?'

It was quite possibly the politest conversation she'd ever had with him, nothing like the camaraderie that had once existed between them.

He'd been forced to marry her. Did he not want her any more? Thinking of how he'd been in the carriage after their wedding yesterday, she bit her lip.

Par Dieu, she hoped that wasn't the case!

Breakfast began as a quiet affair. Dieudonné made sure she was seated before taking his own. The morning light illuminated his features, and she noted the tension in his shoulders.

'I trust you slept well?'

'I would have slept better had you been with me, Dieudonné.'

He'd been about to drink a cup of hot chocolate, but he choked on the liquid. Coughing, he set the cup down and used a cloth napkin to wipe his mouth.

'Evena.'

'Did I say something wrong, husband?'

She stressed the last word, making sure there was no misunderstanding on his part.

'No,' he said slowly.

'Then where were you last night? I waited for you for a long time.'

Dieudonné leaned back in his chair. 'I'm not sure if it's a good idea for us to consummate this marriage yet.'

'Why on earth not?'

His eyebrow lifted into his forehead. 'Are you so eager for the experience, Evena?' His eyes had darkened to that stormy blue.

'Am I wanton for admitting it, Dieudonné?'

There was a heavy silence, one that pulsed and throbbed. His face had flushed for some reason, but then he cleared his throat.

'No. There are many men who would wish they had such an eager wife to welcome their attentions.'

Now it was her turn to feel the blood burn under her skin.

'Then why—'

'Let's not talk about that right now.' The planes of his face tightened. 'Although my servants are discreet, they do listen.'

As if on cue, the servants entered the room and began to serve them.

The meal progressed with desultory conversation, their initial stiff politeness gradually giving way to a more relaxed exchange. As breakfast concluded, Dieudonné surprised her with an offer. 'Would you care to see the estate? When you were here the last time, you didn't get a chance to fully appreciate it. Now that you are mistress here, I expect you'll want to update it as you see fit.'

'Of course I do.'

Her heart lifted. This was a chance to try to make him see her as his wife—one who could manage his home, the servants, and build their reputation.

They strolled together through the opulent halls, talking for what seemed like hours even though she knew barely any time had passed.

It was like they used to be.

Exiting the house, they stepped into a cloudy day.

'It looks like it's going to rain,' Dieudonné said.

'I love the rain. Especially after—'

Her voice stopped, but the affable air that had existed between them had ceased, replaced by a tension between them. She knew why she'd said that. It was because of their first kiss on the mountain slopes of Belot.

A quick glance in Dieudonné's direction showed a muscle in his jaw twitching.

He knew exactly what she was referring to.

They said nothing for a long while as the clouds deepened in colour. Still, Dieudonné walked the grounds with her. Looking around at the manicured gardens unfolding in every direction, with paths leading to different sections, she couldn't help feeling slightly overwhelmed.

'This is beautiful,' she remarked as they came to a gazebo that stood quite a way from the main house. 'Incredible that this all belongs to you and in turn will one day belong to our son.'

A jolt went through him. 'A son?' he whispered.

'*Oui*, a son to carry on your name.' Her hands flitted to

the flat of her belly. A smile lifted her lips as that innate desire, that need swelled in her. She wanted to be the mother of Dieudonné's children as much as she wanted to be the influential wife he needed. 'Or a daughter to give birth to honourable children.'

Dieudonné said nothing for a long minute. When he did speak, it was to say, 'I was told this estate once belonged to my natural father before he passed away. It was kept in order until I became of age. My inheritance came to me then as well, so I have been most fortunate.'

The telltale signs of a storm splintered the sky. Clouds swelled and darkened with rain and then the heavens opened upon them.

Laughing, they dashed into the nearby gazebo and stood looking out as the rain crashed to the earth.

'I feel like we used to feel in Saint-Domingue, don't you?'

He grinned, and her heart leapt.

'Why is it that we're always getting caught in the rain?'

Dieudonné watched her, myriad emotions flickering across his face. For a moment, they stood in silence.

Then, something within her snapped.

With part of her mind screaming that she would regret this, and the other part cursing all restraint, she stalked over to where Dieudonné stood. Throwing her arms around his neck, she ignored the shocked expression on his face, and brought his mouth down to hers.

Dieudonné knew he shouldn't have been so surprised. All this time, he'd held on to his self-control tightly. Last night, he'd battled with himself and won—their marriage would not be consummated until they'd both had time to think about what they wanted from this union.

What it had cost him had been a good night's sleep. This

morning, the look of hurt and confusion on her face had bothered him greatly. She'd resembled a small child who didn't quite understand what had happened to her.

Still, he'd continued to do everything he could to resist her.

It wasn't supposed to be this way. They were supposed to talk over things properly, like a civilised husband and wife, bereft of that uncontrollable madness which had taken over them in growing intensity.

Now it was simply too late. He wanted his wife.

He wanted Evena. Desperately.

How much more could a man take? Well, he didn't want to find out any longer.

He should have known that Evena would take matters into her own hands. For that he was glad as he enjoyed how Evena's tongue meshed with his, surrendering to the fire that had existed between them since that first moment in the mountains, when she'd taunted him and whetted his desire for her. Or had it always been there, simmering beneath the surface, waiting for this moment?

'*La Sirène,*' he murmured against her mouth and, almost without being aware of it, he took her down to the floor.

'Dieudonné,' she breathed into his mouth. 'Please, please, please…'

'I will,' he promised, understanding on an instinctive level what she wanted from him even though she couldn't articulate it.

Above them, Dieudonné could hear the furious tapping of the rain, beating down on the gazebo roof. Around them, the rain deepened the fragrance of the flowers, adding the scent to the heady fragrance of Evena's own delectable aroma.

Her mouth grew wild, sipping and nipping at his lips as if she were trying to taste him like a sweet. It was making him go insane. There were too many reasons why he shouldn't allow this to happen.

He couldn't think of any of them right then.

Instead, he cupped her head and drank deeper of her moist sweetness, trying to rein in the raging beast that wanted to destroy his control and take her. His tongue battled her own in hard strokes.

After all this time, there was no reason to hold back. Evena was his wife, a woman he had wanted for far too long. He was like a man in a desert, finally feeling the fury of a storm. He needed to soak up every drop, every thunderous beat, every part of it that raged between them.

Had he always wanted this with Evena? He didn't know. All he knew was that it was getting harder to harness his passion because she simply would not let him hold back from her.

Her hands were everywhere, her body shuddering, jerking, and moving as if she didn't know what to do with herself. When her legs came up and clamped his hips between her thighs, he thought he'd ignite into a forest fire.

She was trying to kill him.

His hands traced the curve of her shoulders, touching the rain-slicked skin that made her feel like a bolt of silk. He wanted to luxuriate in the sensation. When he came to the end of her gown, halting his enjoyment of her bare skin, he did the most sensible thing he could think of.

He drew it down her arms, nearly ripping it before she eagerly pushed the rest of it away herself.

Drawing his lips away from her, he ignored her protest for a moment to gaze at her body.

'Do you…do you…like me?'

Her shyness surprised him, tempering the rampant desire

that begged for release. Something both protective and primal moved in the centre of his chest.

For all her fiery response, Evena was still an innocent and he wanted to make her first time memorable.

'*Deyès...*' he uttered in Creole, wondering in an abstract way why the endearment came so much easier in his mother tongue.

She truly looked like a goddess.

Her *tignon* had unravelled, revealing her silky black hair spread out behind her. Her slender throat had captured beads of water at the hollow and he longed to drink from it like an offering. Her bronze-skinned breasts filled his eyes, round, high and voluptuous, with rose-coloured areoles topped with hard little apricot peaks begging for the worship of his mouth.

'You're beautiful,' he said simply. 'Everything about you is just so lovely.'

He rested on his forearm and angled himself towards her. With a growl he'd been unable to suppress, he bent his head and drew that turgid, rosy peak into his mouth.

She tasted hot and delicious. Her hissing scream and arching body was an orchestra of sound and sight. His manhood hardened, stiffening like a chair leg, and there was nothing more he wanted than to be inside of her.

But he pushed his own needs to the side, focused on her, and like any worshipper, he longed to idolise her with his mouth, his hands, his fingers, his teeth.

The rain fell harder, louder. Thunder rolled above them. The water slanted against them at an angle, soaking them. He hooked his arm around her and drew her further under the gazebo to escape most of the rain, but it still sprinkled upon them.

The storm around them awakened an expanding passion inside of him. In some way, he felt he'd become one with the storm and his wife was the earth. Evena made gasping sounds, her fingers tangling in his clothes, pulling and tugging at them urgently.

He tore off his waistcoat and shirt, revealing his chest to her. Evena drew her head back to look at him, her dark green eyes almost black as she used her palms to trace the muscled contours of his body. She traced her fingers up the broad planes of his arms as if she were trying to memorise him by touch alone.

Fire seared him from the inside, burning hotter with every pass of her hands. Then she lifted her head and placed her lips on his own nipple, letting her tongue twirl around it, and he thought he'd wither and die from the intense pleasure of it.

'Again,' he choked out.

Without hesitation, she did as he begged her, using her tongue in a clever way to send waves of pleasure through him.

How was it possible he had lived as long as he had without holding her in his arms like this?

'Stop,' he ordered as he gently clasped the back of her head and drew her away from the wonderful torment she was lavishing on his body. If she kept doing that, he'd lose control all too soon!

Her eyes had a glazed look to them, as if she had become lost in her own world of pleasure. When she blinked, he saw the awareness come back to her.

Suddenly, he didn't want her aware. He wanted her mindless, and thrashing, and screaming, and calling out his name so loudly it would split the sky with the same intensity as the thunder all around them.

Dieudonné's eyes had darkened like the storm. Something elemental and primitive and perhaps a little bit dangerous emanated from his half-naked body.

Whatever it was, she wanted it unleashed on her.

He was a masterpiece of a man. It was a silly expression even as it went through her mind, but there was no other way to describe his body. Sculpted and smooth, with lean, defined muscles that made him as intricately formed as any statue. His hair had come undone and it hung around his head, long and dark brown, with hints of blond glowing from the tips.

She reached up and threaded her fingers through it.

He took her hand and pressed it to his mouth, licking the centre of it with his clever tongue.

She shuddered.

One by one, he drew her fingers into the warm cavern of his mouth, sucking on them as if he were sipping honey from them. Excitement curled inside of her stomach, and she shivered at the feeling.

From there, he drew his mouth to her inner wrist, nibbling at the tender skin. She hissed at the sensation, which was not pleasurable in the strictest sense of the word, but not painful either.

She didn't care. He was driving her wild.

'Deyès mwen,' he murmured against her skin.

Bending his head, he kissed her lips again, this time deeper and slower, as if he were trying to draw out her very essence. He continued kissing her while his hands moved over her body, somehow removing her clothes without her being too aware of it, although she shifted and moved when she needed to until only his hands and the rain touched her skin.

She should feel self-conscious. Indeed, part of her did, but the pleased, possessive look in his eyes showed her she had nothing to feel awkward about.

From there, it became an exercise in how much pleasure could a woman take before she went completely mad. There was no part of her that went unexplored by his hands or his mouth. He kissed her until her body arched into his, tangling his tongue with hers before he ripped himself away to lead a moist trail to the hollow of her neck.

He murmured appreciatively against her skin, and she thought she would nearly die from it. When he cupped both her breasts in his hands and drew them both together in his mouth, she almost screamed, the pleasure was so intense.

A growling laugh erupted from his mouth. 'I take it my form of worship pleases you, *La Sirène*.'

It was an onslaught from there. He caressed, licked and nipped every inch of her body. Whatever he did to her, she wanted it. And he did nothing she didn't like.

By the time he'd propped himself onto his forearms again, she was a quivering, mindless mass of sensation. She wanted something just out of reach, but she didn't know what it was.

His fingers trailed through the hair at the apex of her thighs. He whispered in her ear, and she hid her face in his damp neck, suddenly shy. He coaxed her gently, and she slowly opened to him.

When his finger lightly touched the tiny bud hidden between the folds of her flesh, she gasped and clutched at his arm.

'Dieudonné!'

'Look at me, *La Sirène*.'

She did, seeing his darkened eyes gazing into hers with a heated intensity. 'Do you trust me?'

Swallowing, she nodded.

'Then let me please you, *La Sirène*.'

'I don't… I don't…'

'Shh. Let me show you what I mean.'

Bending his head, he whispered again, telling her what he wanted her to do, and encouraging her when she did it. Soon, her hips bucked against his hand freely, and she cried out at the tension building inside of her.

He kept talking to her softly as whatever was within started to stretch her insides—pull, tug and twist. She wanted to run from it. She wanted to embrace it. He laughed at her, and she realised she had spoken those words out loud.

His eyes were hot, but his mouth was tender against her temples. Then he pressed the heel of his hand to her mound and ground it hard.

She screamed out into the storm, her body trembling and shaking as something in her finally snapped and sent wave after wave of intense pleasure rippling through her body.

If there was a more beautiful sight than seeing Evena being taken by *la petite mort*, then Dieudonné had yet to see it.

She slumped against his body, breathing hard.

He knew he should give her time to recover, but his own need beat furiously at him. Yet even now there was a part of him that wanted to pull away, to stop before anything more could happen, before it was too late.

Only what man would want to leave this image before him—Evena sprawled out and naked in his arms, winded, flushed and so achingly lovely that she could tempt a saint to sin?

And he wasn't a saint by any definition of the word.

Then she looked at him. Her lips, swollen from his kisses, were particularly delectable as she murmured enticingly, 'I'm yours, Dieudonné. Aren't you going to take me?'

Every sensible, noble thought scampered away like gleeful, naughty children. When she looked at him like that, how could he resist her?

I'll withdraw, he thought wildly to himself, even as he moved over her. *Before my seed spills inside her, I'll make sure to...to...*

As carefully and slowly as he could, Dieudonné penetrated her exquisitely tight sheath. Her fingernails dug into his shoulders and she bit her bottom lip.

'*La Sirène?*'

She shook her head, and he knew she wanted him to continue.

Her tightness wrapped around him like creamy silk, burning him so sweetly he had to grit his teeth against the delicious agony.

It took all his willpower not to thrust. She had only taken part of his manhood and he needed to be inside her, clamped by those feminine walls and held deep within her so that he could never, ever leave her.

She whimpered as he moved again. He dropped his head to lave his tongue against her rosy nipple before taking it deep into his mouth.

She cried out, and he sank in further, knowing he had finally made her his in a way that couldn't be changed. Something masculine and utterly possessive roared in his breast.

Her body tightened around him, and he pushed forward until he was firmly inside her, feeling her shake and tremble and clasp him closer. He kept still, trying to give her the time she needed to accept him.

Finally, after eons it seemed, she relaxed around him and he began to move once more, thrusting gently at first, and then, as his body clamoured for release, faster and deeper.

Watching her face, he saw her eyes begin to darken in colour, and a delicate flush of blood pervaded her skin. Her nails started to leave grooves on his back. She reached up and drew his mouth to her, nipping at his lower lip, making it sting a little at the same time as she wrapped her thighs around his waist.

It was that…that moment where he lost it.

He surged into her harder and harder, trying to be gentle

but unable to as his need pounded at his control. Yet he saw her face through the flashes of his desire, watched it contorting in ecstasy as extreme pleasure ricocheted through her body and she started to convulse once more.

Blindly, he slid a hand between their bodies to stroke her nub. Once. Twice. She screamed in a strangulated way, which finally shattered him, hurtling him into the throes of his own wild storm.

Chapter Thirteen

The scent of rain-soaked flowers stirred Evena from slumber. Sleepily, she opened her eyes to see the wooden rafters of the gazebo above her. Droplets of water lingered along the edges, shining like crystal gems. She turned her head and sunlight pierced her eyes.

Par Dieu! What time was it?

Then, in a rush, the memories of the morning flowed through her.

She and Dieudonné had finally made love!

That was when she became aware of the heavy weight around her torso and the warmth over her legs.

She glanced down to see that Dieudonné had wrapped his long arm around her, drawing her close to him. One hand cupped a breast, and one leg was thrown over both of hers.

Her new husband lay next to her, fast asleep.

Evena smiled. Of course he would be tired. He'd not only taken her once, but twice, while the storm raged. The second time had been thrilling, a slow, drugging, sensual loving. He'd whispered sweet things in her ear, telling her there was still so much more they could learn about each other.

Glancing at his mouth, she saw where she had nipped him in the throes of passion. A tiny dot of red just at the edge of his lower lip. She flushed.

The breeze blew again, and she shivered. Where his body didn't cover hers, she felt the chill of the wind. From the look of it, morning had turned to early afternoon while they'd been asleep under the gazebo.

Her eyes closed, listening to the sounds of nature resume its activity after the storm that had briefly ravaged it. Everything around her seemed brighter, more vibrant. The faint calls of birds, the humming of insects as they went from one flower to another, even the wind as it blew, created a pleasing melody of sorts.

She was glad Dieudonné had made her his wife in truth—under the clouds, in the midst of nature, surrounded by a sense of wildness and freedom. Even the storm hadn't dampened their passion. There was no one she'd rather have experienced such pleasure with than him.

Dieudonné had been all she could have dreamed about and hoped for. Masterful. Gentle. Giving. Taking.

He was her dearest friend and her fiercest love.

She jolted, feeling goose bumps lift along her skin.

Love? Did she love Dieudonné as a woman loved a man, with her entire heart?

Her mother's words reverberated in her mind. There had to be more to their marriage than desire.

Had she always loved him?

Maybe not in this way as children. That feeling had closer ties to sibling attachment. Back then, he was the older brother she'd never had, a friend who she'd tormented and teased, but got along with so well.

As they'd grown, the bond between them had only increased in potency. She'd simply accepted that change as a sign of maturity, growing from a young girl to a woman. Still, her affection for Dieudonné had remained, deepening with each year that passed, cultivated and growing even when she didn't realise it.

All she knew was that she'd felt she couldn't wait until his family next came to Saint-Domingue and she would have him with her once more.

That was love of a certain kind. At least, that was what she thought. Maybe it had been more, a precursor to this moment.

There was something completely new and exciting bursting through her veins. It wasn't just desire, although she'd be a fool not to admit that it was certainly mixed in there. This was sharper and sweeter, piercing her like an arrow that she cradled to her chest.

This was love. Planted, seeded and rooted from the time they were children to now. Goodness knew she'd had opportunities to explore love with other men, but she never had.

Now she knew why she'd held back. She loved Dieudonné.

A bright smile creased her face. Warmth like nothing she had ever experienced before flowed through her veins. Glancing down at his unruly blond-tipped hair, she carefully placed a kiss on top of his head, not ready to wake him yet.

That day in the mountain, they'd been given a glimpse of how things could be. It was so clear to her now.

She wanted to kiss him again, tell him how she felt. That was why she was so determined to be the wife he needed. Because she wanted to give him a place to call his own.

But what if she couldn't?

A cold hand squeezed her heart. Would it cast a dark cloud over their marriage?

Evena's lip trembled, awash by the strength of this burgeoning love that had started to grow and tower inside of her like a young tree. This was what her mother had been trying to tell her. A woman's love could rival the strongest winds, the fiercest storm. She must succeed in helping Dieudonné achieve his goal. That was the only option.

But he needed to know how she felt. This was one secret she wouldn't keep to herself.

'Dieudonné…'

He stirred and cradled her closer to his body. She basked in the feeling of safety and protection it gave her. Still, now that she was fully awake, she wanted to get up.

'Dieudonné, wake up, *mon cher.*'

He stirred, squeezing her breast in a familiar way, as if reassuring himself in his half-sleep that she was still there. She was thrilled at the idea. His face in repose made him look strangely vulnerable.

Then he came awake suddenly, his ash and indigo eyes stabbing into her own.

'Evena.' His voice sounded deep, roughened by sleep.

She ached to tell him of her discovery, but practicality took over right now. 'We have to go back to the chateau. It's getting late.'

He lifted himself up then and looked around. 'You're right.'

When he removed himself from her she felt cold suddenly, although she wasn't sure if it was because of the lack of his body heat, or for some other reason. An odd expression came over his face and she sat up abruptly.

'Dieudonné, I have to tell you—'

'Let's not talk about it now, Evena—you're cold. Here, let me help you get dressed.'

Her mouth gaped open. The words—he'd spoken them in a bland, almost dismissive tone. He tugged on his breeches, smoothing them up his hard thighs. The movement revealed the prominent musculature of his body.

Her throat went dry.

Standing, he reached down and pulled her languid body to

her feet. She swayed for a moment, her legs nearly boneless and uncooperative. He helped to steady her, an intent look in his eyes that she recognised as masculine satisfaction, before he allowed his lids to lower, concealing them.

Arrogant, wonderful man!

Once she was steady, he helped her to dress. Various aches and pains made themselves known from making love on the hard floor of the gazebo, although she hadn't realised it at the time.

She winced.

'Are you all right, Evena?'

She looked into his face. As he'd helped her dress, she'd noticed his expression becoming more remote, but there was genuine concern in his voice.

'I'm fine, Dieudonné.'

Why was he suddenly looking as if he'd rather be anywhere but here with her?

When they'd finished getting dressed, they stared at each other. Dieudonné was still emanating tension and she felt uneasy again.

'Dieudonné, what's the matter?'

He paused for a moment, and then dragged his fingers through his loosened hair. 'Nothing, Evena.'

Her nostrils flared. 'Don't lie to me. You're acting so strangely.'

He was silent for a long while, and then he sighed. 'I shouldn't have done that.'

Evena wondered if her eyes were going to fall from their sockets, so surprised was she at his words.

'What do you mean?'

Picking up his discarded coat, he shrugged into it. 'We're only here right now because I compromised you at the Duchesse's chateau that night. If I had reined in my desires, you would have been able to marry a man who could help you save your father.'

'That—'

'Let's be honest with each other, Evena. We always have been. I don't have enough influence to try to gain access to the King's physician. I've tried, but there's nothing more I can do.'

'But what does that have to do with what just happened? Dieudonné, you're my husband and what we shared was the most natural thing a husband and wife can share with each other. It was beautiful. How can you apologise for it?'

A muscle leapt in his jaw, his profile becoming hard, implacable.

Evena's heart sank. The magic of those moments in his arms, where he'd made her soar to the sky and become one with the storm, evaporated like dew under a hot sun.

Was he resentful because he'd remembered she wasn't the kind of woman he needed her to be? That nonsense about him not being the man she needed him to be, she ignored. There was something else going on here.

Her throat constricted, but she pushed past the hurt in favour of the anger that flared inside of her. 'Dieudonné, don't you want to make love with me? Don't you want to have a family?'

Her words seemed to erect an even higher wall between them, as Dieudonné's entire body stiffened. 'That is a matter for another time,' he replied, his voice tight.

Evena felt as though she had been struck.

'Another time?' she pressed, her voice rising. 'When, Dieudonné? When will it be the right time for us to discuss this?'

Her voice trailed off, the realisation dawning that no argument of hers would sway him. Dieudonné met her gaze, his own eyes guarded, only reflecting the impenetrable walls he had built around himself.

And yet, for all his detachment, there was a hint of something else there too—was it pain? Regret?

Evena's anger dissipated as swiftly as it had come, replaced by a profound sorrow. How foolish could she be? Of course he would regret what they'd done. This marriage was only a transaction forced upon them, after all. Just because he'd made sweet love to her, it didn't mean his feelings for her had changed.

He must still feel trapped with a woman he'd never have chosen to marry.

All her fine-sounding thoughts of being the wife he needed ricocheted around in her head, accompanied by mocking laughter.

Did you really, truly think he would ever love you like that?

Evena longed to silence that taunting voice, but couldn't.

Of course Dieudonné had made love to her! She'd thrown herself at him, practically begging him to take her. He hadn't reached for her—she'd dragged him into her arms.

Wouldn't *any* man respond like that?

She had hoped to tell him how much she loved him. Even knowing that he'd hurt her in a way she hadn't thought was possible, her love for him dug its roots deeper into her soul.

There wasn't any way now that she could share those feelings with him.

'I see,' she said quietly, the fight draining out of her. 'I had hoped for... But that doesn't matter now.'

With that, they started back to the chateau. She could feel Dieudonné's gaze on her and couldn't help but wonder what thoughts lay behind those shuttered eyes. As the light shifted, casting long shadows on the path, Evena's thoughts were in tumult.

When they arrived back at the chateau, the servants looked at their dishevelled appearance and she couldn't help but see the amusement in their eyes, even though they pretended that she and Dieudonné hadn't returned looking far less put together than when they'd left.

It wasn't until she reached her bedchamber that she allowed herself the luxury of tears.

Every time Dieudonné closed his eyes, he saw Evena's face as he made love to her. When he turned over in bed, he heard her soft sighs, cries and uninhibited moans singing in his ear like the sensuous notes of some forbidden musical score.

When his fingers caressed the material of his bedlinen, he was reminded of the silky texture of her skin, the satiny feel of her moist, creamy heat as he brought her to release over and over. When he licked his lower lip, it stung a little, reminding him of the small bite she'd given him. His back stretched and he felt the marks left from her nails.

Cursing himself, he got out of bed, pulled his banyan around his naked body and went out onto his bedroom balcony. He was supposed to have withdrawn from her body before his seed could spill inside her—prevent a child being created from this union until they were both sure it was what they wanted.

No innocent child should be subjected to the torment he'd faced. It wasn't an outcome he'd ever take lightly, but at the fatal moment he'd forgotten everything but the intense pleasure of being inside her.

The moonlight turned the scenery into day, flowing over the sleeping earth while leaving him awake. A chilly night breeze blew against his body, prickling his skin.

Like a martyr before a holy light, Dieudonné stood there, lifting his face and allowing the moonlight to cascade over him. He tortured himself with the autumn wind as if he were allowing himself to bathe in melted snow.

Anything to cool the hot desire that refused to be suppressed.

There was nothing for it. He'd fought a pitched battle with an enemy he knew very well.

Himself.

And he'd lost.

Even now, in this moment of self-recrimination, he wanted her still.

When she'd fallen asleep under the gazebo, exhausted from his ravenous passion, he'd been unable to pull his eyes away from her sleeping features.

In a stroke of pure coincidence, the storm had stopped soon afterwards, and murky, watery light had flowed over her, dappling her flushed skin.

Along her hips he'd seen slight marks left from his possession. They would probably have faded by now, but the thought of them there still evoked something entirely primitive within him. He'd liked seeing them far too much, and he'd bent his head to place a gentle kiss against each.

At that moment, something inside of him had gripped him mercilessly hard and refused to let go.

He'd fallen in love with Evena.

Granted, he'd always cared for her, but this was different. What he had felt for her when they were children had no comparison to what coursed through his veins as a man, bubbling inside and invigorating him while at the same time sending an odd kind of terror flooding through his system.

He'd become like thousands of men had throughout the years, since time immemorial. Learning that life with the woman he loved was worth every sacrifice.

Sacrifice.

Dieudonné's fist shook. Had he thought about that when he'd sunk himself so deep inside her that he didn't know where he ended and she began? That he might have given her a child that could end up suffering as much as he had? Had he bound Evena to him in a way she didn't truly understand? The pleasure they had given each other had made any other experience pale in comparison. He couldn't, wouldn't regret it.

He snarled. Did that make him a selfish *bastard* in more ways than one?

'Don't call yourself that!'

Evena's voice echoed in his head, and he sighed. No, she wouldn't want him to castigate himself like this.

In the harsh, soul-stripping moonlight, he mentally flogged himself for his lack of restraint. That didn't deter the desire to open the adjoining door of their bedchambers and lose himself in the sweet oblivion between her thighs all over again.

Cursing once more, he spun around and stormed back into his bedchamber, the warmth of it heating his chilled skin. He'd no idea how long he'd been out there, but it wasn't long enough to dampen his need for her.

He didn't think anything would.

What did that mean for their future then? He clearly couldn't trust himself to pull out in the heat of the moment, so if he continued to make love to Evena, she'd end up with child. And he couldn't let that happen when he was still so unsure if it was the right thing to do. She was worried enough about her father as it was. Adding a child would only cause more problems than it would solve.

He stopped in front of the long oval-shaped mirror and looked at his semi-naked form without really seeing it. That vision of his imagined daughter came back into his head.

Would it really be so terrible if you had a child? a tiny voice whispered seductively. *A little one you would do your best to protect from all the harsh realities of the world.*

It was a delightful, evocative thought. A child as a symbol of his and Evena's love.

His heart twinged so painfully that he physically flinched. Then, with a force of will he hadn't known he possessed, Dieudonné wrenched the image from his mind, deliberately sending his thoughts down another path, although it was almost as painful.

The last time he'd spoken with Claude, just before their wedding, the older man had told him that he was glad that Dieudonné was marrying his daughter.

'I have always believed my daughters need a certain kind of man who can understand them fully. My Evena will grow and blossom with a man who will do nothing to restrict her. He will be her tower of strength, her battlements against the world. That Seigneur de Guise Elbeuf may have been well connected, but he would have done everything he could to dampen her fire.'

Claude's eyes had stared into his own. *'You understand her better than most, mon fils. And you will care for her the best.'*

Unspoken was his blessing—that if something happened to Claude, he knew that Dieudonné could be trusted to take care of Evena for the rest of her life.

Some of what Claude had said was true. He did know Evena better than most.

But she'd feel terribly guilty that she hadn't been able to help her father.

An old familiar feeling of worthlessness came over him and his shoulders hunched. Could he not do anything to help her?

'No,' he said out loud, the word a self-inflicted wound to his heart. 'I can't do anything.'

Yes, he had his wealth. Evena, though an heiress with a

substantial dowry of her own, had no need to worry that he couldn't provide for her material needs.

But what did any of that mean if he couldn't help her father?

He forced the gnawing thoughts away with a grimace, inhaling deeply as if to draw strength from the very air that surrounded him. He turned from the mirror. Slowly, he began to pace the length of his room again, each step an attempt to quiet the storm within.

After several moments of aimless wandering, he paused by the window once more, glancing out into the night.

A sense of resignation washed over him. It dulled the sharp edges of his desire. He couldn't allow himself to touch Evena again.

With a weary sigh, he finally turned back to his bed and let his banyan fall to the floor. Sliding under the covers, his thoughts drifted inevitably back to Evena.

If his plan was to work, he'd have to find some way to resist her. He knew instinctively that a single look from those green eyes would be enough to break his promise to himself.

He'd have to try to forget how wonderful their lovemaking had been.

That voice mocked him again. Did he really think it was possible to forget that exquisite pleasure?

No, but he could try. Now that he knew he loved her with every part of his body, he had an obligation to protect her.

Even from himself.

Yes, that was the way he would view it. He was doing this for both of them. If he told Evena why, she wouldn't understand and she'd argue furiously with him. This way was better.

Embracing a newfound calm, Dieudonné allowed himself to close his eyes and drift away into slumber, only to be tormented by wonderful, sensual dreams of the woman he'd given his heart to.

Chapter Fourteen

November 1774

Evena sat in the weak afternoon sunlight that shone through the arched windows.

'Madame la Comtesse, Mademoiselle Moreau is here.'

Evena set aside her book and stood in the centre of the grandly furnished drawing room, the light playing off the subtle silk of her gown making the fabric shimmer with a life of its own.

A glance at the ornate clock perched on the marble mantelpiece showed the other woman had arrived on time. It was the best news she'd heard in a long while.

Trying to calm her beating heart, Evena clasped her hands together. 'Please, show her in.'

The servant curtsied and left.

This was the only thing she'd been able to think of. It was a mad idea, but she was running out of alternatives.

Dieudonné hadn't made love to her since that day in the gazebo, nearly two months ago. No matter how many hints she'd tried to give him, or even blatant invitations, he'd found a way to deny her. It was never by word, but by deed.

But she couldn't forget that time in his arms, which made everything seem worse. How masterful and wonderful he'd been with every touch, every caress, every kiss they'd shared. Every night, she strained to hear him in the adjoining room, pleading silently for him to come through and take her.

She longed to confront him, but she'd decided she really didn't want to know if he regretted marrying her, especially when she knew Agnès regretted not marrying *him*.

Not speaking to him wasn't hard. The few times he was there, he kept his distance, locked in his study, going over the accounts or talking with his solicitors, or whatever it was he did to occupy himself.

But she mourned the friend who had been with her since childhood. He had retreated behind a cool, distant persona and she had no idea how to get him back.

So she kept herself busy. Her own days did not lack for anything. She was determined to make her mark on society as the Comtesse de Montreau. A few weeks after their wedding, invitations to social engagements had started arriving, and she'd accepted all of them.

The theatre, a soiree, a carriage drive, it didn't matter what it was, she'd accepted, using the skills she'd learnt from the Duchesse to skilfully navigate the various nuances of society. Wondering what she could do to make her own unique mark that would elevate her amongst her new peers, and thus her husband. Would being a social success win back Dieudonné's regard for her and lure him to her bed once again?

As time passed, her worry had been replaced by frustration. Why was she working this hard to help him when he was being so distant? Never in all her life had she wished for a man's approval as she did now. Albeit none of those other men had been her husband, nor had they ever made her feel like Dieudonné did.

Give up, a part of her had teased in the quiet of her thoughts. *Stop trying so hard.*

She almost wanted to obey that shrewd voice. It would be so easy just to not care any more.

He's not worth it, that same voice insisted.

But he is, she argued.

This was her marriage she was fighting for. Her heart she was gambling with. This was her life, and it wasn't going to get any better if she just gave up on herself. On Dieudonné.

On them.

It wasn't until late one night, while she lay alone in her cold bed, aching for Dieudonné's touch with a feverish longing that threatened to consume her, that it came to her.

She thought about the Duchesse de Villers-Cotterêt's salon, when the Comte de Novilos had been invited to speak to her guests about Saint-Domingue. It had been a great success.

She'd decided to make her mark by becoming a *salonnaire*, a salon hostess, turning Château Lumières de Montreau into a place to meet and discuss the issues of the day, whatever they were.

It wouldn't be limited to rank or race either. Common or noble, Parisian, English or any other race, all would be welcome and invited to discourse.

After all, no matter what the nobility thought, there was a growing unrest among the citizens. Razor-sharp minds such as Voltaire and others were causing a stir among the aristocracy with their dangerous views that were upsetting the way things had always been.

Just as they were in Saint-Domingue, albeit to a lesser degree.

Change was coming.

As she'd lain in bed, Evena had known she could use the

chateau as a meeting place for such minds. Especially the elite mixed-blood people she'd met here and there.

Maybe then, Dieudonné would...

What? Come to her bed? Tell her that he loved her? That he didn't regret making her his wife?

A wave of dizziness came upon her, drawing her back to the present. She lurched over to her chair and sat heavily, willing herself to stay in control.

Fear ate at her insides. The swooning spells had started a week or so ago. The first time, she'd thought nothing of it as she had been balanced on a small step, trying to reach a book on a higher shelf. She'd thought she'd simply lost her balance. Thankfully, the maid had been there to steady her.

Since then, she'd experienced two more swooning spells.

The same as her father. Although her mother had written to say that her father hadn't experienced any swooning spells since her wedding day. That was a huge relief. Maybe the nightmare was finally coming to an end for him.

But was it starting for her?

Evena leaned her head back against the chair, begging the spinning to stop.

She didn't want to think about the implications, didn't want to suppose that what had happened to her father was happening to her too.

And what it meant for her marriage.

Lately, her appetite had disappeared, and she could barely manage to eat anything. If Dieudonné knew...

No, she didn't want to think about that either.

Evena lifted her head then and pasted on a smile as a woman entered the room.

If she didn't know any better, Evena would think Lilas Moreau had been born and bred on Saint-Domingue. She could have been any of the Creole beauties on the island. The difference was that the woman had the poise and restrained posture of one born into Parisian society.

A woman of mixed blood, Lilas had lovely Armagnac skin matched with rather lovely violet-hued eyes. Her fine-boned features matched perfectly with a retroussé nose and full lips. Dressed in a gown of lavender with a high hair pouf dressed in peacock feathers and small gold medallions placed here and there, she looked the epitome of a woman of status. Ringlet curls framed her long swan-like neck.

The other woman curtsied in deference. 'Madame la Comtesse de Montreau, it's a pleasure to meet you.'

Evena stood. 'The pleasure is mine, Mademoiselle Moreau. I've heard much about your artistic talent.'

The other woman gave a regal nod of acknowledgement. 'You honour me.'

Evena gestured to a seat by her side and then sat when the woman had settled. After giving instructions for hot chocolate to be brought, Evena turned to find Lilas's violet eyes were fixed on her.

Evena cleared her throat. 'You're wondering why I've asked you to come.'

'Not at all, *madame*.' Lilas shrugged in a matter-of-fact way. 'Anyone who seeks me usually seeks my services.'

'That is true. You've come highly recommended by several women I've spoken to. But this would be a special commission.'

Lilas leaned back against the cushion. 'I'm listening.'

Evena had the woman's undivided attention. For all that, she couldn't open her mouth and speak.

Why not? What she was asking for wasn't really all that terrible, was it?

But she wanted to shock Dieudonné into giving her his

undivided attention, and this was the only way she could think of to get it.

'Mademoiselle Moreau, I want you to paint a nude for me.'

'I see.' Lilas didn't blink an eye. 'Is this for an erotic collection, *madame*? If it is, I must inform you I do not produce that sort of work.'

Her face burned. 'No, *mademoiselle*. It's nothing of that sort.' She cleared her throat. 'It's a painting of myself. To give to my husband as a gift for his birthday.'

A gleam appeared in Lilas's eyes. 'Ah, I see. As I recall, Madame la Comtesse de Montreau, you are newly married, aren't you?'

'Oui.'

Though you wouldn't know it, she thought bitterly.

'Very well. If I may, *madame*, can I present you with an alternative idea?'

'Such as?'

A knock at the door signalled the arrival of the hot chocolate. Once it was served and the door closed again, Lilas picked up her cup and took a sip.

'I don't think you should be in the nude, *madame*. Granted, I'm sure your husband would not be at all displeased to find you as naked as Eve, and just as lovely. However, I feel it's rather too obvious.'

She almost replied that was exactly the reason why she wanted it. To make her husband aware of her. But she kept quiet as Lilas continued.

'Yours is a type of beauty that would be best expressed more subtly. I envision you lying on a chaise, dressed in a simple white chemise, but one that is draped in a revealing manner. Seductive yet chaste. Innocent, and yet still sinful.'

As she listened to Lilas's idea, she breathed, *'La Sirène.'*

'What did you say?'

She shook her head. 'It's nothing, but you've captured the image I'd like to give to my husband perfectly.'

'I'm afraid it'll be frightfully expensive.'

Evena barely heard her. Dieudonné wouldn't be able to resist her then, would he? All she could think of was the look on her husband's face once he saw the painting of her.

Eagerly, she looked at her guest. 'When can we get started, *mademoiselle*?'

Dieudonné didn't know how much longer he could hold out against Evena. Nearly two months had gone by, and he hadn't touched her once. Some small, quiet part of him had relished the proof of his ability to control himself for her sake.

The other, larger, much louder part of himself kept calling him a fool. Did he think he could go the rest of his life not making love to his wife? He'd have to come to terms with his fear of having children and risk it, despite the potential social consequences.

Either that or he'd die from sheer frustration!

Dieudonné heard that voice in his head now as Evena entered the dining room for breakfast. Without her being aware of it, he fixed his eyes on her as she walked.

She was always lovely, but to his fevered mind there was something even more hauntingly beautiful about her this morning. An odd frailty tugging at something inside of him.

Frailty?

He squinted, trying to send his raging lust back to whence it came. Studying her more closely, he suddenly noticed that there seemed to be something wrong with her today. Her burnished skin lacked the vitality he was used to seeing. Dark circles rested under her eyes, and her usually lush, full mouth appeared dry and drooped at the corners.

Unease gripped his body. Was something wrong? Was she unwell?

If you stayed home more often, you would know.

He pressed his lips together, shame and guilt making him squirm. That much was true. If he spent more time with her, he would know everything he needed to know. But if he did that, he wouldn't be able to stay away from her. He'd take her again and again.

She sat down and sighed rather wearily.

'Good morning,' he greeted her, his voice betraying none of his inner turmoil.

She barely glanced in his direction. 'Good morning.' Her voice was low.

The servants placed their meal before them. After she'd thanked them, she fiddled with her food. Dieudonné watched as she took a bite or two before setting the dish away from her as if it disgusted her.

Come to think of it, her appetite had waned lately. Worried now, he said, 'You look tired today. Did you not sleep well?'

When her head lifted, he noticed the lines of strain on her face.

Evena scowled at him, a swift flash of irritation sparking in her dark green eyes as she snapped, 'I'm perfectly fine, thank you.' Her voice rang sharply.

Dieudonné blinked. 'Evena,' he said in a deliberate, calming way, 'I don't think you are.'

Then, without any warning, she rose swiftly from her chair, gripping the edge of the table as if she were holding on for dear life.

He stood. 'What's wrong? Where are you going? Aren't you eating?'

For some reason, she looked as if she were going to be sick. He started to walk towards her when her eyelids fluttered.

'No, I'm not—' She swayed, and he darted forward, at her side in an instant, just as she fell into a faint.

He caught her soft weight in his arms. Dieudonné's heart nearly jumped out of his chest as Evena lay there, unconscious. He could tell she was still breathing, but he had never seen her like this before.

She'd swooned—just like her father. He swallowed the rock in his throat. What was happening?

Calling for the servants, he ordered one to go for his father's physician and the other to get a damp cloth. Carrying his precious cargo to the drawing room, he laid Evena on the chaise.

The folds of her *tignon* had unravelled and he removed it, tenderly smoothing back the coils of black hair from her forehead. She was incredibly pale, almost waxen.

Frantically, he called out to her, 'Evena, please...'

He didn't know what he was begging for, but a moment later, she stirred on her own, and his chest caved in relief.

Her eyes were dark and sad when she looked at him. 'I swooned, didn't I?' She sounded like a young girl about to be scolded.

Dieudonné caressed her cheek with his thumb. 'You did,' he answered in a quiet voice. The next part was difficult to say but they had to face it. 'Like your father.'

Although Evena had told him Claude was getting better, the very idea that his swooning spells could have been passed on to his daughter frightened him.

Blinking, her lashes became damp with tears. 'Oh, Dieudonné!' she whispered in a sorrowful way that wrenched his insides.

Lifting her up to his chest, he held her as she cried, feeling utterly helpless. What were they going to do? If she were experiencing the same swooning spells as her father, then...then...

'This isn't the first time you've fainted, is it, Evena?'

She sniffed and shook her head. 'It's happened a few times within the last week or so. I'll be fine one moment and then the next, the world spins.'

Drawing back, he used his finger to lift her chin. 'Why didn't you tell me?'

The minute he asked the question, he wanted to take it back. Why did he think she hadn't told him? He'd made himself extremely scarce for nearly two months, just to avoid the temptation of her.

He waited for her to berate him. After all, she'd have told him if he had been here to make sure of her well-being and health.

She hadn't been able to depend on him because he was so disappointed in himself for not being able to help her. For being afraid to have children with her. So overcome by a love that beat against the cage it was trapped in. Every day it wailed inside of him, begging for release. Praying for a chance to be expressed.

Like any miserable jailer, Dieudonné had locked it up and hidden the key, desperate to keep the prisoner from escaping and wreaking havoc on his world.

How fanciful he sounded to himself. Yet how selfish he'd been, worrying more about his lack of restraint instead of being here with her.

Would her closest friend have ever acted that way?

Was that how a husband was supposed to treat his wife?

Just because he wasn't the husband she'd originally wanted, it did not preclude him from being the husband she needed.

A knot formed in his throat.

'Désolé.'

Something of his anguish must have made it into his voice because she drew away, looking up into his face.

'*Non*, Dieudonné. I should have told you, but I was... was...so afraid I was becoming ill like Papa.'

Her tears had soaked his shirt, but he didn't care. If anything, he felt bathed by them, washed clean even. She tried to move away, but he kept his finger on her chin so he could drown in the depths of her beautiful green eyes.

He cradled her, pressing a kiss on her forehead.

A moment later, the servant came back with a damp cloth, looking worriedly at them. Dieudonné mopped Evena's face, murmuring nonsensical words to her.

How childlike she looked, lying on his chest. It tugged at something vulnerable in him. She was the woman he loved, but he'd treated her badly. Instead of talking to her, just like they used to when they were simply friends, he'd pushed her away. Instead of sharing his doubts about being a father who could protect his children from the vitriol of society, he'd made the arbitrary decision to not give her a voice to decide what she wanted. He should have known better.

A new resolve entered his body, stirring his blood. He would remedy that.

The wait for the physician to come was a torture all of its own, each tick of the clock a strike upon Dieudonné's heart. When at last the doctor arrived, Evena had become quiet and still. Not at all like the woman he knew.

The doctor refused to let him into the room, preferring to talk to Evena on her own. Dieudonné rubbed the back of his neck, trying to ease the tense muscles.

For what seemed like an eternity, he waited for the doctor to return, sending all kinds of prayers to the heavens, begging for divine intervention on his wife's behalf. Would they be forced to live in the same kind of hell as the Baptistes had?

The door opened, and he immediately turned as the doctor came back out. The man looked at him, his expression bland.

'Well, Comte de Montreau, it's a good thing you called me. It is as we've feared.'

He felt sick. 'What do you mean?'

Evena… What would her parents say? How would they react when they found that she was ill…?

'You're going to be a father.'

The room seemed to tilt, all the air rushing out of his lungs as he gasped. A fist slammed into his gut.

'What?' Surely he hadn't heard that correctly.

The doctor grinned, his blue eyes twinkling. 'That's all it is, *monsieur*. Your wife is with child.'

Dieudonné stared at the other man, but his features blurred as the implications made themselves known.

A child!

His face scrunched. 'Why has she been having swooning spells?'

The doctor shrugged and went over to the corner of the room where the spirits sat on a small table. Helping himself to rum, he poured himself a drink.

'It's a symptom of her condition,' he explained. 'In my profession, I've noticed some women experience a variety of ailments that affect them when they're enceinte. Some women are unable to eat certain foods, while others become insatiable for the oddest of cuisines. In your wife's case, she's swooning. If she puts something in her stomach in the morning, perhaps some weak tea instead of the heavier hot chocolate, and a piece or two of day-old bread, it may settle her insides better. When she is further along, the swooning spells will cease.'

Dieudonné took in the words, placing them in the back of his mind to act upon later. The shock of what the doctor had revealed still ricocheted through him.

A child. *Their* child.

His legs weakened, and he floundered until he gripped the back of the chair.

A baby.

There was no going back now. The choice had been made for them.

Was he ready for this? Was he ready to be a father?

The vision of a smiling child flashed into his head once again. Instead of shying away from it, he saw himself reaching down and lifting the child into his arms. He saw himself playing with her—for surely it must be a girl to steal his heart, just like her mother—and guarding her with every ounce of his strength.

He waited for the regret to come. The fear.

Nothing of the sort happened. Happiness rushed through him like warm rain.

It didn't matter if he wasn't ready. He was already a father.

Determination followed the happiness. No matter what else happened, he would never let society ostracise his child the way he had been. He'd take a rapier to anyone who tried to do so!

For far too long he'd let the past rule both his present and his future, wanting society's acceptance so much that it had almost destroyed the most important thing in his life.

His family. His marriage.

Never again would he allow what others thought of him to control his actions. He would raise his child to think the same way. Daughter or son would have his family and Evena's family, who would all love and cherish any child of theirs.

Just as he would.

'Monsieur?'

Drawn out of his thoughts, he saw the doctor staring at him in a quizzical way. The man probably thought he was a lunatic. Until this moment, he had been one. Now, he was finally released from the asylum he'd made for himself.

His voice barely rose from a whisper. 'May I see her now?'

The doctor smiled and poured himself another glass of rum. 'Of course, *monsieur*. And, as most husbands before you have wondered, I will reassure you that you may continue your connubial activities if you wish.'

Dieudonné gulped.

'But give it a fortnight or so first. Just to be certain her strength has recovered.'

He nodded and turned away from the man helping himself to his rum.

When Dieudonné entered the room, Evena was standing by the window, her gaze lost upon the gardens.

'Should you be standing? Why don't you sit?' he pressed.

She turned around, looking much better than she had before the doctor came. There was a definite sparkle in her eyes. A flush to her cheeks.

'I'm going to have a baby.'

He nodded, still unable to believe it himself. 'I know.'

She turned back to the window.

Uncertainty took hold of him. What was he supposed to do? If things were different between them, he was sure they would have jumped into each other's arms, delighted and joyful at the news.

'Dieudonné,' she said suddenly. 'Let's be honest with one another.'

He froze. 'About what?'

She faced him, staring deep into his eyes, her green orbs holding him captive. 'I know I'm not the woman you wanted as the mother of your child, but I—'

'Shh,' he said, walking forward and placing a finger on her mouth. 'Don't speak. You must take your rest.'

His heart sank. How could he blame her for what she was feeling? He hadn't helped the situation at all by keeping his distance from her the last two months. If he told her he was happy and wanted this child with her with every fibre of his being, she would still find a way to doubt him.

There was nothing he could say that she'd believe. All he could do was show her with his actions how much he wanted her and their baby.

Evena could feel Dieudonné's eyes on her.

He was disappointed.

The news of her pregnancy should have been joyful. Indeed, she was ecstatic that she was going to be a mother.

A child that would bind her and Dieudonné together for the rest of their lives. The very reason for her joy must be the reason for his melancholy.

Was he regretting that day in the storm since the baby had been created from their joining? He must be. Now, this news had become a chasm between them. For him, this baby was a burden rather than a blessing.

Well, no matter what he thought, she would love and care for this child with all the devotion a mother could give.

A mother! She was going to be a mother.

Happiness surged through her once more, temporarily overcoming her more sombre thoughts.

'When do you want to tell our parents?' he asked.

'Soon. We'll go there and see them for a few days, don't you think?' she replied.

'Of course. Do you need to rest now?'

How carefully he spoke, as if he were really concerned about her. A flare of anger suddenly sparked. How dare he?

'Don't pretend you're concerned about my health, Dieudonné.'

His brows lifted into his forehead. 'What are you talking about?'

Just as quickly as the anger had flared, it went away. A wave of weariness came over her and she took a step back.

Dieudonné was at her side in an instant, taking her into his arms. 'Evena, you must be careful now. Your condition is delicate.'

'Is it?' She sighed. 'I want to lie down now.'

'As you wish.'

Before she knew what he was about, he bent and lifted her. 'Dieudonné!'

'Shh, let me take care of you, *La Sirène*.'

Her heart leapt into her throat. He'd called her *La Sirène*!

Ridiculously happy at such a small, insignificant thing, she rested her head against his chest and let herself be comforted by the steady beat of his heart. She hadn't been this close to him in such a long time. Whenever she'd accepted invitations for both of them, he always made sure to keep his distance, only ever touching her long enough to assist her in and out of the carriage.

His scent filled her nose, all Dieudonné, with a hint of citrus. The comfort of his strength made her feel protected. Secure.

How she wished he loved her.

She said nothing as he carried her up the stairs, even though she'd offered to walk. When he arrived at the top, barely winded, he still wouldn't let her go until he'd opened the door to her bedchamber and gently laid her on the bed.

He was bent over her and for a moment he lingered. Their gazes latched on to each other and something poignant hovered between them.

She longed for his mouth on hers. Her pulse quickened when his gaze roamed over her face, only to stop on her lips.

'I'll call the maid to see to you.'

She turned her head away, lest he see her tears.

'Evena,' he began, his voice laced with an emotion she could scarcely define. 'I fear my actions of late have given you cause for distress.'

Evena turned back. 'I cannot help but feel that my…condition has become a burden to you.'

'No,' he said in a firm voice that gave her hope. 'Never that, Evena.'

He bent his head and kissed her. She jerked in reaction to the touch of his lips. It had been too long since she'd felt her husband's kiss.

A moan escaped her lips and, without warning, Dieudonné deepened the kiss, coaxing her lips apart, and she eagerly allowed him entrance.

She held his head between her hands, as if she was afraid he would leave again. Maybe she was. She'd wanted this for far too long. If it was only a dream, she didn't want to wake up. All she wanted was to revel in his taste, his mastery, his expertise—everything.

Dieudonné made a sound, and his arms tightened around her. He drew back far enough to nip softly at her lower lip, and she let loose a cry.

Swiftly, he pulled back, his eyes dark and stormy but with a wide smile gracing his face, showing off his dimples. 'I'll have the maid come and see to you, *La Sirène*.'

He unhooked her fingers from his hair, but not before he'd kissed each tip and curled them into her palms. 'You need to rest. I'll make sure to come see you later.'

A silence fell between them, heavy with words left unsaid. She watched as he left her room, leaving behind fears and hopes that danced just beyond her reach.

Chapter Fifteen

Every waking moment, Evena rejoiced in the knowledge that she and Dieudonné had created a new life. She hugged herself at times, overjoyed at the thought of their child entering the world.

The doctor's advice did help with the swooning. Once the servants found out she was with child, they nearly suffocated her with care. The maid always had a cup of weak English tea at the ready and the chef had gone out of his way to make dry bread constantly available.

Yet, after a particularly trying day of being subjected to everyone's care, she'd fought back, telling them she was with child, not suffering from the plague!

To add to her already confused state, a distinct change had come over Dieudonné and Evena didn't know what to make of it. Gone was the cold, distant man who'd made such exquisite love to her. He was replaced by a familiar stranger. He'd been solicitous of her, but underneath the coddling she'd sensed something else and it made her wary.

More than once, she'd caught him staring at her, his eyes intent as if trying to peer into her mind. There was a constant air of tense expectancy around him, as if he were holding back from erupting at any moment.

Was it regret over their marriage? Did he resent the baby?

No, that didn't seem possible. Two days after they'd found out, he had retained the services of an architect to renovate and redesign the nursery suite. Surely a man who didn't want his child would not go to such lengths.

He also stayed at the chateau, spending more time with her. No matter where she went, he was by her side, careful to see to her comfort, observing her every movement.

But at the back of her mind she wondered uneasily if he'd have been happier to have wed Agnès. If their union had produced a child, it would have had a much better chance of being accepted because of the other woman's aristocratic pedigree and her father's influence at court.

After a week had gone by and the swooning spells had ceased, she applied herself to the task at hand. The idea of hosting a salon had solidified in her mind and she wanted to start preparations.

Dieudonné had set aside a small room for her several days after their wedding. It was here she sat now, thinking about where to begin. The maid had already brought a cup of weak tea and she sipped carefully at the brew as she ruminated over her options. For the salon to draw attention, she had to invite people of interest.

'What's wrong, Evena?'

Startled from her thoughts, she blinked to see her husband standing in the doorway.

He stepped further into the room, somehow dwarfing it. Today, he looked more handsome than ever. He'd obviously gone for a morning ride, evidenced by his dark-coloured riding clothes and the crop he held in his hand. The colour of his coat heightened the contrast with his skin, making his stormy eyes more pronounced. As he came closer, he smelled pleasantly of horse, earth and fresh air. It made his own masculine scent that much more potent.

Her fingers curled. How was she supposed to keep on resisting the urge to throw her arms around him?

'What are you doing?' Dieudonné came to stand near her, leaning on the table. Tension rose inside her, and she gulped. He was close enough to touch.

'I am trying to decide who to invite to my first salon.'

'Who did you have in mind?'

'No one yet. I was hoping…you could help me.'

'Of course,' he said without hesitation.

She smiled at his easy acceptance. 'Well, the first person I thought of was Lilas Moreau.'

'The painter?' His brow lifted in surprise. 'Why, what a splendid idea. A fascinating woman. Did you know she used to be a maid in the house of Duc de Languedoc? I am acquainted with his son, the Marquis de Velay, although I've heard he's currently abroad.'

'A maid?' Evena's eyes widened. 'I didn't know that.'

Dieudonné folded his arms. 'The Marquis de Velay is one of the few men who understood my plight. He is also of mixed blood, although, unlike myself, he is of legitimate birth and the heir to a dukedom.' His head tilted to the side. 'How have you made her acquaintance?'

She'd yet to tell him about the painting she'd commissioned, and she still wanted to keep it a secret. Her last correspondence with Lilas hadn't given her any idea as to when it would be completed.

'I was introduced to her at a party.'

'I see. She'll draw people in, for certain. Now, who else do you have?'

Eagerly, she started to name people, and what followed was a pleasant half hour of talking and laughing. It was impossible not to be reminded of their days of childhood. She'd missed this part of her husband very much.

Yes, she wanted his love, and his passion. Without those things, she had always had his friendship, but for a while even that had eluded her.

Later that evening, as she prepared to go out to the theatre, Dieudonné came into her bedchamber. In his hand he carried a small square box. Sitting before the mirror, she watched as he came forward, his eyes intent upon her face.

'You look lovely,' he murmured. 'I do believe I have married the most beautiful woman in the world. You would make Helen of Troy look like Medusa.'

Flattered despite herself, Evena felt warmth spread from the roots of her hair, concealed under her *tignon* to the base of her throat.

'*Merci*, Dieudonné.'

He stood behind her, catching her eye in the reflection of the mirror. 'I have something for you.'

She waited with bated breath as he turned around and set the box onto the bed. When he faced her again, he held in his hand a sparkling diamond and ruby necklace.

Evena gasped. 'Dieudonné!'

A smile lifted his mouth. 'As soon as I saw it, I thought of you. I could imagine it only on you.'

His words made her heart race. 'You didn't have to, Dieudonné.'

'I wanted to.' A certain timbre had come into his voice as he held her gaze. With something like reverence, he slowly placed the necklace around her neck.

The coolness of the diamonds and rubies was a pleasant contrast against her heated flesh. His fingertips brushed her skin as he latched the necklace at the back. She expected him to step back once the necklace was around her throat, but his hands lingered. Smoothing his fingers over her shoulders, he traced a lazy line along her nape.

She shivered involuntarily. Their gazes had locked once more in the mirror.

She was unable to hide the desire in her eyes, her need for his touch.

His face hardened and he bent his head and placed an open kiss along the side of her neck. A soft sigh escaped her lips. Her head dropped back to give him further access to her throat, so glad that she was finally feeling his…

The next moment, he'd stopped and drew back. Jerking her head up, she gazed at Dieudonné's face just as he spun away. His hands had curled into fists.

'I would be honoured if you wore this necklace tonight, Evena.'

He didn't sound like he would be.

She swallowed the rock lodged in her throat, trying not to let her disappointment show. Her skin burned where he'd touched her, leaving a molten impression against it that remained for far longer than it should have.

Three days later, Lilas Moreau sent a note stating the painting was ready if she would like to see it. Without hesitation, Evena sent a note back saying she would call upon her the next day.

Entering Lilas's workroom the following day, her eyes widened at the masterpiece before her. She could scarcely believe that the woman in the painting was her.

'It's beautiful,' she said in awe to Lilas.

'Only because the subject makes it so. I shall have it delivered to you tomorrow. I hope your husband will be pleased.'

How she hoped so, too!

Dieudonné stood by anxiously as he waited for the doctor to come down from examining Evena. He'd just returned from visiting his solicitor on estate business and had been told that the doctor had come in his absence to see his wife. Pacing the drawing room, he fiddled with one thing or another, trying to distract himself.

These past two weeks had been trying. He'd wanted to tell her how much he loved her, but wasn't quite sure how to broach it after having distanced himself from her for more than two months.

He'd heard of the rather mystical transformation impending motherhood often brought to women, but it was quite a different thing to see it for himself. She looked softer somehow, her skin smooth and glowing. There had been times when the sight of her had rooted his feet to the ground, unable to move, or even breathe. That moment in her bedchamber, when he'd given her the diamond and ruby necklace, he'd been hard pressed not to lift her up in his arms, carry her to bed and make love to her until that aching hollowness left him.

The door to the drawing room opened and the doctor sauntered in.

'How is my wife?' he asked without preamble.

The man's eyes twinkled. 'Well, *monsieur*, Madame la Comtesse is doing very well,' he announced, much to Dieudonné's relief. 'The swooning spells have passed and she is feeling much better. I believe she can now resume all her normal activities.'

Dieudonné's face burned. 'Am I that obvious?' Staying true to the doctor's orders had proved to be more difficult than he'd expected.

'There's no shame in loving one's wife. It's a rarity among the nobility.'

The doctor's words lingered in the air long after he had

left. It was a rarity. Dieudonné had once accepted it because it had meant he would finally number amongst the elite.

But did he truly want that? Would he rather give away his heart in exchange for a place in society? Agnès had been willing to use him to legitimise her child's birth. The audacity of that still stung, but he'd found himself increasingly grateful that they had not wed.

If they had, he'd have become a member of that inner circle. But how would it have changed him? It was a question he hadn't really considered before.

Opening his bedchamber door, he glanced around distractedly and then froze.

A painting he had never seen before rested full-length on the chaise. In a stupor, he stared with awe at the exquisite beauty of it.

Evena lying on a chaise, bathed in moonlight. Dressed in a diaphanous shift that clung to her, one could almost detect subtle hints of bare flesh. She'd let her hair down, and it cascaded around her shoulders in a thick cloud of luxurious darkness. Strands rested against the deep cleft of her voluptuous breasts.

Her eyes were bold and defiant, but there was a vulnerability about her mouth as if she were unsure.

Unsure of what? Him? Them?

'Dieudonné?'

He turned, seeing that Evena had come through the adjoining door of their bedchambers and was watching him looking at her portrait.

Wearing the same shift from the painting, her hair flowing down her shoulders.

'Do you like it?' she asked huskily.

'That's too inadequate a word, *La Sirène*.'

He couldn't express what the painting meant to him.

She stepped further into the room, looking ethereal and lovely and sensual like any goddess of myth.

'The doctor said I could resume all my normal activities.'

His heart slammed into his chest, but he answered in an even voice, 'He told me the same thing.'

She took another step, and the scent of lavender wafted to his nose. His body tensed the closer she came. He was trying to hold himself back.

'I asked Mademoiselle Moreau to paint it for you.'

'For me?' He drew back. 'Why?'

Again, she stepped forward until only a hint of space existed between them. It was pure torture, but still he waited.

'I wanted to give you something that would…would… make you want me.'

'Make me want you? What do you mean?'

'You've not touched me since that day in the gazebo, but don't you think, now that I am well, we could enjoy each other again?'

He bit his lower lip. 'Is that what you want?'

She was so close he could feel the heat from her skin enveloping him like a mist. His blood thundered in his ears.

Evena said nothing, but lifted her arms and wrapped them around his neck, exhaled her sweet-smelling breath across his face. 'What do you think, husband?'

Then she kissed him, letting her lips gently tease his mouth while stroking his nape.

He snapped.

His arms crushed her to him as he took over the kiss. Evena moaned and went limp.

Dieudonné lifted her up and carried her to his bed, his lips still entangled with hers. She drew greedily on his mouth like it was a prize she was unwilling to relinquish. Dieudonné obliged her, not parting from her even when he came to the bed and lowered her among the crisp linen folds of his sheets.

Not that Evena would let him up for air. No, her fingers dug into his hair and held on. He wanted to tell her she didn't have to worry. He wasn't going anywhere.

Finally, he ripped his mouth away, grinning a little when she moaned a protest, reaching for him again. There were many men who would kill for a woman to respond to his ardour like this.

'*La Sirène,*' he chided with a low laugh. 'There's no need to rush. We have all night.'

He pulled back, seeing her dark green eyes filled with desire, her flushed face and throat achingly lovely in the candlelit room.

The blood in his veins thickened as he began to undress her. She started to help but he shook his head, and she let her hands fall away.

The first time he'd made love to her had been in the open, secluded and private, witnessed only by the storm. This time, they were together in his bedchamber, enveloped in a world of their own.

When she finally lay before him in nothing but the diamond and ruby necklace he'd bought for her, he took a moment to thread his fingers through her hair as it spread out on the pillow. He undressed himself without being conscious of the act, mesmerised by the beauty that was his wife.

She let out a deep breath he didn't think she knew she'd been holding.

Dieudonné allowed his gaze to roam over her for a long time, revelling in a profound sense of possessiveness.

'*Deyès mwen,*' he murmured.

Much like a goddess, she was physically perfect. Her breasts were as high and round as he remembered them. In the flickering light of the candle, her nipples peaked under his relentless gaze. They still looked like apricots against the golden hue of her skin and his mouth watered.

He wanted to worship her again and have her return his adulation with her long, slender limbs wrapped around him. Her curvaceous thighs clasping his hips and her mouth sighing and moaning his name as if she were bestowing a blessing.

Sweat broke out on his brow.

A wrinkle appeared on her forehead. 'Dieudonné?'

He wanted to ease her worry, but he wasn't sure he could. As his eyes rested on her still flat stomach, a sense of wonder came over him. That day of the storm, they had created a child together.

His breath shuddered as he caressed her stomach. His eyes closed as he realised that a few months from now there would be a child who would make his family complete.

He couldn't think of a better woman to be the mother of his children than Evena.

Bending his head, he placed a tender kiss on her stomach. She trembled, perhaps feeling the same connection to their child. His hands caressed her in languid, sensual strokes. Although his need for her clamoured for release, he didn't want to rush anything about this night.

So he took his time.

Dieudonné shifted back up her body and leaned over to take her mouth with a greedy appetite. Her eager response delighted him. He hauled her to him, her breasts crushed against his chest, her nipples hard and erect. She arched into him, and he devoured her with a reckless, insatiable abandon.

He kissed her again and again until she tightened her arms around his neck in a desperate attempt to get even closer. As if she wanted to press herself into his body so that neither of them knew where the one ended and the other started.

Only then did he let her go, to trail his lips to the hollow of her throat where he lapped and nipped at the sensitive skin, making her jolt and gasp with excited delight before he laved her skin with his tongue.

Something wild was growing inside of him. Only Evena could further heat his blood when he'd thought it couldn't possibly burn more fiercely!

Capturing her apricot-tipped breasts in his hands, Dieudonné drew on them, watching as her head shook back and forth as he took first one nipple and then the other deep into his mouth, circling them with his tongue.

Evena cried out as *la petite mort* took her through its throes. He rode the wave with her, not caring that her fingers had gripped his hair and tugged. At this point, she could pull every single strand out if she wanted to. He had enough wigs to cover up any bald spots.

When she collapsed onto the bed in relief, Dieudonné smiled. '*La Sirène*, you must know we're not done yet.'

Dazedly, she looked at him. 'But I've already—'

He shifted downward, gripped her hips in his hands and pulled her, the sheets, the covers and anything else there to the edge of the bed. 'There's always more.'

'More?'

Saying nothing, he gripped her thighs and spread them apart. 'I have to taste you,' he said.

'Dieudonné, what are you doing?'

'This.' He buried his head between her thighs.

Evena cried out, bucking against his mouth in shock. She clutched at him, pleading with him in one breath while begging him to go on with the next. Then her legs closed about him, holding him fast.

He dragged his tongue over that hooded nub.

Evena emitted a sound somewhere between a whimper

and a scream as she reacted wildly, circling her hips upwards to get even closer to his mouth.

Dieudonné wondered if it was possible to die from pleasure. His manhood was so hard it hurt, but he wanted to hear Evena's pleasured cries even more. She was all hot, sweet, creamy silk and he didn't think he could ever have enough.

Latching on to that nub at the heart of her, he sucked hard.

Evena went stiff and then bucked violently as she broke into pieces before him. Her loud cries reverberated around the room, and he fancied that every person for miles around could probably hear her.

Not that he cared.

Riding out her pleasure, he watched as she finally collapsed on the bed, shuddering and shivering, her body twitching as if she were caught in a violent ice storm.

Her taste went through him like fire and his own body demanded relief. Getting to his knees on the edge of the bed, he grabbed her limp legs and hoisted them onto his shoulders.

Some part of him wondered if he was being too vigorous with her, but when he gazed into her hooded eyes they sparkled with lust and excitement.

That was all the encouragement he needed.

He entered her tight sheath without hesitation, groaning at the almost agonising relief of being inside her again. She clenched around him tightly, and he could barely breathe.

If she kept doing that, this was going to be over before he even got a chance to start!

'I don't care.'

Dieudonné opened his eyes, not realising he had closed them, to see the expression on her flushed face, damp strands of hair plastered along her forehead.

'What?' he choked out.

'I don't care. I want you.'

Realising he had spoken his earlier thought out loud, he gave a pained laugh. 'You have me, *La Sirène*. But just give me a moment to calm down—'

She reached up and grabbed his hips, digging her nails into the flesh of his buttocks, pulling him deeper inside of her.

He shuddered. '*La Sirène*, don't... I won't be able to last—'

'That's what I want,' she told him in a husky voice. 'I don't want your control, Dieudonné. I want the real you.'

All restraint fell away. He began to thrust inside of her, first in short blunt moves and then longer, deeper ones, watching her face as she started to move with him.

It was a dance only they knew, an ancient rhythm, and Dieudonné could tell he was all too quickly getting to the point of no return.

The base of his spine tingled. Twisted.

He gritted his teeth, trying to recapture some semblance of control.

Not yet.

He wanted, no, *needed*, Evena to come undone in his arms once more first. Lifting her legs higher onto his shoulders, he used his hands to hold her steady as he increased the pace, slamming into her faster and faster as it was getting near impossible to hold off on his own release.

Then she screamed, her body shuddering around him, and a split second later he exploded deep inside her, feeling himself fall headlong into the pleasure-filled abyss she'd just dived into.

A week later, Evena was certain that Dieudonné was trying to make up for lost time in the bedchamber.

Unlike those cold weeks after their wedding, it seemed he could barely be apart from her for less than a few hours before he was searching for her and finding whatever surface was available to make love to her. A stroll around the gardens soon turned into a dizzying spell under the speckled light of a large tree. If she were in her private rooms with correspondence, he'd end up making his way there, locking the door behind him.

Twice he'd taken her on her desk, and she could barely look at it now without remembering the things he'd done to her.

The servants all seemed to approve of their employer's behaviour, possibly thinking it was long overdue, looking indulgent when he'd suddenly whisk Evena away from dinner and into his chambers, locking the door behind him until sometimes the next day.

For herself, Evena didn't mind his needy behaviour. She was just as ravenous for him as he was for her. She'd learned what pleased and tantalised him best.

But what she loved the most was the laughter.

Outside of their lovemaking, she'd found humour with him again, something that had been sorely missing. Rediscovering that connection, she didn't know how badly she'd needed it until she found it again.

She was almost happy.

Almost.

Dieudonné had yet to tell her why he had treated her so coldly for so long.

Nor had he told her that he loved her.

Looking at her reflection, she saw herself in all her finery as they prepared to visit the Godiers. They hadn't been back since the wedding, although her mother had written often, giving her the welcome news that her father seemed to have recovered from his swooning spells.

There were times when Dieudonné's lovemaking took an almost…reverent tone. During those times, he seemed to want to draw out every response, every caress for as long as possible. His touch was sometimes hesitant on her skin, as if she were made of the most delicate material, his eyes filled with an emotion she was almost sure was love.

But was it?

He'd not said a word, although his attentiveness to her, in and out of the bedchamber, was such that she could nearly believe he was expressing it to her silently.

Was she being greedy because she wanted him to declare himself to her?

Perhaps, but she needed to know. This marriage had been forced upon him. She longed to know if he'd put aside any regrets and accepted her fully. That even if they were never accepted in society, he would still care for her.

'*La Sirène*, are you ready?'

She jumped at the sound of Dieudonné's voice. Seeing him standing in the doorway of her bedchamber, her heart fluttered once more.

How she loved him!

'Dieudonné, I must speak with you,' she said on an impulse.

'What is it? Is something wrong? Do I need to send for the doctor again?'

'I'm well. It's nothing like that. I need to ask you something important.'

He came into the room. 'What is it?'

Now that she had all his attention, she could barely think. She wanted him to tell her that he loved her, that it didn't matter what she brought to this marriage. That she and their child were what he wanted, that neither of them was just a burden he must accept.

'Why…why were you so cold to me before?'

He didn't pretend to misunderstand. His face dropped and her heart plummeted to the floor.

'Is that something we need to discuss now?'

'*Oui.*'

He sighed and thrust his fingers through his hair. 'Evena—'

'Tell me the truth.'

'What is the truth? I hardly know where to begin. Our marriage wasn't what either of us wanted, but what you don't know is that when we wed I didn't want to be a father. I was strongly against the notion, in fact. I thought it was a—'

Evena had tuned out the rest of what he was saying, as she'd only heard one thing: '*I didn't want to be a father...*'

She should have known the truth. He didn't really want a life with her and their baby. He'd just resigned himself to making the best of a bad bargain.

'I knew it! I knew you didn't want me or our child.'

'Evena, I didn't say that. Please—'

'But you did,' she retorted, anger, hurt and pain flooding her in waves until she could barely think straight. 'No matter what I do, I'll never be good enough for you. I'm not the wife you wanted, and neither did you want our baby!'

'Evena, no. I didn't mean that!'

'How else am I supposed to take your words? You couldn't get what you wanted from Agnès so you settled for me because you were practically forced to do so by your mother. Now, because I'm with child, you have resigned yourself to making this situation tolerable by taking me to your bed again. After all, I'm already with child!'

'I said nothing like that! Why are you twisting everything I say? If you'd only just listen—'

Evena shook her head. '*Non.* I don't want to hear any more. I've tried my best to be the wife you needed. I've done everything possible to woo the nobility to try and gain you the respect you wanted.'

Tears smarted her eyes. 'Personally, I don't think their acceptance matters at all, but because it is important to you, due to what you endured from them over the years, I've been willing to do what I must to make that happen. This salon I'm planning is not for me but for you. I wanted them all to look at my husband and know that he is worth more than any one of them could ever be.'

Dieudonné gazed at her as if he were seeing her for the first time, as all the colour drained from his face.

'Why do you seek the approval of people who have only ever sneered at you, belittled you? They aren't worth a second of your consideration. Anyone who does not care for you, for yourself, for the man you are, as I do, as I have always done, isn't worth befriending. But I see all my efforts to give you what you want have meant nothing to you, so I won't bother anymore.'

'Evena… Please, let me explain.'

She held up a hand. 'There's nothing more I want to hear. Knowing how you truly feel about me, about our baby, I'll never let you touch me again!'

Chapter Sixteen

Evena's words echoed in Dieudonné's head as the carriage swayed down the road.

The pain in her voice, the tears filling her eyes, had been almost too much for him to bear. She was right, if he couldn't be accepted for who he was, what did it matter?

Why? Why had it been so important to him?

He knew that all his life he'd wanted their acceptance, had striven to gain it. At first, it had related to his feeling of being the one who was different. Then it had changed, morphing into a kind of obsession. He'd make them accept him. Make them aware that neither his illegitimate birth nor his Creole blood defined him.

After twenty-six years, he'd not succeeded.

So why was he still trying? What was he holding on to?

Evena sat across from him, her face turned away from his, fixed on the outside scenery. He should have told her before how he felt about her, but for some reason he'd hesitated, afraid she didn't love him back. He couldn't tell her now; her maid was sitting quietly beside her. Evena had insisted on her accompanying them in case she felt unwell.

The salon she'd been so assiduously planning had been for his benefit rather than being a way to introduce herself to society, as most women did, as he'd assumed.

He hadn't realised it was all for him.

He couldn't help but compare her to Agnès, who'd only focused on her own desires. If not for her father's need to maintain his favour with the king, she would have thrust another man's child upon him without a qualm.

So much for using her influence to help him, as she'd agreed. She would have made him a complete laughing stock. People could count—and they could see. Her child could never have been passed off as his.

Now, as he looked back over the course of these past few months, he saw Evena's acceptance of the invitations she'd received in a new light. Very rarely had she turned down an opportunity. How naive of him to think that was due to her outgoing nature, when they were both aware that as a couple they were perceived by their hosts as a curiosity.

She'd done that for him. She'd been trying to become the wife of influence he sought.

Mon Dieu, why hadn't he seen it before?

Because you didn't want to, a voice in his head said.

'Ah, *p'tit fi*, I'm glad to see you looking so well.'

Evena smiled and wrapped her arms around her mother as they all stood in the foyer. At least she hoped it resembled a smile. Inside, she wailed and cried, trying to hold in the pain of Dieudonné's words.

'I'm glad you took my advice to heart,' her mother said with a knowing smile, 'although I missed seeing you both.'

Evena frowned for a moment, trying to think what her mother was talking about. Then her face flushed with colour. Liusaidh had forbidden them to visit for at least two months.

'A man and his wife need time together to bond,' her mother had once advised her.

What would her mother think if she knew the truth?

'I've missed you too, Maman.'

Studying her parents, she saw how well they looked, especially her father. There wasn't any strain on Claude's face. He reminded her of the man he'd been before the illness had stricken him—strong, and full of life.

Dieudonné's parents had also come forward to greet them and for a little while she was able to keep her melancholy at bay. It was just like old times in Saint-Domingue, with the closeness of their families evident in the easy camaraderie they all shared.

She stole a glance at Dieudonné, who was talking to his father. Why couldn't he see the value in what they already had? A family who loved them without question. No amount of acceptance into society would ever compare to the unconditional love of one's own family.

With this child, they could make a life for themselves, shielding them from the cruelties of the world.

Dieudonné, isn't that enough for you?

'*Sé*, what's wrong?'

Sophiette's voice startled her. She blinked and realised she had been staring unseeingly in front of her.

'Why, nothing.'

'Well, that's not entirely true, is it, *La Sirène*?'

Dieudonné had come to stand by her side. His mouth was smiling, but she could see the haunted look in his eyes. She knew what he was about to say. Perhaps he understood how close she was to weeping.

'Evena and I are going to have a child.'

The ensuing cacophony was exactly what she'd expected and more. Their families erupted with joy, hugs and kisses. Their obvious happiness at the coming addition to the family went far to help ease the pain of Dieudonné's betrayal.

At dinner, everyone chatted about the new baby, the conversation loud and boisterous. Ayida was asking her a question regarding the nursery when Liusaidh's voice suddenly cried out.

'Claude!'

Evena watched in horror as her father's eyes rolled into the back of his head before he fell out of his chair and onto the ground.

Dieudonné had thought things couldn't get any worse. Then he saw Evena's pain as her father fell in front of her eyes. After everything she had said to him, the things she'd done for him, the pleasure she'd given him, the one thing she'd longed for was gaining help for her father.

And he hadn't even been able to do that much for her.

Unwisely, they had all allowed themselves to assume the worst was over. They'd deluded themselves. Rage and pain swelled up in him, but he thrust it aside to assist his father in lifting Claude to the nearest chaise.

When Evena's father came to several moments later, he looked visibly shaken.

'Why? I haven't had an attack for months. Why now?'

Liusaidh kissed his cheek and murmured words too low for the rest of them to hear into his ear.

Dieudonné watched as his father ordered the servants to first ply him with brandy and then assist Claude up the stairs to his room, while his wife followed him. That feeling of helplessness goaded him.

'Dieudonné.'

His head jerked at the sound of his mother's voice. '*Oui*, Mère?'

A look of communication passed between her and his father before he nodded. Then she continued, 'I want you to come with me and your father. Evena has gone with her parents. The rest of you stay here.'

Frowning, he followed behind his parents as they went to his father's study and closed the door behind them.

Isadora seemed nervous as she waved to him to take a seat.

'What is it, Mère?'

'I saw your face when Claude fell. I could feel your anger and sadness, my son. Your hopelessness. I know that you asked us to use any influence we might have with the Crown to help, and we told you we couldn't, despite you being so angry and hurt.' A breath shuddered out of her throat. 'It's time you understood why we refused. It's a secret your father and I have kept for nearly twenty-four years.'

Glancing back and forth between them, Dieudonné felt the tension rise in the room.

Isadora opened her mouth, but her lips trembled. Andre went over to her side and clasped her close. *'Mon bijou.'*

'You tell him.'

A grim expression came upon his father's face. 'What your mother is trying to tell you is that she is the King's half-sister.'

The words sucked all the air out of the room.

He whispered. 'Mère?'

'It's true.' She patted his father's shoulder, and he released her but remained close. 'I am the late King's illegitimate daughter. My mother was his mistress for a short while. When she found out she was with child, the King sought out a man who would pretend to be my father. In exchange, he was given significant power and privilege. The only caveat was that he had to remain on the island of Saint-Domingue.'

Dieudonné stared back at his mother. 'I can't believe this.'

'Believe it, *mon fils*,' Andre said heavily.

'My very existence would have caused significant upheaval to his reign if it were ever discovered, especially back then.'

'In exchange for our silence, your mother and I were able

to marry.' Andre paced the room, his face dark and brooding. '*Mon fils*, you have always wanted to know more about your father and mother, but we sought to protect you. Now, I'll tell you the truth.'

Andre stopped pacing and stared at the fireplace. 'Your father, my brother, was a womaniser and a wastrel. He lived purely for his own pleasure. Whatever it was he wanted to do, he did it. He had no interest in taking on the responsibilities due to his title. While he lived, he ran through almost all his money.'

Dieudonné stiffened. 'Are you saying that my father left me nothing?'

'It's true. Your title, your estate and all the wealth you have was given to you by the late King also in exchange for our silence. Not only you, but your sister and brother were equally well-provided for by the Crown.'

Andre scraped his hand through his hair. 'I don't know if the current King is aware of your mother's existence or not, Dieudonné. Even if he is, he will continue the subterfuge for as long as he lives. We gave our vow to the late King that neither your mother nor I would attempt any contact with the royal family, and we must keep it.'

Dieudonné stared at the two people who had raised him, his mind racing with all he had learned. He looked at his mother. The burden of the secret she'd held for so long—how heavy it must have been to bear all these years. Knowing the blood of a King flowed through her veins but forced to keep it secret so that the stability of the Crown could continue.

His gaze shifted to his father. And he'd kept the secret to protect his wife.

Dieudonné's brother and sister also had royal blood. Yet it was clear neither his father nor his mother cared about any of that. Other people would have spent their lives hinting and planting seeds of their dynastic connections to gain favour amongst the aristocracy.

But the Godiers hadn't. His mother had no desire to betray her father. She didn't need the acknowledgement of her place as the King's daughter.

She and his father had made a life for themselves. And they were blissfully happy.

For the first time in his life, he understood the sacrifice they had made because they loved each other...and they loved him. He was their son, no matter what anyone said.

'Can you forgive us for not helping Evena's father?' his mother asked shakily.

He stood up and embraced them both. Holding them close to him, something in his heart shifted. His throat constricted so tightly that he could barely speak.

'Mère. Père.'

Drawing back, he cleared his throat. Evena's contorted face as she saw her father fall unconscious flashed through his mind. After all she had done for him, he couldn't allow her to feel any more pain.

Resolve coursed through every part of his body.

He knew what he had to do. If his parents couldn't approach the Crown, then he would. This time, he would not stop until he had an audience with the King himself.

'I don't know what to do.' Liusaidh wept as she stood by the bed, wiping Claude's face with a damp cloth, although he had protested such coddling.

Sophiette sobbed by Evena's side as they stood at the foot of their father's bed.

'Liusaidh, there's nothing you need to do,' Claude said. 'Whatever happens, I am glad to see my daughters will be well-cared-for and I shall be a grandfather.'

'Claude—' her mother gasped '—I don't want anything to happen to you.'

'Can any man defy the gods?'

Evena's throat tightened. Never had she felt so helpless, so useless. Her father looked as if he was going to die…and there was nothing she could do about it.

'Evena… Sophiette.'

Claude motioned for them to come towards him. Though she was a married woman carrying her own child, in that moment she was her father's little girl, and she and Sophiette crawled up on the bed. Claude's long strong arms gathered them close.

Tears gathered in Evena's eyes as she lay against him, listening as he said, 'I do not want you to worry about me. I have been blessed beyond measure all my life. Men have asked me if I ever longed for a son, and I told them, no. All that I am is because of my daughters.'

She gripped the material of Claude's shirt. 'Papa.'

'*Non*, Evena. Do not concern yourself with me. You have to care for your husband. And you, Sophiette. You must find a husband of your own so your papa won't have to worry about his shy one any more.'

Evena's hand rested on her flat stomach, knowing the child she and Dieudonné had created would have to grow up without their grandfather.

Tears stung her eyes. Here they were, surrounded by the finest things money could buy, and none of it meant anything.

There had to be *something* she could do for her father. He was speaking as if he had already given up. She couldn't let that happen.

As she lay against her father, the answer came to her. It was risky, but what other choice did she have?

What would Dieudonné think if she did what she was contemplating? No, it didn't matter what he thought. He didn't care for her, so why consider his feelings?

A deafening silence blanketed Evena like a heavy mist. It clung to her skin, her hair and her hands as they made their way home in the carriage. Dieudonné hadn't spoken a word to her since they'd left his parents' house.

Her lower lip trembled as she studied his hard profile. Even now, Evena wished she could cross the chasm between them, throw herself into his arms and seek comfort. Her father was dying and the only person she could trust for comfort didn't care for her.

'What's wrong?' Dieudonné's voice broke through the haze of her thoughts, and she looked up to see his eyes fixed on her.

Mindful of the maid, she answered, 'I was thinking of Papa.'

He sighed and rubbed his temples. 'So was I.'

Evena waited to see if he would say anything more, but he lapsed back into silence and stayed that way until they reached the chateau.

After she'd undressed and dismissed her maid, she got into bed and waited to see if Dieudonné would come to her bedchamber. Even though she'd told him that she wouldn't let him touch her again, she'd hoped he would, at the very least, want to talk to her.

She lay staring at the adjoining door, willing it to open and for Dieudonné to come to her. She waited until the early hours of the morning, but he never came.

Dieudonné stirred, the light from the morning sun spilling through the window and piercing his eyes. He sat up and winced, feeling slight aches from his uncomfortable position on the chaise. For a moment, he couldn't remember how he came to be in the library, but then the events of the previous evening came flooding back.

His mother's secret about her royal birth.

His wife's distress over her father's collapse.

His inability to help Claude.

In the carriage last night, despite the maid's presence, he'd wanted to gather Evena in his arms, soothe her mind and then wipe the tears he was sure she didn't know trickled down her cheeks. But the distance between them had been too great.

Last night, despite everything, he'd wanted to go to her bed and lose himself in her, tell her with every touch and caress that he loved her and their baby and didn't regret anything about this marriage.

What had stopped him was the fear of her rejection. She'd always eagerly encouraged his attentions…until she'd told him she'd never allow him to touch her again.

If she'd recoiled from him, it would have destroyed him.

It had been better to keep the whole of the chateau between them last night, but he'd ached for her until exhaustion finally dragged him into sleep.

Dieudonné desperately wanted Evena to know that he no longer sought the approval of society. Those people didn't matter.

Perhaps they never had.

Somewhere along the way, he had allowed his childish desire to be accepted take hold of him and he'd never relinquished it. That stubbornness could have cost him the most important person in the world.

Evena.

Dieudonné pursed his lips. No, he wasn't going to let that happen.

Going over to his desk, he retrieved his writing instruments and paper. Sitting down, he penned a short but direct request to the recipient. Once he'd properly sealed it, he pulled the bell.

Moments later, the door opened and a servant stood there. 'Monsieur le Comte, you sent for me?'

'*Oui.*' He held out the note. 'Have this delivered immediately and please ensure the boy waits for a response.'

'*Oui*, Monsieur le Comte.'

Once the door shut behind him, he went over to the embers of the fire and poked it back into life.

All he could do now was wait and see if the gamble he'd just taken would come to fruition.

Evena paced the floor of the drawing room, squeezing her hands together and trying to keep calm. A glance at the clock showed it was a quarter past the hour of three. Soon, the person she'd asked for help with her father would be here.

For the past three days there had been a strained silence between her and her husband. They ate together but for the most part avoided each other. At night she missed his touch and ached for him, but she knew that it was impossible to go back to how they had been.

No matter how much she wanted to.

A knock at the door startled her. Smoothing her gown, she lifted her chin and said in as clear a voice as possible, 'Come in.'

The door opened and the servant stepped aside to allow her guest to enter.

'Madame la Comtesse, I'm rather surprised you asked me to come here.'

Evena nodded to the servant, who closed the door, and then she extended her hand. 'Please sit, Seigneur de Guise Elbeuf.'

The Seigneur gave her a wary look. 'Where is your husband, *madame*?'

She had no idea. All she knew was that he had left the chateau after breakfast, which was why she'd immediately sent a hurried note to the Seigneur asking him to call on her. She hadn't even known if the man would acquiesce to her request, but she had to try.

'My husband is away from home, but I promise I won't keep you long.'

He sat rather gingerly. 'What is it you want?'

She went to stand by the window, letting the meagre afternoon sunlight flow through. 'I won't waste too much of your time, *monsieur*. My father has suffered another attack, a truly terrible one. I want to know if you can connect me to the King's physician so I can ask him if he will aid my father.'

There. She'd said it. She'd lowered her pride, tossed away all her good sense and asked for his help.

'*Madame*, how can you ask this of me after all that has happened between us?'

A shiver went down her spine at the memory of his unwanted seduction. No, she couldn't focus on that right now.

'Please, *monsieur*. Time is of the essence. I am willing to give you whatever amount you'd like in exchange for your assistance.'

Evena couldn't turn around. She didn't want to see the triumph on the man's face or see the smirk on his lips.

But now she was desperate enough to beg help from anyone, even him. What was pride worth when one's father's very life was at stake?

'Madame la Comtesse, please look at me.'

She wanted to resist, deny his request. Obviously, the man wanted to lord it over her, now she was asking for his help. She straightened her shoulders. So be it. If he wanted revenge, then she would give it to him. Nothing mattered but her father.

Doing as he asked, she turned. Her brow creased. She'd expected to see him gloating, but instead, she saw an almost remorseful look on his face.

'If my mother were here, she would take what money you offered, then lie and give you false hope. That has always been her way.' A steely look came into his brown eyes. 'I can't do what she wants any more. I won't.'

'What on earth are you talking about?'

Sighing, the Seigneur got up and walked over to where she stood. '*Madame*, my mother lied to you all along. We never had any connections or a way to gain access to the royal physician. It's true our family has some standing at court, but we are impoverished, which doesn't sit well with the King or those who surround him.'

Evena thought her legs would collapse. This couldn't be happening. It wasn't true!

'Then why did she say she could help us?'

'Because she wanted your money.' At the frank tone, she winced. The simplicity of the statement made it even more offensive. 'As I told you at the Duchesse's party, my mother tried to sell me to you. Which brings me to something else I must confess.'

'I'm not sure I want to hear it.'

'Perhaps it would be better if I didn't say anything. But my conscience will not allow me to be silent any longer. That night at the Duchesse's chateau—'

'Please, let's not speak of it again.'

'But we must, *madame*. We must, for you see, my mother insisted I attempt to seduce you that night.'

Evena's mouth fell open. 'What?'

His lips twisted. 'My mother wanted me to compromise you so that you would be forced to marry me. I couldn't do that to you, especially when in all your dealings with my mother, you and your family had been nothing other than honest.'

'Marriage is transactional,' she said, hearing Dieudonné's words coming out of her mouth. 'A means to an end.'

'But not for me. I have always wanted more in my marriage. I deliberately paid attention to you that night, knowing that the Comte de Montreau would be watching us closely.'

'Why do you say that?'

'He loves you,' the Seigneur said simply, knocking the wind out of her sails. 'A blind man could see that. That whole evening, he was unable to stop looking at you. I knew then I had to do something that would make him come to your aid.'

'Do you mean to say—'

'I meant none of those things I said to you that night, nor would I have harmed you in any way.'

'You certainly gave a convincing performance!'

'Did I?' He shrugged. 'Perhaps, but I knew it wouldn't take long for the Comte to come looking for us, and he did what I expect any man would do when he sees the woman he loves being accosted. Truly, it was a relief to see him or I would have had to stop my subterfuge and make my true intentions known to you. Thankfully, a man in love, blinded by rage—well deserved, I agree—made it much easier for me to fool you both. I offer my sincere apologies for the distress I caused you.'

Evena stared at the man, her eyes wide. She believed he was sorry, that his apology was genuine, but she'd believed him to be an upstanding gentleman too. Anger rose in her.

'How dare you!' she hissed.

The Seigneur held up his hands in a defeated way. 'I'm sorry.'

'Do you know how much you frightened me that night? I thought you were going to—to—'

'I know.' An expression of deep remorse and disgust came over the Seigneur's face. Evena stared, feeling some of the rage within her starting to vanish away. 'It is reprehensible what I did. I'm not a good man, madame. Yet, I refuse to be a monster.'

His words ended in a low, dead voice. Despite herself, some part of her knew he was baring his soul to her. Still, whatever excuses he had, whatever his intentions, Evena could not see a way to forgive him just now, even if it was the gracious thing to do. 'Why are you telling me this now?'

'Because I wanted you to know the truth before I leave.'

'Leave?'

He nodded. 'I am leaving France for a while. I've heard a lot about the Colonies and the New World. It's said a man can make himself a new life there. I wish to do that for myself.'

Evena goggled at him.

The Seigneur sighed. 'Can you forgive me for what I said and did to you, *madame*? For all the lies my mother told you and the deceit I took part in?'

It was obvious that he was being sincere. There was nothing in his demeanour or actions to show otherwise. After all, he didn't have to tell her anything.

'I just don't understand why you didn't come forward with the truth earlier,' she replied, unable to keep the resentment out of her voice. 'We wasted so much time on someone who never intended to aid us when we could have been seeking help elsewhere.'

'My mother is…' His voice trailed off and he said nothing for a long minute. When he spoke, he said, 'There is no acceptable excuse I can offer you. I know it is impertinent of me to ask for your forgiveness and expect to receive it this instant, but I do beg you to consider it. And while I am confessing all my sins, please also pass on my apologies to the

Comte for my shameful taunting of him in our youth. I've long regretted my childish actions.'

Evena held up her hand. 'It's best if you told him that yourself, monsieur. An apology should not be given by second-hand account. Especially since you did not insult him by second hand.'

He made a derisive sound. 'It would be, wouldn't it? But as well as not being a good man, I am also a coward.' He shrugged. 'At least you know the truth. And now, I'll take my leave, madame.'

The Seigneur bowed and started to open the door when she called out to him, 'Is there nothing you can do to help my father?'

'Nothing, I'm afraid.'

Her heart sank. 'I see.'

'Do not fear, Madame la Comtesse. A man who loves you as much as your husband does will find a way.'

There. He'd said it again. He believed Dieudonné loved her when it was the furthest thing from the truth.

Wasn't it?

'There's nothing he can do,' she said weakly.

'I wouldn't wager on that,' the Seigneur stated with a certainty she desperately wanted to believe. The idea of having Dieudonné care for her as fiercely as she cared for him!

'It wouldn't surprise me at all if he were in the King's bedchamber right now, standing over His Majesty's bed and demanding an audience with his physician. A man will do anything for the woman he loves. I envy you, *madame*.'

Chapter Seventeen

Dieudonné prayed in several different languages as he traversed the corridors of Versailles behind Baron Mercier. Anything could go wrong.

'Remember, *monsieur*, this is an unannounced visit. I do not know how the King will respond. I am at risk as well,' Baron Mercier said over his shoulder as they walked down the Hall of Mirrors on the way to the King's State Apartments.

'I know. *Merci*.'

'There is no need for that. I owe you for what my daughter did, and this is the repayment of that debt. That is all.'

His gamble had paid off. When he'd written to Baron Mercier he hadn't even known if the message would reach him in time.

Taking in the opulence around him, he could scarcely believe he was here. The ceiling, adorned with intricate paintings of gods and angels, reflected brilliantly in the countless mirrors that lined the walls, each gilded frame catching the light, casting a warm glow on the marble beneath their feet.

There was a time when he'd thought he would get to walk these hallowed halls as a member of the court, finally included in the world of the elite that had always been denied him.

Swallowing his pride to ask for Baron Mercier's help after what Agnès had done had been difficult. But he was here for

Claude. And Evena. The woman he loved. There was nothing he wouldn't do for her.

She had no idea he was here. He hadn't wanted to tell her, lest she get her hopes up and it all came to naught. He didn't want to disappoint her more than he already had. Evena's approval and her acceptance of him was more important than anyone else's. In time, he hoped he could gain her love, too.

According to Baron Mercier, the King was in the Apollo Salon. It was one of a series of rooms called the enfilade in the State Apartments, dedicated to the planets and the Roman deities each represented. He passed through the Salon de Mercure, which teased the eyes with lavish furnishings and tapestries. Then the Salon de Mars, a guardroom filled with trophies of war and paintings depicting victories of past military campaigns.

When they reached their destination, Dieudonné's gaze raked over the opulence. For a room dedicated to the sun god of Roman lore, it certainly boasted a well-designed veneration of its deity. On the ceiling, a painting illustrated Apollo on his chariot escorted by four attendants. Alongside was the symbolic figure of France and the personification of the four seasons and other imagery.

'Are you ready?'

He was ready to do whatever it took to procure the King's physician for his wife's father. After all she had done for him, it was time to do something for her.

'*Oui.*'

Taking a deep breath, Baron Mercier knocked on the door, and then opened it.

Inside the Apollo Salon, he was greeted by a number of courtiers who were gathered there. They all stopped to stare at him as he made his way into the room.

No one could fault his attire as he'd made sure to dress

for court. His coat was embroidered with golden threads and large mother-of-pearl buttons. Underneath, he wore a waistcoat made from silk brocade with a floral pattern. His tight-fitting breeches, made of the same velvet as his coat, ended just below the knee, fastened with matching golden buckles that caught the light with every step he took. Silk stockings were tucked into polished black shoes adorned with large rosettes. Dieudonné had gone so far as to wear a wig, for the King liked them himself. A tricorne hat under one arm, edged with the same golden embroidery as his coat, completed his lavish ensemble.

Would it be enough to gain him entrance? He no longer cared for himself, only for what this could mean to Evena.

He could feel many eyes on him, but he kept following the Baron as they drew closer to where the King sat on a gilded throne.

He had never seen His Majesty King Louis XVI up close. From what he'd heard, the King was almost as tall as himself, with a somewhat stocky build, a round face and fair skin.

The King looked up and his blue eyes touched Dieudonné's. He frowned. 'Baron Mercier, what is the meaning of this?'

'Your Majesty, allow me to explain,' the Baron said quickly as the King's guard came forward. 'I would rather throw myself from the highest wall than bring any harm to my King. Besides, I bring you an interesting mystery to unravel. Allow me to introduce you to Dieudonné Godier, the Comte de Montreau.'

Dieudonné wondered if he would be thrown out of the room immediately. Still, he bent his head in reverence. 'Your Majesty, I am honoured to make your acquaintance.'

On hearing his name, King Louis sat up straighter and his eyes narrowed thoughtfully. 'Who is your mother, *monsieur*?'

'Your Majesty, my mother is Isadora Godier, the Marquise de Lyonnais.'

Dieudonné wondered if the King would be terribly upset if he addressed him as Uncle.

The King locked eyes on him for a long while, before he said slowly, 'Baron Mercier, why are you here? You mentioned a mystery.'

Dieudonné could feel the King's eyes boring into him as the Baron spoke, making Evena's father's condition sound like a titillating curiosity. What would cause a Saint-Dominguan man to swoon like that? Such men were well suited to the climate of the tropics. They should be as fit as a horse.

Other courtiers came to listen, but Dieudonné felt the King's eyes on him throughout.

'So that is why I thought it would be a wonderful thing to bring this mystery to your own physician, Your Majesty. I thought it might be an amusing diversion.'

'What is it you expect, Comte de Montreau?'

Dieudonné gave a start. He hadn't expected the King to address him again.

'About what, Your Majesty?'

'You obviously have a strong connection to Baron Mercier, which I admit intrigues me somewhat, but what exactly is it you want from us?'

He sensed the King was asking him something entirely different from what it would appear to everyone else.

Should he tell the truth via subtle clues? His parents had no idea he had come here. He hadn't wanted to cause them any anxiety so soon after their revelation.

Still, there was no time for power play of that sort. He met the King's blue eyes squarely. 'It's as Baron Mercier said, Your Majesty. An intriguing mystery.'

The King sat back on his throne, studying him thoughtfully. Dieudonné didn't know what to think. He felt it was best to reveal nothing, say nothing.

Would it be enough?

'Comte de Montreau, I have heard much about your mother, the Marquise. Tell me, how is she?' Louis asked blandly.

He knew then that the King knew exactly who Isadora was and strongly suspected that something else was going on here. Dieudonné wondered what he would do.

'Monsieur le Comte de Nolivos!' the King suddenly announced.

Surprised, he looked over his shoulder to see the former Governor General coming towards the King. What was the man doing here?

'*Oui*, Your Majesty?'

'Did you ever meet the Baptiste family on Saint-Domingue? You've been telling us so much about the island and I want your thoughts.'

'I did, Your Majesty. The Baptistes are a highly respected family who lived on the island during my time there. One of their daughters is married to the Comte here. I met her some months ago at the Duchesse de Villers-Cotterêt's salon. A beautiful young lady.'

The King remained silent for a long moment. Then he said, 'I'll send my best physician to examine your wife's father tomorrow.' He pierced Dieudonné with an icy gaze. 'I trust the mystery will be solved, *monsieur*.'

Dieudonné's heart seized in his chest at the King's words. A tumult of emotions whirled within him—shock, disbelief, and then a burgeoning joy as the reality of the King's promise dawned upon him. His eyes widened, his breath caught, and for a moment he stood frozen, a statue among the bustling courtiers of the Apollo Salon.

'Thank you, Your Majesty,' he managed to say, his voice

sounding firm, although he had no idea how. His knees felt weak with relief, the weight of worry that had pressed upon his shoulders lifting in an instant, replaced by a hope that felt as light as air.

He'd finally managed to help Evena.

Maybe now, no matter what happened, she would love him for the rest of his life.

After he'd left, the Seigneur's words reverberated through Evena's mind all day.

If Dieudonné truly loved her, then wouldn't everything be all right between them? Especially if she told him she loved him, too?

As for her father...

'Madame la Comtesse, *Monsieur* has returned.'

The servant's voice broke through her thoughts, and she stood. 'Where is he?'

'He's gone to his bedchamber, *madame*.'

Without another word, Evena rushed out of her sitting room and up the stairs until she reached Dieudonné's bedchamber. The door was closed. She gulped. If she knocked on it, would he refuse her entrance after everything she'd said to him?

Squaring her shoulders, she went forward and knocked.

'Come.'

Taking a deep breath, she turned the knob.

He was standing in the middle of the room, but looked over his shoulder at her entrance. When he saw her, he froze. 'Evena?'

'I must talk to you, Dieudonné.'

He came towards her. 'Are you all right? Is the babe in some trouble?'

She shook her head. 'Nothing like that. But I do need to speak with you.'

'Before you do, I must tell you something important.'

Evena waited, her heart stuck in her throat. What was he going to tell her?

'I've been to see the King at Versailles. I've just returned.'

For a moment, Evena was sure she'd heard incorrectly. Then she took in his attire, seeing how well dressed he was and the wig he had set aside.

'What do you mean?'

'His Majesty is going to send his physician to see your father tomorrow.'

Evena stood still, frozen in shock. This couldn't possibly be true.

'Are you sure?'

'*Oui*, I'm absolutely certain.'

Her legs weakened and she collapsed onto the small chaise in front of his bed. 'How did you manage that?'

He sat next to her. 'I spoke with Baron Mercier. He used his influence to get me an audience.'

Of course, it had to do with Agnès. She'd thought that woman was gone from her life!

Evena snarled, 'And what did you have to promise her in return?'

'Her? Who?' He drew back. 'What are you talking about? Do you mean Agnès? I haven't spoken to her for some time. This was something between her father and me.'

'Why? Why would he do that?'

'Because he owed it to me.'

She listened as Dieudonné told her about Agnès's plan to bring a child into the world and have him raise it as his own, without his prior knowledge or agreement. When she heard that, anger surged through her. How awful he must have felt, knowing she would do such a thing to him after everything he'd been through.

When he finished, she shook her head. 'I can't believe it.'

'You can, *La Sirène*. You can. Do you know why?'

There was a look in his eyes that made her heartbeat a speeding tattoo against her ribcage. 'Why?'

'It's simple. Because I love you, Evena. I always have. From when we were children to now. There has never been anyone else who has held my heart.'

Evena's eyes watered. They were the words she'd wanted to hear for so long.

'Dieudonné…'

'I never wanted to hurt you, Evena. It was my own anxieties about my capability to protect my child from the cruelty of our society that I myself had endured. It wasn't because I regretted our marriage or had resigned myself to it. I wanted us to talk about it before you became with child. To see what we both wanted from this marriage. But I struggled to make a decision and I stopped communicating with you, and for that I'm sorry.'

'Do you mean that?' She had never properly considered it from his perspective. But of course he'd worry about his inability to shield his child after all he had gone through.

'I wasn't going to touch you until we were both sure of what we wanted, but then you kissed me with such passion, and it was impossible to resist you.'

She thought about that day in the gazebo, the rain beating on their bodies and all around them in the storm. 'It was wonderful.'

A heated look came into his eyes, but he said, 'When I realised what had happened, that's why I stayed away from you. We hadn't yet had a chance to discuss things properly. I was ashamed of my lack of control and worried you might end up resenting me for it. Bringing a child into this world felt like too big a risk…'

'Resent you? I wanted our child, Dieudonné. I thought perhaps you believed I wasn't a good enough wife for you. I couldn't bring you the sort of influence at court like Agnès could. That you regretted marrying me.'

'No, I don't regret marrying you. But you are a woman who belongs in the sunlight, Evena. You love company and people. I was aware that once you had wed me, you would likely be ostracised from the upper echelons of society, just for being my wife. I didn't want that for you.'

Her heart melted. Now she understood what had been driving him.

'I've felt so helpless, having to stand by, knowing I couldn't help your father. I hated seeing you with Seigneur de Guise Elbeuf, but I thought at least he could do for you what I couldn't—'

'Speaking of him, there's something I must tell you.'

Quickly, she told him about the conversation she'd had with the Seigneur, seeing his eyes and mouth fall open.

'He was pretending all along? And he apologised?' he exclaimed.

'It's all true. He also said he knew you loved me,' she said rather smugly.

'What about you, Evena? Could you love me? Even if it's just a little?' he asked.

Her eyes shone like emeralds. 'Of course I love you, Dieudonné. So much that it hurts. You are my dearest friend. My greatest love. The best and only husband I'll ever want.'

He grabbed her hands and drew them to his lips before his arms wrapped around her. In an instant, their lips met in heated bliss.

Dieudonné started to tug at her gown. Evena immediately pulled at his clothes.

'I think, *La Sirène*, we're going to kill each other.'

'As long as you're with me, I'll die happy,' she breathed.

Love shone in his eyes, and she heard the promise in the deep timbre of his voice. 'I'll always be with you.'

Epilogue

A year later...

The guests milled about in the ornate, luxurious salon hosted by Evena Godier, Comtesse de Montreau. To receive an invitation from her was a coveted honour that many among the elite sought. It wasn't just because she was a beautiful, interesting Saint-Dominguan *salonnaire* who had married into the wealthy Godier family, but also because she always had the most interesting of guests to grace her home.

Among the attendees were people of high status from France and England, as well as the West and East Indies, the Orient and other far-flung places. She hosted a wide variety of guests, from poets and writers to political speakers and more of various races.

The food and drink were delicious and in excellent supply, and a string quartet added a wonderful ambience to the evening. But, for all of that, one did have to wonder where their hostess was. Some of them would be quite scandalised if they knew she was currently occupied with trying to keep her husband's hands from taking off her gown.

'Really, Dieudonné. We have guests!'

'What does that have to do with us, *La Sirène*?' His voice thickened as he bent his head and kissed the side of her throat, sending fire streaking through her as it always did when he touched her.

'Everything. We're supposed to be down there greeting people.'

His hands roved over her gown, trying to untie the ribbon that held it together. It wasn't that she didn't want her husband. Far from it. If she could tell those tiresome people downstairs to go away, she would.

Her salons had grown in the past year to become highly sought-after. No longer did Dieudonné wish for their approval to feel as if he belonged in their circles. Now, everyone wanted to be a part of theirs.

Especially after the King had shown such special favour to her father, who had all but recovered from his swooning spells three months after the royal physician had visited him. Dr Beaumont's advice on what he should eat and drink to combat what he'd said was an imbalance in Claude's blood, coupled with severe anxiety over his family's well-being, had been followed to the letter by Liusaidh. Claude had gone from strength to strength and he and Liusaidh were at their happiest when they were coddling their granddaughter, Marie-Charlotte, and fighting with Dieudonné's parents over whose turn it was to look after her.

It was a wonderful thing that they still lived with the Godiers, who'd insisted they had more than enough room to spare. Charlotte was able to stay with both sets of grandparents whenever Evena hosted a salon.

Which Dieudonné saw as his opportunity to make love to his wife whenever he wished. Even if they did have a house full of guests!

She started to protest again, when he brought his mouth down on hers and kissed her in that fierce way she loved, taking away her resolve one drugging kiss at a time.

'I love you, *La Sirène*,' he whispered against her lips. 'You've given me the life I've always wanted. And it doesn't include those people down there. You and my daughter are all that matter to me.'

Her head dropped back as he placed more heated kisses along her collarbone and she shivered. It was beautiful to hear, and her heart soared with love for him.

'I promise you may have me to your heart's content later,' she pleaded as he started to touch her in all those places that made her resolve weaken further.

'Very well, *La Sirène*.'

He drew back reluctantly, and she smiled at his obvious aggravation. Smoothing her gown, she looked up into his face, happiness making her almost float up in the air. He had been by her side for her entire life.

And he always would be.

* * * * *

While you're waiting for the next book in
Parker J. Cole's
Proposals in Paris miniseries,
be sure to check out her previous great reads

The Duke's Defiant Cinderella
A Marquis to Protect the Governess

Harlequin® Reader Service

Enjoyed your book?

Try the perfect subscription for Romance readers and get more great books like this delivered right to your door.

See why over 10+ million readers have tried Harlequin Reader Service.

Start with a Free Welcome Collection with free books and a gift—valued over $20.

Choose any series in print or ebook. See website for details and order today:

TryReaderService.com/subscriptions

RSBPA2409